In 2002 Karl Cullen volunteered at the Elephant Nature Park in Northern Thailand, spending four months with two orphan elephants; Ging Mai and Hope - the hero of this story. The experience changed his life and in 2003 he moved to the park full time and took on the role of mahout - elephant carer - of an elderly bull elephant named Maximus. The privilege of spending so much time around Max, Hope and the thirty odd other elephants who make up the extended family left an indelible mark, and Karl now hopes to do what little he can to ensure that those elephants lucky enough to spend their lives living free in the wild, continue to do so; while those forced to live in captivity live a life deserving of their noble and majestic being.

Feel free to contact him at;
kcullen75@gmail.com

ELEPHANT KINGDOM

The Search for the Giant
Sun Throwing Elephant

For The Elephants

The beginning of everything

It was very early in the morning and deep in the jungle all was still and silent. Everyone was sleeping and even the trees seemed to be making an effort not to rustle or creak in the wind and so not disturb any of the creatures that sheltered in or under them. Of course the trees never slept; they were the ever silent, ever watchful guardians of the land, and everyone took comfort in that.

The young elephant Hope walked softly along a well worn path through the jungle. This was his favourite place and he knew every tree, every flower and every rock by sight, by sound, by smell and by name. He silently greeted them all as he passed by. This was his own little kingdom. He had walked this path many times, but recently he had done so more than usual. It was only seven days until his tenth birthday and he was becoming worried - and when he was worried, he walked.

You see, on his tenth birthday, Hope would be crowned "King of the jungle", and even though his real responsibilities wouldn't come until much later he could already feel the burden of growing older. The freedoms of the valley, of the jungle, of calfhood, were slipping away, and he didn't understand why.

He thought back to last night, to the dream; the

same dream that had plagued his sleep since he had first learned of his auspicious future all those months ago. In this persistent dream, there was first blackness. Nothing but impenetrable blackness. This never had any effect on the sleeping Hope, it neither worried him nor comforted him; it was just there, as was he.

He would simply be aware of the blackness, and of himself engulfed in it. How long this would go on for in his dream was impossible to tell, as all things of the dreaming kind are, but inevitably the neutrality would be invaded. First by a tiny point of white light in the centre of what Hope would imagine to be his vision, and a feeling of joy would become embedded in the pit of where Hope imagined his dreaming stomach to be; but this would immediately be replaced by an overwhelming sensation of dread and anxiety, accompanied in tandem by the appearance of two blue orbs, larger than the first light and positioned as if they formed the base of a triangle with the point of white light as the apex. The blue orbs would stare at Hope with what Hope felt in every part of his sleeping body as the worst kind of dislike. It made his insides want to curl up tighter than his outsides could ever manage.

How long this would go on for, Hope had no way of knowing, but what he did know was that for him, it was way too long. As much as he would struggle and fight to get away, to will himself awake once he inevitably realised he was in fact dreaming, he never could. The dream would take him to its invariable conclusion, whether he liked it or not. And where the dream always took him was to a point where Hope felt with every fibre of his being that he just couldn't resist the malevolence of those blue spheres any longer, that he wanted to crumble to dust in front of them, to turn himself to nothing rather than suffer their malicious gaze another moment. It was at that point, at that same moment each night, that the tiny speck of light would again come to Hope's attention, growing in size, surging forward it would seem at a great speed. A buzzing vibration would tickle Hope - his real or dream body he couldn't tell - and start up his legs. The light would quickly grow to fill almost half the blackness that surrounded him, while the blue dots, oblivious to what was going on behind, stayed locked on Hope.

The massive ball of light would then change colour to a deep red, the vibrations would fill all of the little elephants body, the buzzing having taken complete control of his ears, and the feelings of angst would retreat to a spot somewhere at the back of his mind. The light would continue to grow, changing colour again to orange, then to yellow and finally, once more, to a searing white, at which point Hope would hold his breath, while the light overtook and engulfed both the blue eyes and Hope in one blinding explosion. That was the exact moment, the same moment every night, that Hope would wake up, breathless and gasping as if he had just escaped from drowning. This morning had been no different.

What had been different this morning was that Hope, for reasons not entirely known to him, had made a decision on waking. He had decided that today he was going to climb to the top of the largest of the mountains which loomed protectively over his valley, which was where he was making his way to now.

He had walked through the jungle on his own before and, except for when he started thinking about pigs, of which he was very frightened, he had never felt afraid. The jungle was his friend. But he *had* been afraid of climbing that mountain, because it was so high and so far away from his family and all of the comforts of the valley below. He was afraid of the unknown. Hope had no idea what he would find up there. What was on the other side? Elephants were almost never afraid of things they knew about, but they were almost always afraid of things they knew nothing about.

Hope had decided that he was going to do it, he was going to climb that mountain, and he had crept stealthily past his still sleeping family very early in the morning because he wanted to be there before the sun came up. The sun always came up from behind the largest mountain in the valley, and Hope imagined he might see where it was that it came from. He quickened his pace, but kept his steps as soft as he could. He knew of course that his family would be worried when they woke to find him gone, but Hope felt this was something he had to do; and he had to do it alone. *It's funny,* thought Hope to himself, *how as a young calf he seemed to often know what he wanted to do without thinking too much about it, when the grown ups seemed to split themselves in a hundred different pieces trying to make a decision sometimes.* It was another reason he was anxious about growing up.

He quickened his pace once more.

Hope was about halfway up the mountain when he saw the first sign of the morning sun. A faint glow spread over the edge of the mountaintop and for the first time that morning the trees at the top became visible. They leapt up as giant black shadows against the dim light of morning. It seemed to Hope as if they had just noticed that he was climbing their mountain and they had jumped to attention to stand guard against this intruder.

And *he* was the intruder!

Well that just doesn't seem right, thought Hope, allowing his imagination to take over. *After all, this will all be my kingdom very soon. How dare they treat me as an intruder in my own land!* And so Hope imagined instead that the trees had jumped up to salute their new king and show their respect. He felt much better about this and marched towards the mountaintop with his head held high, speeding up a bit more to make sure that he reached the top before the sun did. He really wanted to see where the sun came up from every morning. Hope imagined that maybe there was an enormous giant elephant on the other side of the mountain which would pick the sun up in its trunk and throw it as hard as it could into the sky every morning. The elephant would be so big and so strong that it would be able to throw the sun from one side of the land to the other.

When the sun fell back down behind the mountains on the other side, everything would go dark again. While everyone was asleep, the giant elephant would then sneak around behind all the mountains until he found where the sun had landed - usually within the same 50 or 60 mile radius, which meant it was very, very rare that he wouldn't find it after a short while -

and he would sneak back again in time for the next morning, whereupon he would do it all over again.

It sounded like a lot of fun to Hope. He hoped that maybe the giant would take him with him that night to help find the sun, and he started running now, excited to see the giant sun throwing elephant.

The light was getting brighter and the jungle was stirring. The birds had started their cheerful morning songs and two squirrels had come running out of a tree trunk and were chirping at Hope. They seemed curious as to why he was so far from his home, but Hope paid them no attention. He was near to the top now. He came up over the crest of the mountain and through the trees that stood between him and the vision that awaited.

This was it. Hope was about to see what was on the other side of the largest mountain in the valley. He would see the enormous giant sun throwing elephant who must have only a moment ago sent the sun hurtling into the sky. He thought of the story he would tell his family when he got back home, and how they would all forgive him for disappearing and causing so much worry.

As Hope came out through the far side of trees a huge trumpet blast burst from his trunk without him even meaning it to. He was so excited about all the things he was about to see.

Then he saw it.

Hope stopped right where he was. His trunk, which he had raised high over his head when he trumpeted, now just flopped down to the ground like a bird that had only now realised it was of the flightless variety, and those wings were really just for show. He couldn't believe what he saw, and he had to rub his eyes to make sure he was really seeing it.

The sun was just peeking up over the mountain, only it wasn't the mountain that Hope was standing on. There was another mountain, way off in the distance, and the sun was coming up from behind *it*.

Or maybe there's another mountain behind that one, and the sun's actually behind that, thought Hope. He turned around to look at where he had come from and that's when Hope realized something. Everywhere he looked, for as far as the eye could see, there were more mountains, more valleys, more forests and large open plains that filled every space between.

Behind, he saw the small valley that he called home, which before this morning had been his whole world. But now, from the top of this mountain, he saw that the land stretched out forever, and the blue sky followed it wherever it went.

'Well,' said Hope to himself, 'if I am going to be King, then I really should get to know my kingdom. Besides, if I go back to my family without any fantastic stories then they will be angry with me for disappearing the way I did.' Hope decided that as King, he should really know where the sun came from every morning, and so he decided that would be the direction he would follow; and if it ended up being incredibly far, then when he got there he would simply ask the giant sun throwing elephant to throw him all the way back to his family.

Hope smiled to himself. That sounded like a lot of fun.

As he took his first step down the other side of the mountain, Hope's entire body was filled with a strange sensation. It was like excitement and fear mixed together, and Hope thought that he liked the feeling. It was what we might call a sense of adventure; although we might be wrong.

Later, Hope would remember it as the beginning of everything!!

PART ONE

Chapter Two

The other side of the mountain

Hope's first step down the mountain quickly became his second, and then his third and his fourth. Before he knew it, Hope was charging down the mountain as hard and as fast as he could. His legs swung wildly around his little pot belly and his trunk swung from side to side, always swinging away just as his front foot threatened to come squashing down on top of it.

Hope tried to concentrate on his legs, thinking to himself: *Front left foot goes there, and now back right foot there. Now the front right leg comes forward and the trunk swings left out of its way, followed by the back left foot swinging past the belly, making sure it doesn't kick into the front left leg.*

But when he tried to concentrate on how he was running he almost tripped himself over. So he thought it was best to let his legs think about what his legs were doing and let his trunk think about what his trunk was doing, and he would simply think about how much fun it was to be charging down the mountain. Especially a mountain he had never charged down before.

Despite the fact that with every step he took it looked as though he would either kick his own belly, trip on his own feet or stamp on his own trunk, he never once did any of those things and anyone watching might have said that he was the most graceful animal they had seen. Or they might have said that he was the clumsiest; and they would probably both be right.

As Hope charged down the mountain he trumpeted and squealed and yelled at the top of his voice. Any animals that were in his path had to quickly scurry out of the way. Many of them scrambled up the nearest tree, only to find that Hope was charging straight for that same tree. Hope had become well known for crashing into trees for fun, and so the trees knew better than to get in his way.

Even though Hope had never been in this part of the jungle, the trees here knew of him. You see every time the wind blows through the treetops and the branches creak and moan, that's actually the trees calling out to all the other trees. They tell each other of all the things that have happened around them, and the wind carries their story from tree to tree and from jungle to forest, whispering tales of distant places and strange happenings, always gathering more pieces to add to its story of no beginning and no end. And as the trees never sleep, and so see everything, are ever silent and so hear everything; and as they have been here from the beginning of memory, and also because the wind never stops, but blows from land to land, so the entire history of the world is carried forever on every gentle breeze or raging storm, depending of course on which part of the story is being told.

But that's another story, and we should get back to ours.

So, because the trees knew of Hope's reputation for crashing into them, as he charged toward them they would bend and sway at just the right moment so as that Hope would simply brush past them. When Hope noticed this he suddenly felt very big and powerful. He started charging even faster down the mountain, and the trees had to move very quickly to keep out of his way. Because he was running so fast, he very quickly came to the bottom where the valley opened into a wide grassy plain that stretched from the end of this mountain to the beginning of the next.

Just before Hope reached the bottom and plunged into that ocean of lush green grass that spread out before him, he spotted a large grey rock at the edge of the path. He adjusted his direction mid charge so that he was now heading straight for the rock.

If those trees all knew who I was, and so kept out of my way, thought Hope, *then surely this rock will also have heard, and will roll to one side to make way for me.*

He was coming upon the rock at full speed now - only the rock didn't move.

Hope was filled with a sense of might and power. He wouldn't stand for a mere rock being so disrespectful that it couldn't simply roll over to make way for its future King, and so he continued to charge at it head first. He was within a few metres now and still the rock stood as still as a ……… well, as still as a large rock would be expected to stand, really!

'Get out of my way,' yelled Hope at the last second, and at the same time he suddenly realised a few things.

One - the rock was *not* going to get out of his way.

Two - now that he was so close, he saw that the rock was much bigger than he had thought. It was quite a bit bigger than he was actually.

Three - it was too late now for him to stop or change his direction.

The last thing he realised just in the moment right before he crashed head first into the rock, was that just after he had yelled 'get out of my way,' and just before the collision, he had seen the rock lift its head and look at him with great big round eyes. Before he had time to ponder this, Hope smashed into the rock and flew into the air, somersaulting over the rock, through the trees, and out into the wide open field of grass.

The last thing Hope heard before he thudded back down to earth was the rock yelling, 'Why don't you watch where you're going.' And the last thing Hope thought before his short life as a flying elephant came to an end, was that rocks don't yell at you, they don't have heads that they lift up at the last moment, and they certainly don't have eyes that watch you as you complete your collision course.

The only other thought Hope had was, 'Hey, this is kind of fun.' But all of these thoughts had to leave Hope's head as quickly as they came in because Hope's head was about to have the whole world come crashing down on it.

Or was it the other way around?

Hope had tumbled through the air so many times, he wasn't sure what was up and what was down, or whether he was falling onto the ground, or was the ground falling onto him? In the end it didn't matter. All that mattered was that one of them, either Hope or the ground, was moving very quickly towards the other and there was nothing either of them could do about it.

Hope hit the ground - or the ground hit Hope - very hard, and he tumbled through the grass, eventually coming to a stop some distance away from where he first took flight. He sat in the grass for a moment trying to collect up all the thoughts that had spilt from his head and were now fluttering around him like butterflies before a storm. He remembered the rock; how he had charged into it and how the rock had refused to make way for him. He remembered that at the last moment the rock had looked up at him, and as he flew through the air the rock had said something, only he couldn't remember what it was it had said.

'Why don't you watch where you're going,' called out a voice.

'That was it,' exclaimed Hope, and then realised that it was the same voice that had said the same thing before, only now it was a lot closer.

Hope was a little scared and a lot confused. He wasn't used to rocks looking at him, or yelling at him or, even more so, coming towards him. But this was the other side of the mountain after all. Maybe this was what rocks did here.

He got up on his feet and could just see over the top of the long grass. He could see the big grey mass of the rock pushing its way through the grass towards him. The rock stopped suddenly and something lifted up out of the grass, turning this way and that way as if it was looking for Hope. He suddenly realised what it was. It was a trunk. The rock wasn't a rock. It was an elephant!

The trunk stopped as its end turned towards Hope. He knew how an elephants trunk was much better at seeing things than its eyes, and while he was really happy to see another elephant, he wasn't sure if the elephant would be mad at him for crashing into him and so decided to wait quietly in hiding to see what happened.

The rustling grass crept closer and closer. Hope was sure that soon enough he would be face to face with this other elephant, when suddenly the rustling stopped. There was silence.

Hope inched forward and hesitantly pushed the grass aside with his trunk. But it seemed as if the elephant had disappeared.

'That's impossible,' said Hope to himself, and as he said it a large grey head eased up unseen from behind and settled in, peering into the empty space alongside him. Hope continued to stare straight ahead.

'What are we looking for,' said the head.

'Ahhhh!!!!,' screamed Hope in reply as he disproved the notion that elephants can't jump by jumping several feet in the air.

'How did you do that?'

'Do what?' asked the elephant, seeming genuinely confused.

'One minute you were there,' explained Hope excitedly, his heart trying to thump its way out of his chest, 'and the next you were here.'

'I believe it was less than a minute,' answered the elephant, with a very serious look on his face that suggested he was thinking very hard about something.

'What?' blurted Hope, the confusion helping to

distract his heart from its escape plan and return to its normal place and speed.

'Well, from there to here is really not very far at all,' the other elephant explained, 'and if I don't mind saying so myself, I can move quite quickly, so I can't see how it would take me a whole minute to move such a short distance.' The elephant was quite satisfied with his explanation, but Hope was not.

'It wasn't a whole minute,' said Hope, 'you simply disappeared from there, and reappeared here.'

'Did I really?' asked the elephant, his face brightening and looking impressed with himself. 'How did I do that? I mean, did you see it? What did it look like?'

'How should *I* know how you did it?' Hope was becoming more confused and a little annoyed. 'All I know is that one minute you were there, and the next you were here.'

'Me?' asked the elephant. 'You must be mistaken. I would go from there to here much quicker than a minute. I'll show you if you like,' and the elephant started to move off into the grass so he could better illustrate the point he was trying to make.

'No!' yelled Hope in exasperation. 'I didn't mean to suggest that it would take you a minute to go from there to here.' He was becoming tired of this conversation. 'What I meant was that somehow you seemed moved from there to here; without actually moving.'

'Well, no, I think you are mistaken,' replied the elephant, looking extremely thoughtful again. He stroked his chin with his trunk. 'That would be

21

impossible, and I've never done something impossible before. You see it's impossible to do something that's impossible, because if you did it, it would mean that it was possible, not impossible, or else you wouldn't have been able to do it. You see.'

Surprisingly, Hope did see, but was still bemused and a little fed up by the whole thing.

The other elephant seemed to have also become perplexed and had turned away from Hope muttering to himself. Hope couldn't hear what he was saying but could make out the occasional word such as 'possible' and 'impossible', or 'one minute' and 'disappear' and also, for some reason, 'bananas.'

The two elephants stood like that for some time until Hope decided he should say something. He thought that if he didn't, then the elephant might still be trying to figure things out when the sun came up tomorrow; and he was getting hungry.

'My name is Hope,' he tried gently so as not to startle the elephant who was concentrating deeply on what was or was not impossible. It didn't work!

The elephant spun around wildly with ears flapping, trunk swinging, and tail pointing straight up. 'Where did you come from?' demanded the elephant, his eyes almost popping out of his head.

'What are you talking about?' answered Hope. 'I've been here the whole time.'

'I think not,' stated the elephant confidently. 'Why, I was right here just last week and I didn't see you at all. If you were here for the whole of time, I would surely have bumped into you many times before. Not to mention the fact that you would look a lot older than you do.' The elephant nodded knowingly at Hope to emphasise the impeccable logic of his argument.

Hope, for his part, put his trunk in his mouth and sucked in deeply. He had had just about enough of this nonsense, but he tried to stay calm.

'I didn't mean the whole of time,' he said coolly. 'What I meant was that we both came here at the same time, just a minute ago.'

'Where from?' asked the elephant.

'Well, I came from the other side of this mountain........,' started Hope.

'No, no, no, ' interrupted the elephant. 'That's impossible. Now, I can move pretty fast, if I don't mind saying so myself, but even I couldn't get from the other side of the mountain to this in less than a minute. Unless of course you had a tunnel, and you ran really fast, and it was downhill and.....'

The elephant continued on like this, but Hope had stopped listening. He was contemplating simply walking away, but that would be rude, and not very king like. Instead he decided to once again state loudly and clearly his name.

The elephant stopped in the middle of an explanation of how you could never be in one place before you were in another, because at that time it wasn't before at all; it was simply now, and it only became before, afterwards. And how could now be before, as now is now, before is before, and afterwards hasn't even happened yet; and every time he thought of where he was, it was always now, never before, and certainly not afterwards. He had almost become clear on all of this when Hope had interrupted him.

23

'My name is Hope,' he tried again, seeing an opportunity in the blank look that had spread over the others face, and to his surprise, the elephant regarded him with a great big warm smile.

'Well it sure is a pleasure to meet you,' he cheerfully replied. 'My name is Pu-pa.'

Hope was so relieved to have gotten one sensible sentence in reply that he suddenly burst out laughing.

'Oh, I love to laugh too,' exclaimed Pu-pa, and they both remained there for sometime, laughing uncontrollably. Hope, because of the ridiculousness of it all, and Pu-pa, simply because he loved to laugh.

Once they had finished laughing, they stood regarding each other slightly awkwardly. Hope had an expression on his face that suggested he was thinking hard about what he should say next. He didn't want to get Pu-pa started on another long explanation on something that made no sense whatsoever, yet at the same time somehow seeming inexplicably correct.

Pu-pa wore an expression that suggested he was thinking of nothing at all, and was simply waiting to see what happened next.

'Well,' ventured Hope, 'Um, I should probably get going. I need to get to the top of that mountain before the sun comes up tomorrow.'

'Why?' asked Pu-pa.

'So I can see the giant sun throwing elephant,' replied Hope.

'Okay,' was Pu-pa's surprisingly short response.

'Ooookay,' said Hope slowly, and he turned into the field of grass and started walking towards the mountain. He walked a short while before he noticed that the sound of his footsteps wasn't the normal 1-2-3-4, but instead they continued to 5-6-7 and 8. He turned, and saw that Pu-pa was following behind him.

'What are you doing?' asked Hope, turning to face him.

'Well, I believe I'm off to see the giant sun throwing elephant on the other side of that mountain,' said Pu-pa. 'Would you like to come?'

'But I'm already going,' snapped Hope.

'Perfect,' exclaimed Pu-pa, ' we can go together.'

Hope gave up. He had wasted enough time already talking in circles, and so the two elephants headed off towards the mountain, tearing mouthfuls of grass with their trunks as they went. For the most part they walked and ate in silence, but at one point Hope made the mistake of asking Pu-pa why he had been pretending to be a rock.

'Pretending?' queried Pu-pa. 'I never pretend! I *was* a rock. Now I am an elephant, but perhaps tomorrow I shall be a bird, or a star, or perhaps a raindrop; who knows?

'Perhaps I shall even be you, and you will be me. Anything is possible, you see, and nothing is impossible, and if it was, then you could never find out for sure anyway. I mean, just because something didn't happen today doesn't mean that it definitely won't happen tomorrow, right, and so if……….'

Pu-pa continued like this for a long time. Hope had trouble following it all and wished he hadn't said anything, but really he was glad of the company.

The sun was high in the sky now, and the two elephants walked and talked and ate their way towards the next mountain.

The mountain, for its part, stayed exactly where it was and waited patiently for the elephants. But it was watching them, and it was certainly listening. For a while anyway, before it too became confused and a little annoyed at the nonsense that continued to float from Pu-pa's mouth. The mountain gave up listening and started counting the trees on its back instead.

But it kept watching!

Chapter Two
This side of the next mountain

The two adventurous elephants strode purposefully toward their destination. The sun was shining, the birds were singing, the grass was delicious and the company was ……. well, the grass was delicious.

Hope had to admit that things were going pretty well so far. They had almost reached the bottom of the mountain, and the sun had just begun its descent towards the far horizon. They should easily make it to the top by nightfall, in time to see if the sun did in fact come up over the far side of this mountain.

They reached the mountains foot, stopped and looked up. There was no real reason for doing this; I guess it's just what you do before you start climbing a mountain. It wasn't a particularly big mountain, and Hope was glad for that. He had been walking since very early that morning and was looking forward to getting to the top and having a rest.

'Are you ready?' he asked Pu-pa

'Ready for what?'

'To climb to the top,' said Hope

'The top of what?'

'Oh just come on,' snapped Hope, and set off on the path up the mountain. Pu-pa shrugged his shoulders, smiled and followed Hope.

There was a well worn path leading up the

mountain and the elephants accepted its invitation. It was a good deal narrower than the paths that Hope was used to, and so he figured that it hadn't been made by elephants. Either way, it was a lot wider once Hope, and more particularly Pu-pa, had made their way along it. Although the path seemed to be making a great effort not to go in a straight line, even when it very well might have, Hope and Pu-pa made very quick progress up the mountain.

It was a very beautiful and friendly mountain. The trees stretched gracefully towards the mountaintop and swayed rhythmically in unison with the soft breeze that squeezed through their branches. They were all evenly spread apart so as not to crowd one another, and in the spaces between their bases, flowers of every colour and description covered the forest floor. They too danced to the same tune that had set the treetops in motion; only their dance was light and playful, while the trees dance was heavy and sombre, because it carried the weight of every story ever told, and if you watched it for a long time, you found that there were tears in your eyes and a smile on your lips.

But we should get back to our two adventurers.

They didn't spend too long watching the forest dance, but they did appreciate its beauty. They enjoyed seeing birds of every variety chase each other through the treetops, swooping in and out and up and down, always looking as if they were about to crash into something, but never really coming close. Butterflies fluttered from flower to flower so that it seemed as if the flower petals themselves had taken flight and were swapping one stem for another, never settling for any in particular. There were animals and insects of every kind, and everywhere they looked there was movement.

The beauty and energy rubbed off on the two pachyderms and put a spring in their respective steps. Presently, they were about halfway up the mountain and the sun was still reasonably high in the sky. They had come so far so quickly, it seemed as if they had been walking in a dream. Neither of them had spoken since they had started up the mountain, but now Hope came to a stop under a large tree.

'I think we should rest for a bit,' he said.

'But I'm not really tired,' answered Pu-pa.

'Me neither, but it seems like we should be. Besides, we still have plenty of time to get to the top.'

'I suppose,' agreed Pu-pa.

They lay down on their sides, and before their trunks even hit the ground, they were both fast asleep. They were obviously much more tired than they realised.

Hope woke to a chattering sound in his ears. He jumped to his feet. The light had turned to a pale orange. How long had he been asleep? he wondered. Not long enough for his recurring dream to take hold, thankfully. The chattering had stopped, and he turned to Pu-pa who was snoring loudly beside him. Hope nudged him gently with his foot.

Pu-pa leaped to attention yelling, 'Two two's are four, four two's are eight; I eight all my bananas befour it was two late.'

'What?' said Hope.

'What?' said Pu-pa.

They looked at each other.

'What's that?' asked Pu-pa.

'What's what?'

'Flap your ears,' suggested Pu-pa.

'Why?' demanded Hope. Hope couldn't see what Pu-pa saw. What Pu-pa saw was two large furry tails peeping out from behind Hope's ears.

Hope decided that it was best not to question Pu-pa too deeply about it, and so just flapped his ears. When he did, two small squirrels fell from behind them, hit the ground and rolled out in front him. They unfurled themselves, scrambled around each other a couple of times, and turned to look up at Hope with big brown eyes that seemed too big for their small oval faces. In one chirping voice, barely more than a squeak, they said, 'Boo!!'

Hope, of course, wasn't at all frightened by two small squirrels who yelled 'Boo!!' at him, and he simply stood staring at them, unsure what to say or do next.

The squirrels however, thought that it had been a very fine joke and were rolling all over the ground in fits of laughter, slapping each other on the back and re-enacting the scene from start to finish.

Hope became a little annoyed with this, and even more so when Pu-pa joined in the laughter, even taking on the role of Hope in the ensuing re-enactments, which became more extravagant and greatly exaggerated with each telling. When it came to the part where the squirrels had yelled 'Boo!!' at Hope, Hope - being played by Pu-pa, remember - would leap up into the air, eyes bulging, trunk flailing, and then roll over onto his back, all four legs pointed stiffly at the sky, as if he had completely fainted from fright.

Hope (being played once more by Hope) was losing his patience. 'Enough,' he yelled. 'As your future king, I command you to stop.' They ignored him. They were having too much fun.

This made Hope incredibly angry. Not just because they were ignoring him, and not just because they were having fun without him, but because they were having fun because of him, without his intending them to. He didn't like that one bit.

He tucked his trunk under his belly, curled his head to his chest, and then flung the whole lot at the squirrels so that his trunk shot out directly between the three performers, continued with great speed up and over his head, paused there for a dramatic second before finally dropping back to the ground and coming to rest between his feet. Hope didn't do it to hurt anyone. He only wanted to get their attention and stop them from laughing at him.

It worked. They stopped laughing instantly and looked up at Hope. Hope looked back with an air of quiet satisfaction at having regained some of his dignity.

It was then that Hope realised that there was now only one squirrel standing where previously there had been two, and the thought occurred to him that maybe he had sent the other squirrel flying to the far side of the mountain with a flick of his trunk. Before he could worry too much about this, Pu-pa and the remaining squirrel burst into another fit of laughter. With tears streaming down their faces, they pointed at something

31

down near Hope's feet. Hope looked down and saw what it was that was so amusing. At the end of his trunk, staring up at him with a great big cheesy grin, was the other squirrel. It had somehow managed to stuff its entire tail down one nostril of Hope's trunk and was dangling there waving back up at him.

'Aaaaaaagh!!!,' screamed Hope, and he started to flail his trunk all around himself, trying to dislodge the squirrel. He threw his trunk left and right, and up and down with great gusto, until it became a blur - and even Pu-pa backed away, not wanting to be caught in the crossfire.

After Hope had made quite a spectacle of himself, he came to a halt some distance from where he had started. He stood there panting from his exertion, only to hear an enormous ball of laughter burst out of Pu-pa as if it were in a great rush to be somewhere else and had to depart immediately. The force of it almost knocked Hope backwards, but he kept his footing long enough to see what had caused this latest outburst.

At the end of his trunk, holding hands and cheerfully waving and smiling at him, were both of the squirrels, each with their tails firmly lodged in each of Hope's nostrils.

'Boo!!' they said.

This time Hope did scream. Not from fright, but from frustration. He lifted his trunk up in the air, sucked in a deep breath through his mouth until his lungs were filled with air, and then blew it out through his trunk with all of his strength.

The two squirrels shot out of Hope's trunk with such force that they went from being two furry little creatures stuffed into Hope's trunk, to being two tiny brown dots sailing over the trees in next to no time.

If you're worried that the squirrels were hurt by such a long flight and big fall, rest assured that they landed safely in a large eagle nest. To this day they talk about it still as the most fun they ever had; although the following days that they spent trying to convince a poor mother eagle that they were her chicks, and that she should teach them to fly, would have been a close second.

But back to our story.

The two squirrels were quickly disappearing into the distance, but before they did so completely, two small squeaks came scurrying back through the air to Hope's ears. In his left ear he heard a minuscule voice chirp the words, 'Careful blue eyes,' while in his right a similar voice said, 'Wooohooooooooooo!!' and both voices quickly faded with the squirrels who delivered them. Hope, mystified by the words - the ones in his left ear that is: the one in the right made perfect sense - glared hard at Pu-pa while Pu-pa tried hard to bring his uncontrolled laughter back under control.

'Right!' said Hope sharply and with purpose. 'After them.'

'Huh?' managed Pu-pa between two large chortles that shook his whole body, but Hope was already charging off into the jungle in the direction that the two airborne squirrels had taken, (or had been given, we should really say!).

'Why are we going after them?' asked Pu-pa once he had caught up with Hope.

'I'm going to catch them and take them home with

me,' answered Hope, 'and when I'm crowned king, I'm going to turn them into a nice warm pair of ear warmers for the winter; and if you don't wipe that smile from your face,' added Hope, turning to Pu-pa, 'I'll make you into my court jester, and we can all spend our days laughing at you.'

Hope didn't want to mention the real reason, which was of course what he had heard the squirrel cry out on departure, and wasn't actually serious about the ear warmers and jester. Pu-pa, on the other hand, was never serious and, try as he might, he could not wipe that smile off his face. In fact, it seemed to get a little bigger.

The two elephants charged through the thick undergrowth; Hope leading the way and Pu-pa a couple of steps behind. They came upon a large growth of tall grass. Neither of them could see what was on the other side, but they could hear a thundering sound that was unfamiliar to them. Hope, however, was still too occupied with the thought of finding the squirrels to think of anything else. Without pause he disappeared through the long grass. Pu-pa followed, but when he emerged the other side, Hope wasn't there. He quickly looked left and right, then up and finally, down. It was when he looked down that Pu-pa realised what had happened. You see, down didn't stop at Pu-pa's feet the way down normally did, but continued much further into the distance.

Pu-pa realised that he was in mid air, having run off the side of a ravine, and he could see Hope's tumbling figure plummeting towards the water below.

'Oh!' said Pu-pa, and decided that the only decent

thing to do was to plummet down in the same fashion.

The elephants splash-landed into the river at the bottom of the ravine, plunged to the bottom, lightly touched the river bed and then surged back to the top, breaking the surface with great bursts of air, water and trumpet blasts from their trunks. They bobbed at the surface of the river, greatly relieved that they had taken such a large fall and come away with little more than a smile on their faces. It was then that they again noticed the thundering sound, only it was much louder down here. They turned in its direction and saw what it was.

There was a great waterfall pouring down directly behind them. Looking at the force with which the falling water of the waterfall met the flowing water of the river seemed to increase the volume of the roaring thunder pounding on Hope's ears, and he stared motionless in awe.

Pu-pa on the other hand yelled 'Wey-hey!! or something like that, and surged toward the point of impact. When he reached it, he threw himself directly under it, and the falling water pushed him down with such force that it seemed to Hope as if Pu-pa simply vanished. Moments later, however, Pu-pa shot up out of the water next to him yelling 'Woo-hoo!!' or something along those lines.

When Hope saw what fun Pu-pa was having he was spurred into action. He immediately started swimming towards the bottom of the waterfall as quickly as his little legs could push the water behind. When he got there, he threw himself under the full force of the falling water without hesitation. He was plunged downwards with such force that his head quickly moved to where his tail had been, and his tail moved to some place else altogether. He tumbled over and over, and lost all sense of what was up or down or left or right; or what was himself or not himself for that matter. He allowed the water to decide where it wanted to take him, and before long he bobbed to the surface again yelling 'Woo-hey,' in imitation of Pu-pa, but without quite so much enthusiasm.

He *would* have been just as excited as Pu-pa, but he had very quickly realised that he had not come up in the same place as he had gone down. This place was much darker, and the sound was a lot duller, as if it was being swallowed up by something before being allowed to find its full voice. That something was more than likely the cave that Hope had just noticed behind him, its great mouth stretching over the little elephant as if it meant to swallow him too. Just then Pu-pa appeared in the water next to him. He too saw the cave mouth and turned to Hope. Hope turned to Pu-pa.

'Shall we?' suggested Hope.

'I think we shall,' smiled Pu-pa. Climbing up and into a pitch black cave entrance hidden behind a wall of water and striding confidently into its darkness seemed like the only thing for our two intrepid explorers to do.

And that is exactly what they did!

Chapter Three
The cave

As Hope and Pu-pa ventured further into the cave, the sound of the waterfall retreated into the distance, it not being as brave as the two fearless elephants. The darkness, which at the beginning had been as dark as Hope or Pu-pa had ever known darkness to be, now became closer to what we might simply call black. For now though, we shall still refer to it as darkness, and it surrounded Hope and Pu-pa so completely that they really felt as though they had been swallowed up. Although they couldn't even see each other, and although they would never admit to it, in the darkness they leaned closer and had to strongly resist the urge to reach out and hold each other's trunks. They felt their way through the cave, testing each piece of the ground with their trunks before they ventured to put a foot forward. To ease the tension, Pu-pa started to sing. This was his song.

'Oh what it is to be an elephant.
To roam free and far and wide.
With always a song upon your lips,
and a companion by your side.
Our footsteps they have fallen down,
on every piece of land.

37

From wherever you,
have come from to,
wherever you now stand.
The sky it rests upon our backs;
the ground is held beneath our feet.
If ever the elephant should disappear,
the sky and ground shall meet.
The stars will all fall into the sea.
The fish will all fly away.
"Where have all the elephants gone,"
is what everyone will say.
So remember this, if you see us pass,
singing our song with pride.
Oh what it is to be an elephant.
To roam free, and far, and wide.'

Hope was moved by the words of the song. He lifted his head and lengthened his stride, suddenly not as fearful of the surrounding darkness. It had the same effect on Pu-pa, and the two elephants plunged deeper into the mountain.

After they had walked a distance, Hope turned to Pu-pa, (or at least he thought he did; it was hard to be sure in the dark), and asked him, 'Where did you hear that song?'

'In my ears,' replied Pu-pa matter-of-factly.

'I beg your pardon?' queried Hope.

'In my ears,' repeated Pu-pa firmly. 'I'm pretty sure that's where I hear everything. Why? Do you hear things in your trunk, or perhaps your tail?'

'My mistake,' conceded Hope. 'What I meant to ask was, where did you first hear that song?'

'In my ears,' answered Pu-pa cheerfully.

'………..?' was about all Hope could think of to say. He had never heard the song before, yet it seemed somehow familiar, as if it was buried deep in his mind as some long forgotten memory.

The elephants continued on for a while, Hope remaining silent while Pu-pa whistled cheerfully. Hope didn't say anything, but he was becoming worried that this cave was going on forever, and they would never get to the top of the mountain before morning.

Neither he nor Pu-pa had thought of this before they had stepped into the cave. They had simply seen an opportunity for discovering something new, and taken it. Now Hope was having second thoughts, and was about to voice these to Pu-pa, when another voice interrupted.

'What's all this noise abou' then, hey?' asked the voice firmly. It was a small, fussy kind of voice, but it made Hope and Pu-pa stop dead in their tracks, their backs stiffening. Pu-pa immediately stopped whistling and Hope held his breath.

'Well?' demanded the voice, echoing from wall to wall and back again, making it impossible to pinpoint its source. 'What do you mean by trampling' through someone's home, singin' an' whistlin' at the top o' your voices. Don' you know that any sound that gets loose down here travels roun' an' roun' through all the differin' tunnels lookin' fer a ways out? Sometimes it takes days 'til it finds one you know. Quite a maze it is down 'ere. Very easy to get lost.'

'I think we already are,' said Hope quietly, almost to himself. He realised that they had no idea where they were going, or even where they had come from.

'Who are you?' slipped in Pu-pa, wholly unconcerned as to whether they were lost or not. 'Oh, and also; *where* exactly are you?' he added. 'You see, we can't see a thing down here, so for all we know, you could simply be a voice in our heads. Although,' he continued, 'if you think about it, no matter how a voice starts out, by the time it travels over to you and goes in through your ears, it always ends up as a voice in your head, doesn't it?'

This worried Hope. He hadn't considered the fact that the voice might in fact be inside their heads, but it was a prospect that didn't appeal to him; but then again neither did the idea that the voice belonged to something much more solid that might be standing right behind him. Right now. Lurking....watching...... waiting........Hope spun around on the spot as an uncontrolled shiver shot through his body and out his mouth as an unwanted 'uuehhh' sound.

'I'm righ' 'ere,' said the disembodied voice, answering Pu-pa's second question first, and wisely choosing to ignore the last. 'But knowin' tha' I'm righ' 'ere an' you're righ' there ain' gonna help any of us now is it, seein' as you two can' see where righ' here is, while I would see very well where righ' there is, excep' for the fact that I'm blind. So what I'm gonna do is walk forward 'til I bump into one o' ya, alrigh'?'

Hope wasn't all right with this at all. He leapt to behind where he thought Pu-pa would be standing, instead finding the hard wall of the cave with a dull thud and wondering if Pu-pa had turned himself into a rock again. His fears in that regard were quickly dispelled.

'Oh, stop, that tickles,' giggled Pu-pa in reaction to something soft, wet and pointy that was twitching against his ankle. It was a nose.

'There you are,' came the voice. 'Big fella aren' ya.'

'Well, yes. One of the biggest actually,' said Pupa proudly, adding enigmatically, 'though I'd be a lot bigger if the sky weren't so heavy.'

'Hmm, indeed,' answered the voice absent-mindedly. 'My name is Mole. That's wha' I am an' that's wha' I'm called. I created all of these 'ere caves an' can fin' my way around blindfolded, so to speak. You two wouldn' be the firs' tha' I've helped fin' their way ou'. That's why I kep' makin' the tunnels bigger an' bigger; so as foolish creatures wouldn' keep getting' stuck in 'em an' I wouldn' have to keep rescuin' 'em, but turns out gettin' stuck is only half the problem. Gettin' out is the other half.'

Hope and Pu-pa introduced themselves and explained how and why they wanted to get to the top of the mountain in time to see the giant sun throwing elephant. If it was in fact on the far side of this mountain and not the next. Or the next.

Mole set off, talking as he walked, and Hope and Pu-pa followed the sound of his voice through all the twists and turns of the labyrinth that led upwards through the heart of the mountain.

'I wouldn' know anythin' about the giant sun-throwin' elephan', what with being blind 'n' all,' offered Mole. 'Never even seen the sun 'ave I? Not sure I'd like to anyways. I've lived my whole life in

41

darkness; inside or out, it's all the same to me. Thing is, when everythin' is dark, then everythin' becomes light. No difference, you see? So you can 'ave your sun throwin' whatsit, I'll stick to wha' I knows. Darkness an' the coolness of underground; that's wha' I likes. But I'll take you to the overground, no harm in that. Not sure why you'd wan' to go to the top of this 'ere mountain though. Nothin' up there but monkeys and their monkey ways.'

'Monkeys?' queried Hope.

'Oh, I like monkeys,' joined Pu-pa. 'They like a good joke do monkeys.'

'Aye, they do indeed,' agreed Mole. 'Only trouble is, in the end, the only ones laughin' are them. Things 'ave changed 'round 'ere since they set up their little kingdom up there. An' not for the better, I might add. All the more reason to stay down here, I reckon. What goes on up there, stays up there. Don't bother me too much. So, I'll takes you up an' out; no harm in that, but then you'll be on your own. Agreed?'

'Agreed,' said Hope.

'Agreed,' said Pu-pa.

They were suddenly not so sure it was where they wanted to go at all, but there was no turning back. The tunnel had started to brighten, and they could see their exit from the underground. Or entrance to the overground, depending on how you looked at it.

Chapter Four
The wall

Hope and Pu-pa emerged from the dark tunnel into the dim light of the setting sun. They had reached the mountaintop, or somewhere close to it, before nightfall, and so things had worked out. So far!

Mole stopped just short of actually leaving the tunnel.

'Righ' then lads,' he called out. 'Just a little further up that way and you'll get to where it is you're wantin' to get to. Mind you keep an eye out for them monkey fellas though. Tricky lot, they are. 'Ave you stuffed in one of their little boxes if you're not careful, they will, an' there's not much else up 'ere 'cept monkeys these days, so you'll be pretty much on your ownsome.'

Mole turned and scurried off into his dark world, leaving the two anxious elephants to ponder over his departing words of warning.

'Good Luck,' they heard him call out just before he disappeared. They kind of wished he hadn't.

Hope and Pu-pa turned towards their goal. They could see the outline of the mountain peak silhouetted against the soft pink sky. *Just a little further*, they thought to themselves, and headed off. As they trudged up the final ascent, it occurred to both of them that the jungle up here was much quieter than down below. Admittedly, night was falling, and a lot of the animals would be turning in, but it seemed *too* quiet: *too* still.

Another thing that became more and more apparent the further they walked on, was that the trees seemed to grow less and less. There definitely seemed to be fewer trees than there should be, and as they drew closer to the top, the trees disappeared completely. Where exactly it was they had disappeared to became clear to the two elephants as they clambered over the final ridge.

There, on the mountaintop, was what appeared to be every tree that should have been growing below; only here, they weren't growing at all! They had been taken from their birthplaces, their homes, and they had been stripped and broken, they had been halved and quartered, and then they had been placed back into the ground, all squeezed together in one long line.

What Pu-pa and Hope were looking at was a wall, erected from all the trees that they had already noticed as missing. It was their first encounter with a wall, and they stared at it dumbfounded. They didn't understand the purpose of it. It seemed strange to them to take something from one place and move it to another, just to divide one side of the jungle from the next. That was the only purpose Hope and Pu-pa could see for it.

It was getting darker, and the two elephants wanted to solve this mystery before they settled down to await tomorrow's sunrise. They walked to the far end of the wall to see what was behind it, but found that at the end the wall simply turned left and continued on for a good distance. They followed it again, too perplexed to speak, but found that at the end it again took a left turn. They followed it to two more turns and found them selves back where they had started.

It was a great big square wall. Of that, Hope and Pu-pa were certain. Only one question remained. What was inside?

There was no question in their minds that the jungle was not responsible for this mystery. They knew the jungle, and this, despite being constructed of trees from the jungle, felt very much separate from it. It seemed absurd that there was a section of the jungle that was now closed off to them. The jungle surely belonged to everyone and everything in it.

Hope stood looking up at the monstrosity, thinking what he should do next. Pu-pa, on the other hand, went ahead and did it.

'Hey,' he yelled out, in a voice more authoritative than Hope expected. 'If there's anyone in there who can let us through this thing, I suggest you do so now, or else, after the count of three, I'll be coming through my own way.

'One…….Two……..'

As he said, 'Three,' and spread his ears out ready for the charge, a voice called out from behind the wall.

'Who is it?' and then, 'What do you want?'

'My name is Pu-pa,' he called back. 'My friend here is Hope. He is soon to be crowned king of all this land, so I would suggest letting us in this instant, or you will be forced to face his …….' Pu-pa looked at Hope, seeming to notice for the first time that Hope was still very young, and really quite small. '………fury,' he finished anyway.

There was much muttering and discussion on the other side. Just as Pu-pa lost his patience and took up his charging stance once again, a group of the, well, what once were trees, creaked and groaned in a way that Hope and Pu-pa had never heard before. It was a lifeless sound, so different to the sound normally produced by trees, which spoke of so many different things.

The section of wall swung back on itself, opening up a passage into its centre. Hope and Pu-pa stepped inside.

Immediately upon entering, a shiver ran through both elephants. The air around them seemed to be trying to whisper something in their ears. Hope felt that it was telling them to leave, and he had to fight every muscle in his body to convince them that this was indeed the direction in which he wanted to go. Once inside, the opening swung shut behind them with a frightening - or perhaps frightened - bang. The elephants swung around, but there was no one there. There was no one anywhere!

The moon was coming up, and in the dim light they could vaguely make out some shapes around them in the shadows, but they were lifeless shapes. They started toward one of these to get a closer look, when all of a sudden, out of the night sky, a large shadow rushed down on top of them. Or rather I should say it rushed down around them, because they found themselves surrounded by another wall. This one, however, was much smaller, and was constructed with bamboo. The bamboo was spaced apart, so they could still see outside. Not that they could see much anyway.

'What on earth is going on here?' Hope whispered, feeling that he should. 'What is this place?'

'Questions tomorrow,' came a voice from the darkness. 'Tonight you can rest, and in the morning our king will decide what fun we'll have with you two.'

'I think they're our first elephants,' added another invisible voice. 'The first that we've taken whole at least.'

'I believe you're right, brother,' agreed the first voice. 'The king will be pleased.' The voices retreated into the night, leaving Hope and Pu-pa alone and trapped inside the small bamboo cage.

'What should we do?' Hope asked anxiously, turning to Pu-pa, but Pu-pa was already laid out on the ground, snoring softly. Hope marvelled at how Pu-pa remained so relaxed and unconcerned, no matter what the circumstances. He laid down next to him as an enormous wave of exhaustion swept over him. Even still, it took him a long time to fall asleep. Where there should have been the sounds of frogs and crickets, owls and cicadas and all the creatures who saved their voices for the night time, there was instead complete silence, and it echoed around Hope louder than any sound ever could.

Eventually he did drift off , and he dreamed a new dream for the first time in months. He dreamed of being curled up asleep, back in his valley surrounded by his family while dreaming of adventures in far away lands.

Hope opened his eyes slowly the following morning. The light of the morning sun had slipped quietly through the gaps in the bamboo cage and gently nudged him awake. The events of the previous night, and the realisation that he had missed the sun coming up, all rushed together to the front of Hope's mind, causing him to jump to his feet much quicker than he should have.

'Pu-pa,' he called out as the blood rushed to his head. His head almost exploded as the rush of blood collided with the rush of memories, and his vision blurred. His knees wobbled slightly beneath him. His eyesight slowly settled into focus, initially on the grey mass standing beside him, which was of course Pu-pa.

'It's horrible,' breathed Pu-pa softly just as Hope's vision cleared. On Pu-Pa's face, Hope saw an expression he had never seen Pu-pa wear before. Not only was it not a smile, but it was an expression that threatened never to become a smile again. Ever!

Hope followed his line of sight and immediately his expression perfectly and unintentionally imitated Pu-pa's.

All around them, scattered across the enclosed courtyard inside the wall, were cages just like the one around them. There were big ones and small ones, some stacked one on top of the other, while some stood alone. One was even suspended in the air by vines attached to more of those lifeless trees that stood tall over them. Inside all of these cages was enclosed all of the life, all of the movement and all of the sounds that had been so noticeably absent from the jungle outside.

There were cobras and eagles and lizards of every kind. There were rabbits and squirrels and owls stacked on top of one another. There were small cages with beetles and scorpions and butterflies of every shape, size and colour, and there were bigger cages with rhinos and leopards and crocodiles baking in the sun.

There were creatures of every description, and in every cage they were slumped across the floor, or cowering in a corner, trying to hold onto the last shadows before the sun chased them all away. Some were partially squeezed through the gaps in the bamboo in abandoned attempts at escape, never bothering to pull themselves back in. It was the strangest and most disturbing sight ever to confront our two innocent prisoners.

All of the animals that Hope and Pu-pa were so familiar with from their time in the jungle now seemed so foreign to them. They were the same shapes, sizes and colours, but whatever normally filled them with such life and purpose was gone. There was only one cage that showed any sign of movement. It was the large one that hung in the air next to theirs. It constantly rocked back and forth and occasionally a low and fearsome growl spilled out from the sides of the cage and forced its way across the courtyard causing everything in its path to shrink away from it ever so slightly, whether they wanted to or not. Hope tried to get a glimpse of its occupant, but the cage was too high.

All attention was pulled from this as there was a sudden outburst of movement and sound. From every side and every corner dark shapes scurried, leaped and swung into view. They clambered down the walls and sailed over the top, clinging to vines. They somersaulted from the tops of cages, and poured out of other self-enclosed walls, which they were obviously free to come and go from at will. All the while, as they filled the area with an unrivalled display of acrobatics, they hooted and screeched in a perverse and sinister imitation of what Hope would have normally called laughter.

'Monkeys,' pronounced Pu-pa, though they were not exactly like monkeys Pu-pa had known before. For one thing, their fur seemed much thinner than Pu-pa remembered, and some seemed to be losing it altogether; and they moved, not with the playful, meaningless grace of monkeys he had seen before; but with a menacing purpose in every movement.

Pu-pa shivered.

Hope agreed.

The monkeys were spread throughout the courtyard now, and they surrounded the cages. Some of them appeared to be holding onto something in their curled up fists, and it was these that approached the cages first. The others looked on in expectation.

At every cage the same scene was repeated, with slight variations. The monkeys that approached the cages held out their fists and revealed what they had hidden in their palms. It was food. Some held grains, some had fruits of different kinds. Some presented leaves and grasses, and some held small creatures that wriggled and squirmed over and through their fingers. The food, which wasn't necessarily relevant to the animal within the cage, but selected completely at random, was delivered in different ways.

Some was thrown to the animals; some was thrown at them. Some was tied to different parts of the cages and some was left outside on the ground, often just out of reach of the animals inside. Some was held out, only to be snatched away if the animal ventured over to sniff, taste or reach out for the morsel. The reaction from the monkeys outside was the same no matter which scene they were watching. Laughter.

It wasn't the kind of laughter that spread out and infected anyone that it touched. This laughter excluded everyone and everything outside of it. It existed solely for the one who was laughing.

Hope and Pu-pa watched on in an air of increasing anger. An anger that threatened to burst the walls of their cage in every direction. But then silence fell from nowhere, and the monkeys all visibly stiffened. The only sound was the growling that still rocked the cage suspended above their heads. Its menace seemed to have increased.

From the centre of the courtyard a gap started to open up. The monkeys in that area all cowered away, their eyes cast to the ground, and into the gap stepped three more monkeys. The two on either side looked the same as all the rest, and they cowered just the same. They each carried a large bunch of bananas on their backs.

The monkey in the centre was different. He was bigger than the others, and he walked more upright. His coat was thick and the fur was pale, taking on an almost yellow appearance. His eyes were a clear icy blue.

Hope stared straight into those eyes as they approached, and felt a chill in the centre of his chest.

They made a direct path over to Hope and Pu-pa, and all the other monkeys fell in behind them, completely surrounding their cage. A large roar erupted from the cage above, and its unseen occupant must have thrown itself to one side, as the cage tilted violently down for a moment. It was the side closest to the large monkey, and he and every monkey there ducked instinctively away from it, their eyes shooting up nervously.

The pale monkey recovered his composure first, followed by the rest, then threw his head back and released a chilling, screeching laugh. The others joined in and the sound drowned out the roar from above. The cage tilted back up and resumed its gentle but insistent rocking back and forth.

The head monkey, for that is certainly what he appeared to be, glanced quickly upward once and then, seeming satisfied with this outcome, turned his attention back to Hope and Pu-pa.

'Well,' he addressed to Hope in a sincere voice that dripped with insincerity. 'This is a pleasant surprise. Not one, but two elephants. Quite a catch I would say, wouldn't you?' He reached his wiry arm towards Hope's face, his eyes drifting to some far away memory. 'Too young perhaps,' he muttered to himself, 'but they might grow in time.'

Snatching his arm back and snapping back into the present, Maad's face took on an expression of vague disinterest.

'So, I'm told that you are to be the new king of all this land, is that right?'

Hope stared back but remained silent.

'Not big on speeches I guess,' the monkey said over his shoulder to his horde behind him. A constrained ripple of laughter spread out, seeming unsure of the level of appreciation appropriate for this joke. 'Well, let me introduce myself,' he sneered, turning back to the two captive elephants. 'My name is Maad, and I am king of THIS here land.' He spread his arms out indicating all that was inside of those walls.

He continued. 'And it would seem that so long as you are within these walls, then you shall be under *my* rule: and given that my…*our*...intention is to move these walls outwards in a never ending expansion of my kingdom, it would appear only a matter of time before EVERYTHING is under my……*our*…control.' Maad's lips curled back to reveal large canine fangs dripping with saliva.

'However,' he went on, 'it would be terribly rude of me not show a noble one such as yourself our warmest hospitality.'

A look of utmost warmth came over his face, masking his genuine expression of disgust and contempt. He held out his hand to the monkey holding the bananas next to him. The monkey picked a banana from the bunch and placed it nervously on Maad's palm. Maad held the banana up and slowly peeled back each corner of skin. He popped the banana in his mouth with a look of utmost pleasure, and then flicked the empty peel into the cage. It landed at the feet of Hope and Pu-pa.

Hope glowered. Pu-pa stared at the ground.

Maad held out his hand again and repeated the process.

'These are our very best banana peels,' said Maad in mock indignation, 'It will do your reputation no good to refuse our generosity.'

All the monkeys howled with laughter. They jumped up and down on the tops of the other cages. They did back-flips and handstands, and beat their chests in a rousing display of appreciation. One leapt up in excitement and grabbed the underside of the suspended cage before remembering what was in there, letting go with a frightened yelp. The cage growled in return.

Maad repeated the performance again, and looked set to go through both bunches of bananas in this manner, when something extraordinary happened.

Hope heard Pu-pa say something like, 'Right. That's enough of that', but he only really heard it later, when he was thinking back on it. At the time Hope's brain didn't register it at all because it really didn't seem to be the right thing at all to say at that particular moment.

But it was!

'Right. That's enough of that,' said Pu-pa, and he took three steps forward. The thing about that is, he only had room inside the cage for two steps. The third step took him outside. He had passed straight through the bamboo bars. Now, when I say straight through, I'm not talking about some kind of magic. You see, those bars had enough respect and good sense to bend, break, splinter and shatter in a way that left a nice hole for Pu-pa to pass through.

Hope watched on in awe. He had momentarily forgotten how powerful an elephant could be. *He* was an elephant. He followed, though not through the hole already made by Pu-pa. Instead he made his own, smaller hole right beside it.

Pu-pa moved straight towards Maad, whose mouth had fallen open, a half eaten banana hanging limply from one of his teeth. The peel fell pathetically to the ground in front of him.

In the blink of an eye, the entire troop of monkeys, apart from Maad, transformed themselves from a leering mob into a perfect display of how not to act in a crisis. Screaming and squealing monkeys scattered in all known directions, and even made up a few of their own. They tumbled and flew over the cages, over the walls, and over each other. They bumped and collided, and scratched and clawed one another. Some of them cowered in any shadows they could find, mumbling about how they always knew it was all going to end badly.

Pu-pa was now almost on top of Maad, who had not moved a single muscle. He seemed entirely unable to understand what had happened: what was *happening*!!

Pu-pa continued forwards until he was literally head to head with Maad. They stared into each others eyes. Maad's gaze had lost all of its cool now. Pu-pa kept edging forward, and Maad folded backwards, given no choice in the matter, until he was completely flat on his back. Pu-pa stood directly over him, his trunk resting lightly on Maad's chest. I say lightly, but its strength was still enough to pin Maad hard against the ground. Then, Pu-pa stopped.

He stood perfectly still, like a statue, holding Maad in place, staring straight through him to the ground below. Maad didn't move a muscle. His mouth was still hanging open, the piece of banana still dangling from it. To Hope, they looked like a moment in history that had been frozen; captured and pulled out of the flowing river of time, to be observed by all of the future generations of the jungle.

Hope shook his head to break the spell. He had to do something. He walked over to one of the cages. There was a squirrel inside, curled up in a corner, eyes open but seeing nothing. Hope was reminded of the two squirrels he had met earlier. They were so lively and full of fun, it was hard to believe this was the same animal. He opened the cage. The squirrel remained motionless so Hope shook the cage gently. Nothing. He reached inside and pulled the squirrel lightly out of the cage by its tail and held it in front of himself.

'Boo,' said Hope quietly.

The squirrel snapped to attention instantly. It looked at Hope for the first time and seemed to immediately realise what was going on. It began chirping. It chirped at the top of its little voice. It chirped with complete and utter joy and abandon. He placed the squirrel on the ground, and it was up and over the wall before Hope even had the chance to smile. He did anyway.

The effect of this spread throughout the compound. All of the animals sprang to life. They hissed and roared, and fluttered and scratched in their cages. This spurred Hope into action.

He charged from cage to cage, not even bothering to open them, but instead smashing holes in them with a swing of his trunk. He roared and trumpeted as he did this, and soon the entire place was alive with sound and movement. The surrounding jungle was for one moment alive in that one confined area before it flew, jumped, crawled and slithered back to where it belonged.

Silence crept in once again.

Pu-pa and Maad were still locked in their pose. They hadn't even blinked. Even the hanging cage had stopped rocking and fallen completely silent. It was waiting.

It was to this that Hope turned his attention.

Chapter Six
The cage

The cage was motionless, and if he hadn't seen it rock, and earlier heard it growl, Hope would have assumed it was empty; but he knew it wasn't. He could feel a presence throbbing inside it. There was a length of vine stretching from the top of the cage down to the ground.

That must be the way to lower it, thought Hope. He grabbed the vine in his trunk and started twisting it round and around. The vine tensed and stretched in Hope's trunk until it reached a point were it simply couldn't stretch anymore.

It snapped.

The sound echoed inside the walls. Maad, who had remained motionless under the weight of Pu-pa's trunk, swivelled his eyes in the direction of the sound.

'NO,' he squeezed from his pressed lungs.

Hope turned to Maad. Pu-pa gently but forcefully increased the pressure in his trunk. The vine was still wrapped around Hope's trunk; the cage suspended from it remained still. Hope chose to ignore Maad's plea and raised his trunk up, causing the cage to lower itself. It hung just above the ground. Hope released the vine, and the cage landed with a dull thud, raising a cloud of dust from the ground below. The dust momentarily obscured the view inside the cage.

Hope watched and waited. Maad stared wide-eyed, holding his breath. Pu-pa simply stood over Maad and continued to stare straight through him.

The dust settled, and inside the cage Hope saw the most beautiful, awe inspiring and fearsome animal that he had ever seen. A barely audible wheeze escaped from Maad's throat and fell lifeless in the dust.

The animal prowling from end to end inside the cage was a tiger. It was huge; almost as tall as Hope. Its mouth was held half open revealing a set of teeth that were as sharp as they were long and they *were* long. Barely contained within the tiger's jaw, they stood in a row like palace guards with spears raised, and you could be sure that nothing got past them without being thoroughly checked over and examined first.

The tiger's eyes were ablaze. They glowed red in the sun, divided down the middle by dark slits that contained a depth that threatened to engulf anything that looked into them for too long.

Hope's eyes moved along quickly and fell on the tiger's most astonishing feature; its fur. The tiger's coat was the purest of whites that Hope had ever seen. Broken only by some narrow stripes of black along its back, the white fur stretched from the end of its nose to the end of its tail. It was breathtaking.

Hope remembered to breathe again.

He was captivated by the stunning creature, and he really wasn't sure if he wanted to release it. He knew he should, and that he would, but he hesitated. That's when he noticed another figure inside the cage. It was another monkey.

The monkey was sitting against the back wall, its

head slumped against its chest. His chest was slowly rising and falling, so Hope knew the monkey was still alive, and something told him that this monkey was different to the others. For one thing, it had all of its fur, and its fur was completely white, like the tiger, only not so pure. It seemed to be more from old age, and held streaks of grey throughout.

Hope sprung into action again. He pulled the bamboo bars off one by one until there was a hole big enough for him to step inside. The tiger watched and waited patiently. The monkey never moved. When the hole was big enough, Hope stepped back.

The tiger moved. It moved with such grace and power in each step, such agility and potential violence in each sway of its back, that Hope could only look on in admiration.

And a little bit of concern, if he was honest about it.

The tiger moved toward Pu-pa and Maad. It stopped short, and seemed to be deciding on something. Its eyes were locked on Maad's, and Maad seemed to be struggling with all the energy he had left to turn his gaze away. He couldn't.

Flames danced in the tiger's eyes and were reflected in the icy blue pools of Maad's. The tiger bared its teeth, stretched its jaws wide; and roared.

I mean; it ROARED!!

Everything shook. The air throbbed. Cages that were still loosely held together rattled and collapsed. Hope's legs vibrated in rhythm with the air around them and then gave up altogether. He sat down. The old monkey lifted his head and seemed to recognise the world around him for the first time in a long time. Pu-pa appeared to ripple slightly, but remained in position. Hope wondered if Pu-pa had become a rock again. Maad, for his part, rolled his eyes back into his head and went completely limp. He had fainted.

The tiger's roar finished and a cool wind swept in to take its place. The tiger seemed to be pondering what it would do next. It made its decision.

It turned swiftly, glanced once at Hope, who had to turn his eyes to the ground, and then, in a single leap, it was over the wall and disappeared swiftly and silently into the jungle.

'You're welcome,' said Hope to the cool breeze that followed the tiger over the wall.

He smiled to himself.

Chapter Seven
Temi's story

The old monkey had come around, and had slowly and very stiffly raised himself. Hope went inside and helped him out of the cage.

'Thank you,' he said in a cracking voice that seemed to hold the weariness of the world within it. Hope bowed in return, feeling that it was appropriate. The monkey's body was bent and twisted, and his eyes were dulled by a sadness that Hope found difficult to look at.

'You don't realise what a thing you have done here today. For me, for all of the animals; and for yourselves. If you will indulge an old monkey, I would like to explain, though my story is a long and sad one. I would like to tell it so it will be remembered and retold, and hopefully help to stop the same thing from happening again.'

Pu-pa had left Maad unconscious on the ground and joined Hope to listen to the tale. The scattered monkeys peered over the rubble of the cages, and they too crept a little closer to listen.

But not too close.

The old monkey cleared his throat and began. This is his story.

'My name is Temi. I am as old as memory itself, and that's where my story begins. At that time, I was the leader of all monkeys, although there is not one amongst them now who was born at that time. We lived happily in the jungle and, except for when we had to search for food, we spent our time in play. We swung from the treetops and hung from the vines. We swam in the rivers and leapt from the waterfalls. It was a good life and we never wanted for more than that. We lived like that for a long time, and even though I was their leader, I spent my days in the same way as all the rest.

'One night, a ferocious storm blew through the jungle. We were shaken from our treetops and scattered all over the jungle floor. Branches broke in the wind and rained down on top of us. Our lives were turned upside down overnight and we were left homeless, frightened and confused. Some monkeys started to whisper of a curse. "We have been punished for spending our days in idle play," they said. The whispers spread, and soon many believed it.

'I tried to calm them and tell them that it was only a superstition; that there was no curse. "Who is it that has punished us?" I asked, but they wouldn't listen. They said that as their leader I should have protected them.

'I was cast out, and sent to live alone in the forest, but I still watched over them, unseen in the trees.

'They never returned to the treetops, and took to living on the ground. They were without the safety of the tall trees, and so they decided to live inside them. At first, they simply found trees with hollow trunks, but soon they ran out of these, so they started to hollow them out themselves. They used pointed rocks that they found on the riverbed, to scrape the flesh from the trees.

'They became serious, and worked day and night. They became clever and found that scraping one rock against another, harder rock, could make them sharper. They tore the hearts out of countless trees, and some of the trees died under the assault. When these dead trees toppled, they soon had the idea of cutting them up with their sharpened stones and replanting the pieces around themselves, in miniature versions of the wall you see around us now. They divided themselves into small groups, each within their own walls.

'I watched from the treetops as the years passed, a great sadness growing in me that threatened to pull me to the ground under its weight. They never stopped working. They were determined not to be idle again, and soon the whole area was stripped of trees. Then a new curse befell them.

'Babies started to be born with large patches of fur missing. Some were almost completely bald. The monkeys wailed and moaned and threw their heads back to the sky, as if an answer might be forthcoming from somewhere up there.

'The sky remained silent.

'They decided that they hadn't worked hard enough, and so they set about building a wall so big they would be able to completely shut out the outside world, and they could remain safe within. The wall took many, many years to finish. It was almost completed a number of times, but then they would tear it down for being too small, or too short. They didn't seem to want to finish it. It kept them occupied.

'It was around this time that a baby was born; a

remarkable baby. For one, it was the first in a long time that was born with all of its fur, but that wasn't all. Its fur was a golden yellow, and its eyes, a crystal blue.

'No one had ever seen a monkey like it before. No one, except me.

'When I was young, still clinging to my mother's back, there had been a monkey just like this one. He disappeared when I was still an infant, but his appearance had sparked the first upheaval in the jungle, and this one was to do the same.

'The monkeys took it to be a sign that the curse had been lifted, that their endeavours had paid off. They rejoiced. They finished the wall and shut themselves inside. Their pride swelled at their achievements. I remained in the treetops, watching. My hair was turning grey, my body bending under the weight of sorrow and time. I watched the pale young monkey as he grew. I didn't share the other monkey's opinion of him. He made me feel a great unease.

'They named him Maad.'

Hope and Pu-pa's eyes turned to the limp body of Maad next to them. Temi's eyes remained on the ground in front of him as he continued his story.

'The monkeys had finished their wall now and lifted the curse. They were left with the problem of what to do next. They had forgotten all of the old ways, and life inside the walls became stale and dull. It was Maad, who was reaching maturity by that stage, who came up with the idea. The monkeys were constantly reminded of the free and joyful life of the jungle outside. They could hear the animals playing all around them.

'Maad decided to bring the jungle inside.

'Under his command now, they set about building these cages, and then they took off outside, armed with traps and snares. In the beginning only the bravest monkeys would dare to step outside the walls, and even then they would only remain outside for short periods. Despite this, everyday they returned with more and more animals that they locked in the cages.

'The monkeys took delight in observing all the different creatures, and soon there was silence in all the surrounding jungle. All of those sounds became trapped in here. Soon, the sound disappeared from here too.

'Things became worse.

'The monkeys were bored, and so they invented new ways of entertaining themselves. Spurred on by Maad, they started to tease and taunt the poor animals. They made them do awful things that I will never speak of; all for their own amusement. They had forgotten the simple pleasures of their former life, and so had to invent these new and horrible ones.

'I couldn't watch any more. I had spent many generations observing from above. My hair was almost completely white, and I knew my time was short. I came down from the trees and allowed myself to be captured by their trappers.

'They brought me before Maad. He seemed curious of me. I told him this same story; tried to make him see how things had gone wrong. He listened, seemed almost interested, but when I finished, he just laughed that horrible laugh. He knocked me to the ground and two monkeys dragged me to this cage.

'I was left in here for weeks. When another monkey came to bring me food or water, I would try to convince them of the error of their ways. Most refused to listen, but one or two seemed moved.

'Maad must have noticed this, and he ordered that the cage be lifted off the ground and food thrown up to me. I only had rainwater to quench my thirst. I stopped eating. They stopped bringing food. I stayed like this for days.

'One night, the cage was lowered. There was the sound of a great struggle, and a large shape, wrapped in vines, was dragged to the cage by too many monkeys to count.

'It was the tiger. Her name is Queen Freassel. She was thrown in with me, and the cage was snapped shut and quickly pulled up. I think Maad had hoped that I would become her dinner, because he never sent any food for her. I would say that he also wanted to weaken her, as I suspect he was greatly fearful of her power.

'We were in there together for three nights before you arrived, and apart from giving me her name, she said nothing. She just prowled back and forth, waiting for her time. She never seemed to waiver for one moment in her belief that she would get out and, I imagine, get her revenge.

'I stayed sitting on one side. I never took my eyes off her. She was the most beautiful animal I ever saw in so many years in this jungle. Last night though, my eyes dropped. My spirit was fading. I heard your arrival, and all the events after, but they were in the distance, as if I were already some place far away. It was only when the Queen roared that I was jerked back by an invisible thread to the here and now.

'And so, that is my story.'

These last words floated from Temi's lips on a long and gentle breath that continued on past Hope and Pu-pa and out into the jungle. The breath never returned.

Temi sat motionless, eyes to the ground, his spirit already chasing that last breath through the treetops. Tears rolled down Hope and Pu-pa's cheeks.

All the monkeys had come out of their hiding places, and some also had tears in their eyes. They had listened intently to Temi's tragic story, and they looked now as if they had woken from a dream. They surrounded the two elephants. One stepped forward and approached Hope.

'Please, Your Highness, ' he said. 'Please forgive us. Show us the old ways. Show us how to live the way we once did.'

Hope was embarrassed.

'Please don't call me Your Highness. I am not a king yet. As for showing you the old ways, I'm not sure I know how. And besides, I really need to be getting to the next mountain before tomorrow's sunrise.'

They looked disappointed. They were lost and totally unsure of what to do next.

'I'll do it,' said Pu-pa suddenly.

'What?' said Hope.

'Sure,' Pu-pa went on. 'It sounds like just my kind of thing; teaching monkeys how to have fun, and I'm sure they can teach me a thing or two.'

Hope smiled. It seemed right. 'Well then,' he said.

'I should really get going if I'm going to make it in time.'

The sun was already climbing to its peak.

'We might be able to help you there,' said one of the monkeys to Hope. 'Follow me.' The monkey started off into the jungle. Before following, Hope looked to Pu-pa.

'If I'm ever feeling down or bored, and I need you to cheer me up, how will I find you?' he asked. ' I mean, how will I know if you're an elephant, a rock, or even a shooting star.'

'You'll find me,' replied Pu-pa. 'Or I will find you.'

Hope smiled and turned to follow the monkey. As he headed into the jungle he heard Pu-pa's voice behind him.

'What do you mean impossible? Nothing's impossible, because if it was, then…….'

Hope laughed to himself. He caught up to the monkey at the edge of the mountaintop. He was standing beside another large cage. There was a vine attached to a tree behind it, that then passed through the top of the cage and off into the distance towards the other mountain.

'It will take you to the next mountain very quickly,' said the monkey.

'Great,' said Hope, already climbing inside the cage. 'Thank you.'

'No, thank you,' replied the monkey, and he lifted the stone that held the cage in place.

The cage moved off.

'One more thing,' called out the monkey. 'When you reach the other side, smash the cage to pieces.'

Hope nodded in reply.

The cage picked up speed, and soon the mountain behind him pulled away into the distance. Hope turned to face his new destination. The next mountain was approaching very quickly.

Perhaps too quickly, thought Hope.

PART TWO

Chapter One
Coming in to land

Hope was approaching the mountain in the bamboo cage at an incredible speed, just the way he liked it. What he didn't like was the speed at which the mountain was approaching him!

There was going to be a terrible collision, and there was nothing he could do about it. He had considered jumping, but he was too far above the ground. Even toward the end of the vine it was not an option, because the vine disappeared into a group of trees, hiding the safety of the ground from view. He would have to take his chances in the cage.

Hope planted all four feet against the cage floor and held his ears out. He lowered his head as if he was in fact charging at the mountain.

In his mind, that was exactly what he was doing.

This was it! The mountain was upon him now, filling his whole vision. The cage followed the vine through the group of trees. Hope kept his eyes open, but things were moving so fast that all he saw was a blur. Streaks of green flashed past. He could hear branches snapping against the side of the cage, rocking it from side to side, but it continued surging forward; perhaps even picking up speed. Tears streamed from his eyes as they met the on-rushing air. He saw a white bird in clear focus directly in front of him for a split second before it ducked to one side with amazing agility, transforming itself into a white smear down one side of the green sheets that whizzed past on either side, before flying away once again into the distance. Spots of grey appeared, speckled amongst the green blur as the trees thinned. They grew more and more prominent until, suddenly, there was only grey.

The cage shot out of the trees, and directly at a jagged outcrop of rocks. There was only enough time until the cage smashed into the rocks for Hope to say; 'Oh!......Rocks,' and then …….. nothing!

Well, of course, I don't exactly mean nothing. But it certainly wasn't the very messy and possibly very painful meeting of rock and elephant that it had promised to be. Instead, just as Hope was preparing himself for a very brief but memorable introduction to the large rock in front of him, the cage jolted to a halt. It stopped so abruptly that it swung forward and knocked lightly against the large and menacing looking rock.

What had happened was very simple. The vine was tied at the end around the jagged rocks, and a little back from this, it had been tied into a large knot so that the cage couldn't pass over it. This stopped the cage just before it became a pretty decoration on the mountainside.

'Those clever little monkeys,' smiled Hope to himself, but then he remembered how that cleverness had been used, and why that cage had been built at all.

He stepped out of the cage, which now suspended only inches above the ground, and in an incredible display of strength that surprised even himself, Hope tore the cage from the vine above and hurled it down the mountainside. It smashed into so many different pieces you could never have guessed what it once was. In time the jungle would swallow any evidence that it ever existed.

Hope turned to the mountain. He had been dropped off about halfway up and so had saved a lot of time. Now he just had to find a way to get to the top. In this, the mountain turned out to be of very little help. All it offered was a steep climb up and over the rocks. The only other option was to head back down. For Hope, as I'm sure you would have guessed, this was not an option at all.

He started the climb, muttering to himself about how the last mountain was much more helpful and friendly.

The mountain mumbled something back about how it was impossible to please everyone, and if he wanted to get to the top, he should just use the path on the other side like everyone else.

Hope didn't hear. He was too focused on his own problems, and he had started to think once again of the giant sun throwing elephant. He thought of what might happen if for some reason the giant sun throwing elephant had trouble finding the sun one night. Would there be no morning at all?

Maybe they would all just keep sleeping and the night animals would rule the jungle forever. The jungle would eventually grow over all the sleeping animals, and soon enough, everyone would forget that they had ever been there. They would forget that there had ever been a daytime. One night, a curious owl would head out on a journey to find the giant moon carrying owl, which Hope reasoned must be the way the moon sailed through the sky at night. In time, the owl would come to this mountain in their search and would find Hope sleeping on the rocks, where nothing could grow over him. The owl, being curious what this strange animal was, would wake Hope up. Together, they would go and help the giant sun throwing elephant find the missing sun. With their help they would find it quickly, and sunlight would return once more to the land. Hope would uncover all of the sleeping animals who would once more be waking. For them, it would only be the next day, and only Hope would know the truth of how he had rescued the land from the never ending night.

Yes, thought Hope, *that's exactly what would happen*. He felt proud of himself, even though he had only imagined the whole thing. Boosted by his imaginary heroics he reached the top in no time.

The top of the rocks that is, not the top of the mountain.

Things are never that easy!!

Chapter Two
The jungle fight

Hope stepped over the last of the rocks and his feet once more rested on soft grass and earth. That was much more to his liking, but the way that presented itself was much less so. The jungle that loomed up before him was thicker and less inviting than any jungle that Hope had ever come across. The trees were all crowded in on each other, their highest branches a tangled web of limbs, jostling each other for what little space and sunlight they could find. Amongst it all, small animals and birds scurried and fluttered out of view whenever Hope's eyes came upon them. Beneath it the tree trunks shot down to the ground and seemed to stab themselves into the mountainside. The bark was smooth and dark, offering no easy means of climbing up.

Not that Hope had any intention of doing so, of course, but he was used to trees that said, 'come on up,' whereas these seemed to say; 'stay right where you are, thank you very much.'

The undergrowth that spread itself beneath was no different. It was a thick wall of vines and ivy and brambles that poked you with their sharp thorns if you were silly enough to think that they would graciously allow you to pass.

Hope took all of this in, and a voice from

somewhere deep inside his head said, "Don't be a fool. You've had your fun and adventure already. Now it's time to go home to the comfort and safety of your family." It was a voice Hope knew well. It was his voice of reason; the voice that always told him what was the sensible thing to do. Hope had never listened to that voice before, and he saw no reason to start now. 'Well,' he boomed at the jungle in his most commanding voice. 'If you won't invite me in, then I shall just have to invite myself.' With a mighty roar worthy of any king, Hope charged straight into the undergrowth.

'Well, well,' replied the dense jungle, 'if it's a fight you want, then it's a fight you shall get,' and it pulled itself tighter into the area that Hope was charging through. Unfortunately, Hope wasn't paying attention. He was full of confidence after all of his adventures and all the obstacles he had overcome. He had burst through plenty of jungle before, so why should this be any different. At least that's what he thought.

He was wrong!

Hope tore through the jungles first line of defence. Vines that hung across his path stretched and snapped against his sheer weight and momentum. Thorny brambles reached out to try and get a grip on his thick hide, but were brushed aside by the little elephants strength and determination. The tall trees watched passively as he charged past, only occasionally stretching out a branch to block his way, which Hope would dispose of swiftly with a swing of his trunk. He was progressing impressively. He thought that he must have worked his way through the worst of it by now, and it would soon get easier.

That's exactly what the jungle wanted him to think. Hope had been allowed to get this far, and now he was in so deep there was no option of going back. The jungle crept in closer around him.

Hope continued to press on, but he was growing tired. The effort of bursting through all those thick vines had worn him down. The brambles with their needle sharp thorns hadn't stopped him, but they had left him covered in scratches, and even though the blanket canopy of twisted and tangled treetops stopped most of the heat of the midday sun reaching the ground, it was still very warm. All of this was pressing on Hope, and he started to slow down. At the same time, the jungle's attack became more serious.

A length of vine laying across his path became entangled around Hope's front ankle. His leg was pulled backwards and he stumbled to his knees. Without coming to a stop, he regained his footing, snapped the vine with a violent tug of his leg, and continued charging forward. But he was staggering a little.

He burst through an innocent looking bush covered in large, soft leaves; but the leaves were hiding something more sinister. Hope passed through its gentle exterior and immediately let out a startled and pained scream. The bush's central stem was armed with rows of spiky protrusions about two inches long. When he came out the other side he looked like a hedgehog who had gotten dressed in a hurry and put its spikes on the wrong way around. He was all out of energy and in a lot of pain, but he let out a defiant roar that shook the jungle and made it think twice about what it was doing.

Hope made one last charge using all his remaining energy; and a little extra he borrowed from some place else. His little legs were almost a blur as they propelled him forward. His eyes strained to see through the thickness, unblinking and focused on his destination. He didn't even see the branches and vines, the bushes and brambles, or even the small and sometimes large creatures that broke, tore, scrambled and flew from his onslaught.

The jungle was reeling. It was on the back foot. Hope had regained his momentum and, together with his anger at the ill treatment he was receiving, he felt that nothing could stop him now. He could see small strips of sunlight squeezing through the gaps in the trees ahead. He was almost there. He smiled to himself, and his eyes softened, the anger and determination no longer necessary - but he wasn't there yet.

Hope had lost his focus. A large tree shifted ever so slightly sideways just as Hope ran past. He didn't even notice until it had already happened. The tree glanced off Hope's shoulder. It wasn't a big bump, but it was enough to send Hope a few feet sideways. The thing about that is, a few feet sideways was the same as saying, "down a slippery slope," because that's what lay a few feet to Hope's side, and the tree had known it.

Hope started sliding down the embankment. It was wet and muddy, and Hope couldn't get a grip with his feet. He was picking up speed. In a last ditch attempt to stop the downhill slide, he planted his two front feet as hard as he could in front of himself. This had the effect of stopping his front legs exactly where they were. Unfortunately, the rest of his body didn't agree, and continued on. Hope was catapulted into the air and he really had to wonder where all this was going to end.

He didn't have to wonder for long!

Stretched between two trees, as if for this very purpose, was a large, thick web woven of ivy. Hope flew straight into the middle and was immediately engulfed, wrapped, swallowed, tangled, trapped, tied; whatever word you want to use – he was stuck!!

The jungle fell silent, waiting for applause, or at least some acknowledgement for a job well done. Getting none, it turned its attention back to Hope, grumbling about how one day it would trap the whole world and then everyone and everything would have to show their respect; or it would never let them go again.

Chapter Three
The dream?

The ivy had wrapped itself so completely around Hope he could not move. He kicked and squirmed and pulled against it, but that only made it tighten its grip, and Hope's final store of energy was spent. His body slumped inside the trap.

This is it, thought Hope. *I'll never be able to get out of this myself, and there's no one around to help.* He thought of Pu-pa and how if he were here he would no doubt tear the ivy into hundreds of little pieces and release Hope from its clutches. Either that or he would stand there laughing.

But Pu-pa was a long way away, and Hope's family even further. He was alone and for the first time since he set out he seriously doubted whether he had done the right thing.

The sun was still high in the sky, but was about to begin its descent. Even if Hope somehow found himself free now he might not make it to the top in time to see the giant sun throwing elephant: if there even was such a thing. Nobody that Hope had spoken to had seen, or even heard of it.

Hope had felt so sure when he started his journey that it was something that he had to do. He knew in his heart that the giant sun throwing elephant was real and his journey wouldn't end until he found it. Unless of course his journey ended right here and he was swallowed up by the jungle and never seen or heard from again.

He shivered.

The seriousness of the situation struck Hope. All of a sudden the jungle seemed darker, more threatening. The ivy that gripped him seemed to constrict tighter and Hope felt he was being strangled. His breath quickened and his heart was beating fast. Eyes peered at him from unseen faces hidden in the shadows of the thick jungle. He heard the sound of scrambling creatures scurrying around him, as if trying to get a better look at the proud future king's premature demise.

'I've gotta get myself out of here,' gasped Hope to himself, and anyone who was listening. 'Now!!!!'

He summoned all his remaining strength. He forced his shoulders apart and the ivy strained against his might. He pushed his head forwards, the muscles in his neck bulging with the effort. His eyes were clenched tight in concentration. Every muscle in his body was expanding outwards in opposition to the green netting that had enveloped him. He heard the twang of the ivy starting to break. He pushed harder and started to thrash about, as much as his confinement allowed. The ivy started to give. It popped and twanged all around him and he felt its grip slacken. He regained some of his movement, and he used it to increase the ferocity of his attack. His body kicked and trashed in every direction while he flung his head and trunk side to side with great force. He finished with a great blast from his trunk and came to a complete rest. With such a display of ferocity you might imagine that the ivy would be a tattered mess around his feet, but it was not so. He had wounded it greatly, and indeed, a lot of it was in tatters around him, but the rest had simply rearranged itself around Hope. He was still stuck. There was simply too much of it, and he had to give up. He had nothing left to fight with.

Hope stood limp in the web, suspended by the ivy wrapped tight around his body, like a lifeless puppet waiting for someone to pull the strings and bring him back to life. Indeed, if it wasn't for the ivy holding him up Hope would have slumped to the ground and fallen into a deep sleep. Even in his present predicament, his eyes grew heavy and his lids started to fall.

It seemed strange to him that he should be falling asleep when he was in such a vulnerable position, and he fought to keep his eyes open, but his brain was already on its way into a dream, and it wasn't waiting for his eyes to catch up.

This left Hope in the very strange situation of being in a dream while his eyes were still open, even if only slightly. The effect was that Hope was left staring at his surroundings, while his brain, just for its own amusement it would seem, would add strange and random images to what Hope was seeing.

This is what he saw.

The trees around Hope loomed closer over him, their branches stretched wide as if they meant to snatch him up. Dark shapes scurried from tree to tree, their eyes unblinking and glowing red. The light faded and everything became different shades of grey. Hope was terrified. He didn't know if he was awake or dreaming.

He was paralysed with fear and, even without the ivy trap, he couldn't have moved at that moment no matter how hard he tried.

A large black shadow emerged from the half-light to Hope's left. He couldn't actually see it, but he could sense it. Its presence filled him with dread. He couldn't turn his head to look directly at it - he wasn't sure he wanted to anyway - but he could feel it bearing down on him. It was directly over his shoulder now. He imagined he could feel its hot breath on his neck. His heart was racing. The trees bent menacingly closer. The grey darkened and Hope felt he was being smothered by the jungle and, more than that - by his fear.

He had stopped breathing.

His heart pounded in his chest.

The dark shadow floated over Hope and enveloped him. His blood turned cold and his heart seemed to leap from his chest to his head and start pounding on his ears as if it meant to burst from his head and run screaming into the jungle.

He held his breath.

He could feel the presence of the dark shadow crawling over his skin and his hairs stood up in response. His eyes were threatening to leap from his head in the hope that they might see through the darkness to the comforting sunlight that had been there only moments before. The moon appeared from nowhere in the sky just above the trees and as Hope watched on, it split itself into two smaller moons. They stared down on Hope; two eyes in the sky looking on the world for the first time.

Hope continued to hold his breath.

As suddenly as they had appeared, the two moons disappeared and reappeared once more, and to Hope it was as if the sky had blinked, only now the two moons had changed to a piercing blue hue, and they slowly grew larger in the dark sky.

In fact, they were not growing larger at all; they were plummeting straight at him. Every muscle in his body tensed, if they hadn't already done so. The dark shadow had replaced the ivy as Hope's captor. He could feel it sinking into his bones, into his veins, and he felt its coldness becoming a part of him.

The two crystal blue orbs now covered almost the entire sky, and Hope couldn't pull his gaze away from them. They paused their descent and hung in the air for a moment, taking everything in and then, in a flash, they plunged over Hope, merging back into one complete, frozen blue light that engulfed him; that swallowed the entire jungle. Hope was simply surrounded by the light. Everything else vanished, except the dark shadow that now seemed to fill Hope's body more than Hope himself did. His heart slowed almost to a stop, the blood in his veins froze and Hope at last let the breath he had been holding onto for so long burst from his throat.

The breath that raced from Hope's mouth should have carried with it a blood curdling, spine tingling, hair raising scream. That's certainly what Hope had expected of it. Instead, the only sound that was heard was ……… "oink!!"

Hope snapped awake immediately and his surroundings returned to their familiar form. The ivy that he had struggled and fought against only moments ago now greeted him like an old friend. Warmth returned to his body and he was relieved to discover he had been dreaming; or something like dreaming anyway. The one strange thing that remained with him was that last sound he had made. The sound that had jerked him from the terrifying nightmare that had overtaken him.

The sound had of course been "oink", which was, as we know, the sound of Hope's most feared animal - the pig.

I am not at all sure why Hope was so terrified of pigs, but perhaps in the telling of this story we shall find out. For now, what's important is that Hope had just realised that he, in fact, had not made that sound at all. He came to this realisation after he once again heard an "oink" coming from the jungle, and this time his mouth had not even been open. This meant only one thing. There were pigs nearby.

He had awoken from one nightmare, only to find himself in another, scarier one.

Chapter Four
The pigs

Hope shrank back into the protective custody of his ivy nest. The only part of him still visible was the tip of his trunk and, if you looked very closely, his two squinted eyes, undecided as to whether they should stay open to see exactly what was happening, or shut tight and pretend that nothing was happening at all.

The protruding tip of his trunk wiggled up and down and side to side, nostrils spread wide and vacuuming the surrounding area. He caught the scent he was reluctantly seeking. To Hope it was the smell of pure fear. To anyone else, it was simply the smell of a pig. Hope heard another oink, followed by two snorts. Some bushes nearby started to rustle and shake.

The pig was coming!!!!

Hope was perfectly still. His trunk tip carefully and silently slipped back into the darkness of the ivy's interior to join the rest of Hope's cowering body parts. He peered through the small gaps in the ivy at the bush that was threatening to expel that animal which Hope feared above all others.

The bush smiled knowingly at Hope, aware of the influential position it had unwittingly found itself in. As future king, Hope would promise it anything it wanted if it could somehow persuade the pig that it held within to turn and head the other way.

The bush thought of what it might like. Perhaps a place of its own, out in the sun and away from all these big trees that always pushed it around. Maybe it could be in a field of those miniature trees that only grew to a foot or so, and the bush could look down on them all from its towering four foot height.

That would be sweet, it thought. *Oh; and no bloomin' caterpillars ………….*

As the bush continued dreaming of its perfect life, and Hope watched on anxiously, the pig concealed within simply stepped out and into the open.

Hope gasped.

The bush muttered angrily to itself about how it had blown its one big chance by getting carried away with its fantasies and being too greedy; how it would have settled for a good pruning and some decent fertiliser, but now it would get nothing. It went on like this for a long time because, well, for a long time it really had nothing else to do.

But back to Hope.

Hope gasped. It was the biggest pig he had ever seen, around half his size, and sticking up from its bottom jaw were two large and very sharp looking tusks. Hope had heard of elephants having great big tusks, at times as long as the elephant was tall, but there were very few of them left, and he had never seen one. He had never heard of a pig *ever* having them.

The pig stopped as soon as it stepped out into the open. It was sniffing the air and Hope was worried that it had caught his scent. It was a fearsome looking pig and it took all of Hope's willpower to stop himself from trembling and giving himself away.

'What next?' he asked himself. The answer was not long coming.

Another, bigger pig with even longer, sharper looking tusks stepped out beside the first.

'O-kay,' was all Hope could think to say to that, but he forgot to keep his voice in the safe confines of his head and it spilt from his mouth before he could stop it. The two pigs heard and turned in his direction.

'Oh-no, Oh-no, Oh-no,' Hope frantically repeated to himself over and over. The pigs were edging towards him, snuffling furiously. Hope had given up on the whole willpower thing and he trembled violently, with no control and only a little shame.

'I thought I smelt something out of place,' muttered the first pig to the second.

'Elephant, if I'm not mistaken,' replied the second, larger pig. 'Looks as if the jungle caught itself a big one today.'

The pigs snorted to each other. Hope took it as them laughing at his predicament. They were right up against the ivy and Hope was sure that they could see him, or if not, then at least the trembling foliage that betrayed his position.

They started to tear at the ivy. With their freedom of movement and their long, sharp tusks, Hope could see that they would reach him in no time. It was too much. He could control himself no longer, not that he had been doing so well up until that point anyway.

'PLEASE DON'T HURT ME!!' he screamed at the top of his voice. 'I'M ONLY A LITTLE ELEPHANT, AND SOON I WILL BE KING. I CAN GIVE YOU ANYTHING YOU WANT, JUST PLEASE DON'T

HURT ME.'

The pigs stopped instantly, stunned by the outburst.

'I beg your pardon,' said the bigger pig, 'but it would seem that you're well and truly stuck there, and if you'll just……'

'Oh no,' interrupted Hope. 'I'm not stuck at all. I'm playing a game with a friend, you see. This is my hiding place; I could get out any time I like, but if you keep pulling on that ivy, you'll give me away. It's probably best if you just continue about your business and forget I'm even here,' and he added, 'please,' trying not to sound desperate.

The two pigs looked at one another with sinister grins spreading across their faces.

'Well now,' took up the bigger pig, 'we *could* do that, but then what will we feed to the little ones tonight? It's a long time indeed since they've been served elephant for supper, and from what I can see of you, you'd feed our little family for a few days at least. Wouldn't you say Ma?' he asked to the smaller pig.

'Oh indeed Pa. I think the boys would be most pleased to be dining on some elephant steaks, some trunk sausages; perhaps even some elephant tail soup. Oh yes, yes, yes. My mouth is watering just at the idea.' Ma licked her lips to emphasize her point.

Hope almost fainted. All the blood in his body drained away to wherever it is that blood goes when it no longer wants anything to do with the conversation.

'Well it's settled then,' continued Pa. 'Let's stop with the chit chat and get our little smorgasbord here home before sundown.' The mention of sundown distracted Hope for a moment, and he quickly glanced up to notice that the sun was indeed on the way down. There was almost no hope now of reaching the top in time, but he had more urgent matters to attend to and he turned his attention back to these.

The pigs had resumed tearing at the ivy, their tusks now within inches of Hope. If he'd had any strength left, and wasn't so frozen with fear, he would have burst through what little ivy was left and made a run for it. I use the word if, because he had absolutely no strength left, and he was so completely frozen by his fear that he may well have been mistaken for a beautiful ice sculpture had our story been taking place in a colder part of the world.

The pigs tore away at the last strips of ivy that held Hope. He was totally exposed and vulnerable now. His eyes were wide and manic, darting furiously from left to right at the pigs who stood guard on either side of him, their tusks held threateningly close.

'What do you think Ma?' spoke Pa. 'A couple of mouthfuls now for the road.'

'Oh, indeed,' replied Ma cheerfully. 'I can't imagine the boys would deny us the first taste,' and she chomped her teeth to illustrate her enthusiasm for the idea.

That was it for Hope. He let out a blood curdling cry of 'Nooooooooo', and charged past the two pigs, summoning strength from some unknown source.

Birds shot out of the treetops, and the trees themselves seemed to recoil from the scream. Rabbits dived for the nearest burrows, whether it was theirs or not, and turtles pulled their heads and legs into their shells so quickly that they were left spinning on the spot. In a faraway place Hope's scream vibrated inside an iceberg, and a nearby penguin looked to the horizon and said, 'Oh stop your complaining. At least you have a warm bed for the night', but nobody heard him and he turned back to the hundreds of other penguins huddled together in a circle trying to get warm.

Back in the jungle, where it *was* warm, even with the sun on its way down, Hope had just charged past the pigs in an escape attempt. At least, he had intended on charging past the pigs in an escape attempt. What he hadn't realised was that the pigs had left some ivy tied to his two front ankles. The result was that when Hope rushed forward, his legs refused to follow, and his scream was cut short from his falling flat on his face in a dramatic anticlimax.

The pigs burst into laughter. Hope felt just about as humiliated as he had ever felt in his life. He started to cry. He was suddenly and totally overwhelmed by all of the recent events, and now it seemed his short life would come to a tragic end before he had even become the king that he had always dreamed of becoming. The pigs stopped laughing and moved in closer.

'Please,' sobbed Hope through his tears. 'Just make it quick and painless.'

The pigs looked to each other. Ma pig pressed her snout against Hope's ear. Hope paused his tears and tensed. This would be the first bite, he imagined, and he readied himself, but the bite never came. Instead, Ma nuzzled his ear and spoke softly to him. 'Oh little one, we wouldn't hurt you. We were just having a little fun. Tell him Pa.'

'Of course,' Pa agreed. 'I'm terribly sorry if we

went too far, but it's not very often that you come across an elephant who is afraid of pigs now, is it. It's usually the other way around, so you see, it just seemed too good an opportunity to pass up.'

'Come now,' added Ma. 'Stop your crying and we'll untie those legs of yours.'

Hope pushed himself back to his feet.

'You really don't mean to hurt me?' he asked, wiping his eyes with his trunk and shuddering with relief.

'Of course not,' chuckled Ma. 'Elephants are much too tough to chew,' and she laughed heartily to show Hope that she was still joking. Hope nervously joined in the laughter, and Pa giggled along as he pulled the last of the ivy from around Hope's feet.

'Thank you,' said Hope. 'If there's anything I can ever do to repay you, you only have to ask. I mean, as king, I should be able to get you almost anything you want.'

'So you were telling the truth about becoming king then?' queried Pa, his eyebrows raised.

'Oh, yes indeed,' answered Hope, pulling himself up to his full height. Then he remembered the humiliating position he had been in only moments ago, and he let his shoulders slump a little.

But only a little.

The pigs looked to each other, and then back at Hope. 'If you'll come with us, I think there's someone you should very much like to meet; and I would think he should very much like to meet you too' said Pa, and Ma nodded in agreement beside him.

Hope's curiosity was raised. He glanced up at the

sun, never forgetting the purpose of his journey, and asked the pigs, 'Is it up the mountain or down.'

'Up,' replied Pa, unsure of the reason for the question.

'Okay then,' smiled Hope with renewed enthusiasm. 'Lead the way.'

Chapter Five
Hope's story

The unusual threesome made their way up the mountain. The tusks of the pigs made short work of the thick jungle and Hope found himself wishing that he had been born a tusker, but there were very few tuskers born these days. In Hope's part of the jungle there hadn't been a tusker seen for a very long time, although they were still spoken of with reverence. (I should perhaps mention that a tusker is simply an elephant born with tusks, though you probably already know that). Anyway, it was well known that the greatest elephant warriors were always tuskers and while the king was sometimes tuskless, he always had a great tusker alongside him. It was never spoken of openly, but Hope had heard whispers of concern that there were no tuskers around at the time of his impending coronation.

There was one tusker, spoken of above all others, who was believed to be still around in those parts, but nobody knew where, or if he was in fact still around at all. All Hope knew of him was that something terrible had happened and the tusker had disappeared immediately afterwards. No one had seen or heard from him since. That's all that anyone would ever tell Hope, and they would change the subject immediately if he pressed them further. They would not even speak his name. In any event it didn't matter, as Hope wasn't looking for the tusker. He was searching for the giant sun throwing elephant, and his search was back on track, thanks to the two pigs.

Who would have thought it? Hope's most feared enemy had saved him from a near certain and very unexpected end. Hope looked to his two companions and smiled to himself. What had he been so afraid of? he asked himself. Then he remembered.

He didn't like thinking about that day. He always tried to forget and pretend that it never happened.

What day? I hear you ask. Well Hope would never volunteer that kind of information. He had never spoken of it to anyone. Someone would have to drag it out of him; and luckily for us there were two pigs just as interested in the answer as we are.

'So, Hope,' said Pa suddenly. 'I am curious about something. Why is it that a big, brave elephant like yourself; a king in the making, no less, is afraid of two little old pigs like me and Ma here?'

'Oh no, you are mistaken,' stuttered Hope to the unexpected question. 'You see, I didn't realise that you were only pigs. I, um, thought you were, ah…..well … something much scarier. I can't remember exactly what, but…..um..it was really, you know, something really…uh…….scary. But not pigs. No; not at all. I mean, why would a future king, no less, be afraid of a pig. I mean, that's just ridiculous.' He tried to laugh confidently, but made a complete mess of it.

Ma and Pa smirked at each other.

'Fine,' said Pa. 'If you wont tell *us,* who, I might remind you, just saved your life, then maybe we shouldn't take you to see this friend of ours after all. I mean, I'm not sure he would want to meet the future king, who is not only afraid of pigs for no apparent reason, but will not even admit to it. I'm not sure he would like that at all.'

Ma and Pa had stopped, as if they meant to go no further until the matter was resolved.

Hope grew even more curious of this friend that they were dangling in front of him like a banana that promised to be something more than a banana, if he could just get his hands on it. He sucked in a deep breath. If he was honest with himself, there was a part of him that longed to share the story with someone.

'Okay.' He let the breath loose in a long sigh. 'But can we walk as we talk? I still want to reach the top of the mountain before tomorrow's sunrise.'

'Fine,' replied Pa, and they resumed their trek.

The sun had almost descended onto the mountain peak behind, and soon darkness would settle in. They quickened their pace as Hope began his story.

'First of all,' started Hope, 'it must be agreed that this story is never repeated again. Understood?'

'Of course,' agreed the pigs.

'Okay,' continued Hope, checking all around himself to make sure no other ears were listening in: and of course, all of the ears that were in fact listening in, made themselves scarce as Hope's gaze fell on them, and reappeared eagerly as it passed.

'It was a long time ago and I was very young. It was before I lost my mother, and I hadn't ever strayed more than a few trunk lengths from her side. One day we were walking through the valley, just the two of us. My mother had spoken to me many times of the past, when elephants roamed together in large families; but then something had happened, something that divided the elephants and scattered them over the jungle. Nobody seemed to agree on exactly what it was, but there were whispers and rumours of all kind, or so my mother told me. One thing they all agreed on was that they were without a king, and they were vulnerable and without direction. It had happened suddenly, and soon after the elephants started to leave the jungle. My mother was determined to stay, and so we travelled most of the time on our own.

'I was too young to really understand all of this, but at night my mother used to tell me all kinds of stories of the "better days", as she used to call them.

'I am only telling you this so you can better understand the relationship I had at that time with my mother. You see, because for the most part it was only the two of us, we became dependent on each other. We were all that we had.

'So this one day, and it was a beautiful day, we were walking through the jungle and my mother was talking of her days as a young calf. I remember her mentioning how she was often left in the care of her mother's friends, or her aunties, as she called them, and how she always felt as if she had as many mothers as she could ever want. I think I remembered that because after I became an orphan I was taken in by another family who always treated me as their own. The sudden sound of breaking branches nearby interrupted our daydreaming. At first it was just a few, and far away, so we were unconcerned, but curious. The sound moved closer, and then closer again; and it became more and more intense. We had stopped dead in our tracks, my mother facing the sound with her ears spread wide and her trunk held tight around my body, pressing me close to her.

'I was a little worried, but only really because I could sense that my mother was. A much bigger part of me was curious to know what it was, and I pulled against her trunk to try and move closer for a better look.

'It was really close now, and through the sound of countless branches breaking and bushes rustling we could now hear the sound of "oink, oink, oink", which at the time I didn't recognise at all. I was even more curious now and I strained harder against my mother's trunk. Just at that moment, the pigs burst through to where we were waiting. There were so many of them, maybe hundreds, and they were in such a panic they didn't even notice us. They just poured in all around us and swept past.

'My mother let out a startled trumpet and her trunk relaxed, only for a second, but just enough so as that when I pulled against her, I was released from her grip. Only, right then, I wanted nothing more than to be wrapped in her trunk and held close, because I was caught up in the stampeding pigs and swept away from her. I screamed and squealed but the frenzied "oinks" of the pigs drowned me out, and because I was still so small I became lost in the sea of pigs. I could hear her calling for me, but she couldn't see or hear my calling back. Soon I was so far away that I couldn't hear her any more, and I became terrified.

'The pigs didn't slow down for some time and there was nothing I could do but be carried along by their momentum. When they did finally come to a stop they were completely exhausted, and so was I. I was alone amongst all of those pigs, and I didn't know if I would ever see my mother again.

'In all the chaos the pigs hadn't even noticed me among them but now that we had stopped, I became fairly obvious. They surrounded me, looking at me as if I was the most horrible thing in the jungle. I was too frightened to move, or even to speak. I heard them whispering to each other that I was an elephant, and something else about the elephants abandoning everyone. They muttered angrily about how all of their troubles had come about because the elephants had allowed everything to fall out of balance. I didn't understand, but I could see from the look in their eyes that they meant to take their anger out on me.

'They moved in closer and I let out a deafening scream, as only a baby elephant desperate for its mother can, but my situation seemed hopeless.

'But my cry didn't go unheard. Just as the pigs were about to descend on me, my mother came charging through the trees with a mighty roar. She came straight for me, and I tell you, there's no more fearsome or beautiful sight, (depending on which side you're on, of course), than a mother elephant defending her young. It didn't matter that there were hundreds of pigs; there may as well have been one or one thousand, the outcome would have been the same.

'The pigs resumed their stampede, squealing with

renewed panic. I was never more proud of my mother as I was then. She had sent all of those pigs away, but she had not harmed a single hair on any of their heads. She had just made it very clear that she would have, if it had come to that.

'From that day on, I never tried to pull away from my mother; and I never forgot about the pigs. I shivered whenever I thought of them.'

Hope finished his story there. Ma and Pa had listened intently.

'That is a strange story indeed,' said Pa. 'I have never heard of pigs behaving like that, but it certainly explains your fear.'

They had been walking for some time, so Hope guessed they must be close. The sun was perched on the very tip of the mountain, taking one last benevolent look over its domain before retiring for the evening. The jungle cast its shadows wider, filling the space left by the retreating sunlight.

'There is one thing I don't quite understand,' continued Pa. 'You said that you had never strayed more than a few trunk lengths from your mother, and I imagine that became even more the case after the incident with the pigs; yet here you are, still very young for an elephant, and you're all on your own, and a long way from home.'

'Well that's very true,' replied Hope, 'but you see, not very long after that story I lost my mother. Forever. And so I was left to look after myself from a very young age; before I was really ready to, but I managed. Then I met another young elephant, Ging Mai, who had also lost his mother, and we became best friends. Brothers, really. Soon after that, I lost Ging Mai and was on my own again. I was lucky to be taken in by another family of elephants, and they raised me as if I was their own son, but I had already come to realise that everything around us comes and goes, and at some time we will all have to leave as well, and in the end, we are always alone. But we are alone, together, and so, I think, never really apart.

'From then on I decided I would never be dependent on anything or anyone again. I would roam free and alone, amongst everything and everyone.'

There was silence after Hope's story. All three travelling companions were lost in their own thoughts. After a short time Pa whispered to Ma, 'He has a lot of wisdom for one so young. He may well be the future king that he says he is.'

'Indeed,' replied Ma thoughtfully. 'And he may be exactly what our friend needs,' she added.

They both glanced at Hope.

The sun was behind the mountain and the air had cooled down. It wasn't quite dark yet, but some of the animals that roamed the night had started stirring. The jungle stretched and yawned all around Hope. New eyes were watching him now.

He hoped it wasn't too much further.

Chapter Six
Three little pigs

'Well, here we are,' called out Pa cheerfully as he stepped into a small clearing. 'Home at last.'

'Home?' whispered Hope to himself. 'There's nothing and no one here,' and indeed there wasn't. It was a small clearing just like any other.

'Come on out boys,' called Pa. 'We've brought you some supper.'

Hope froze.

'Just kidding,' smiled Pa to Hope.

Hope relaxed; but just a little.

From a small hole in a slight mound to one side came the sound of excited squeals and snorts echoing from deep inside. The sounds burst into the open, followed closely by three perfect little replicas of the two pigs stood next to Hope; though minus the tusks.

There was a frenzied greeting of the reunited family and Hope smiled as he watched Ma and Pa fussing over their three little boys. When they had calmed down, the piglets noticed Hope for the first time. Their eyes spread wide and their snorts fell silent.

'This is our new friend, Hope,' explained Pa to his boys. 'He's going to be the King of the jungle very soon you know. Why don't you go and say hello while we go and fix your supper.'

When they heard of Hope becoming the King of the

jungle the piglets eyes grew even wider, if that were possible. They rushed towards him with renewed excitement, as Ma and Pa disappeared into the hole.

The smile vanished from Hope's face. Pigs were one thing. He had made enormous progress in overcoming his fear of pigs that day. In fact, he felt as if the fear was completely gone: but piglets! That was another thing altogether. It wasn't that he was afraid of them, I mean, that would be even more ridiculous than his fear of pigs. It was just that he found them kind of creepy, if he was honest about it, with their little, little snouts and their tiny curled up tails and all their snorting and squealing and scurrying around. He drew back from them as they came closer, but these piglets weren't the least bit shy.

'Hello Mr elephant.'

'Hello Your Majesty.'

'Hello Hope,' they each greeted him. They ran around his feet and between his legs, darting to and fro, and Hope had to strongly resist the urge to send them off with a swift kick. But instead, he stood there patiently.

'Eh, …… hello …um…….piglets,' he replied, but they weren't really paying attention. They were chasing each other around Hope's legs, which to them, were as big as trees.

'When you're king, will you remember us?'

'Will you make us princes?'

'Will you make us a new mound, as big as a mountain?' they each asked at the same time.

'Well …….' started Hope, but they were already talking again.

'Have you been on any big adventures?'

'Have you travelled over the sea?'

'Have you walked under the mountains?'

Hope paused a moment before answering, to make sure that they were finished. They were staring expectantly at him, waiting for a response.

'Well ....'

'Tell us a story before supper,' they cried in unison.

'If you would just shut .....' began Hope, but they were already interrupting and paid him no heed.

'A story where pigs and elephants rule the jungle together.'

'A story about a pig who travels from the top of the world to the bottom searching for treasure.'

'A story of three little pigs who…'

'WHAT'S THAT!!' interrupted Hope, suddenly shifting his attention to the bushes behind the piglets.

'WHAT!!' cried the piglets in one voice, and they spun around to face the bushes, huddling closer together.

With their backs to him now, Hope reached out his trunk and grabbed a hold of all three of their little curly tails. He pulled back so that the tails became straight and taut; and then let go.

The piglets tails snapped back hard against their bottoms. Their bottoms responded in kind by tucking in, and the piglets shot forwards with a startled yelp.

They spun back around to face this new danger, only to find Hope standing there, chuckling to himself.

'What's going on out there,' came a concerned voice from the mound, and Pa's head emerged from the hole.

'Oh, nothing,' offered Hope before the piglets could say anything. 'We were just getting to know each other, isn't that right lads?'

'Uh-huh.'

'That's right.'

'Well, not really. We were….'

'That's right,' Hope finished for the last piglet. 'Really a great family you have here Pa. You should be very proud.' Hope grinned sheepishly.

'Hmmmm,' said Pa, looking unconvinced. He turned to his three youngsters. 'Supper's ready. Give yourselves a quick bath, and then it's inside with the three of you.' Pa disappeared back into the hole.

The three little piglets jumped to attention at the mention of a bath, and they disappeared hurriedly out of view behind the mound.

Hope remembered how reluctant he had been at his first bath, and how his mother had to gently convince him to take his first steps into the cool water. Since then however, he has been the first to charge headlong into the water. He followed after the piglets, thinking how he could maybe show them how much fun a bath could be, but as he approached the mound he heard the sound of laughter and splashing. They sounded as if they were enjoying their bath perfectly well already.

Hope came around behind the mound and there were the three piglets, splashing and rolling and climbing all over each other. They were having a lot of fun, only they weren't bathing in water; it was mud.

They were having a mud bath, and indeed, it was difficult to tell where the mud ended and the piglets began. As the piglets dived in and out of the mud, it seemed as if the mud was churning itself over and over, occasionally taking on the shape of a small pig. There was of course only one thing that Hope could do when faced with a scene such as this.

'OUT OF MY WAY!!' he bellowed, as he charged directly at the mud bath. At its edge, he leaped up into the air, momentarily eclipsing the light from the moon. The piglets, plunged into the darkness of Hope's shadow, stared up at this new danger from above as if the sky itself were falling.

'Oh-Oh.'

'Oh my!'

'What the…..?' was all they could manage before Hope impacted with the wallow. Mud flew from the bath in all directions, taking the piglets with it, squealing half in panic and half in delight at their first, and most likely last journey through the skies.

Hope was left sitting in..... well, what could only be described now as a hole in the ground. It had been vacated, courtesy of Hope, by piglet and mud alike. He had one big smear of mud, which hadn't been quick enough to get out of the way, across his backside, and as he sat there he acquired another dollop which had somehow shot straight up and come back down on him with a vengeance, covering the top of his head. It hadn't, however, hit Hope with the same impact with which Hope had hit it, and now it simply sat on his head wondering what to do next.

Pa came rushing out of the mound once more to see what had set his sons squealing. He found Hope sitting in the now dry hole, looking for all the world like an elephant in a chocolate bun. Not that Pa knew what a chocolate bun was. To him Hope looked like a big clumsy elephant who had been playing in a mud bath meant for little piglets, about ten times smaller than him. Which of course is exactly what he was.

'Where are the boys?' asked Pa looking all around.

'Ah……..' started Hope, not sure what the next word should be.

'We were flying,' came the voice of one piglet from the bushes to the left.

'The first flying pigs in history,' came a second voice from the bushes to the right.

They waited for the third voice.

Silence!!!

'Where's your brother?' asked Pa sounding worried. In response, Hope started to squirm in his seat, then lifted himself to a standing position. There, underneath him, was the third piglet, coughing and spluttering in the mud that had been trapped under Hope along with him.

'Are you all right?' asked Pa.

'I think so,' replied the piglet between coughs. 'But Hope just jumped right on top….'

'Here,' interrupted Hope. 'Let me help you up,' and he placed the end of his trunk over the piglet's snout, covering it completely. The piglet continued to tell Pa how Hope had jumped right on top of him, but all anyone heard was, 'mmhmnplmmflmnunpnunbrmm.'

Hope picked him up by the snout, keeping it covered, and carried him over to the hole in the mound. He dropped the piglet down the hole and turned back to Pa.

'Great kids, really,' he offered. 'It's a shame they

have to go to bed now. We were having so much fun, heh-heh.' He tried to sound sincere. Pa glared at him.

'Right boys,' said Pa, still glaring at Hope. 'In you go and get your supper, then off to bed, right?'

'Yes Pa.'

'Yes Pa.'

The piglets trotted past Hope and into the hole.

'Goodnight boys,' he offered as they passed, but the piglets didn't even look up. As the second piglet was entering the mound, Hope flicked his tail out behind himself and tapped the piglet's front leg. The piglet tripped over the tail and tumbled head over feet down the hole.

'Sleep well,' Hope called down the hole after them. He turned back to Pa and grinned. 'Really. Wonderful lads; I mean that.'

Pa pushed past Hope.

'I'll be back in a minute,' he said sternly, and disappeared into the hole.

It was a beautiful night. Hope walked to the centre of the clearing and sat down. He gazed up at the clear sky. The moon was almost full, and it illuminated the surrounding jungle with streaks of silver light. The stars shone from one end of the sky to the other and back again. It seemed to Hope as if there were almost more stars tonight than there was empty space around them. Thinking about it, his attention was drawn to that empty space. Every time he had looked at the sky he had noticed the moon and the stars, and perhaps any birds flying in the night, but he had never given any thought to that empty space. After all, it took up more of the sky than anything else in it. Was it really empty, or did it just seem to be from so far away. It seemed impossible to think about, and as Hope continued to stare at the vast emptiness that surrounded him, his thoughts slowed down to a stop, finding nothing of interest for them in the vacancy.

Hope continued to gaze at the space between all the things he normally gazed at. Suddenly, he felt as if he was becoming empty himself. He was disappearing into the nothingness, and the empty space was now being filled by him. All the things of the jungle dissolved around him, and it too filled the emptiness so that the emptiness was all that was left; and it was filled with everything.

'Well, the boys are all asleep now. I imagine you must be getting tired yourself.' The sound of Pa's voice broke the spell. Hope poured back into himself and everything returned to where it had been moments before.

'What? Uh…..yeah, I guess,' replied Hope, coming out of his daze. Then he remembered where he was.

'But what about your friend? Are we not going to see him tonight? I was still hoping to get to the top of the mountain before sunrise, in time to see the giant sun throwing elephant.'

'The giant sun throwing elephant hey?' said Pa thoughtfully. 'You mentioned that before, but I have to say I've never heard of such an elephant. Still, if you want to get to the top of the mountain tonight, you should get going, but I'm going to get some sleep, and I wouldn't recommend going up there alone; especially at night. There's not many who have gone up there alone and come back to tell of it. As for our friend; he prefers not to be disturbed at night, and I for one would rather not be the one to upset him. So, my suggestion would be to get some rest tonight and gather your strength for tomorrow's journey. At first light we'll go and see him, and then we'll work out a way of getting you safely to the top before the following morning. But I wouldn't dare to tell our future king what he should do, so the decision is yours.'

'Well,' started Hope, 'I'm not at all worried about going to the top on my own, night or day. I've faced much worse I'm sure, but I am curious about this friend of yours, and one more day won't make much difference I guess. I just hope it's worth it,' he finished with what he hoped was an air of carefree bravado.

'I think it will,' replied Pa. 'Good night then Hope.'

'Good night Pa.'

Pa headed back into his hole.

Hope lay back down under the stars, and once more took up gazing through the empty space that surrounded him: that surrounded everything.

He very quickly drifted off to sleep and dreamed that he was a massive cloud that stretched across the entire sky, blown around to wherever the wind chose to take him. As he was floating on the breeze, he would break apart into a number of smaller clouds, and these would break again into even smaller clouds, but to Hope, he was always that one massive cloud that stretched across the entire sky and, given enough time, the wind would blow all the smaller clouds back together again. It was a very strange dream, but Hope smiled as he dreamed it.

Hope awoke very early the next morning. The moon had gone down, but the sun was yet to replace it and it was still dark. There was no sound or movement from the hole so Hope decided he might go for a short walk before everyone woke up. He chose a direction, it didn't really matter which, and strolled off through the trees. He walked aimlessly, lost in his thoughts of all the past and future events, paying little attention to where he was going. It was because of this that he didn't see the large bamboo cage in front of him, just like the one he had arrived in. He walked straight into it and when he lifted his head and saw what it was, he gasped in shock.

'What's that doing here?' he whispered to himself. He looked all around, expecting a troop of monkeys to descend on him at any moment. That's when he noticed that the cage was attached to a piece of vine, just like the other, that stretched down into the darkness towards the other mountain.

'This must be how the monkeys got back to their mountain with their captured animals,' said Hope.

He decided that he must smash this cage, the same way he had the other one. As he was about to grab onto the cage with his trunk, he noticed that the vine was moving. There was no wind that morning, so what

111

could be making the vine move, he asked himself.

His eyes followed the line of vine out into the darkness. As his eyes adjusted better to the little light, he thought he saw something. There seemed to be a shape, suspended on the vine, out in the dark space between the two mountains. As Hope watched, trying to make the shape out more clearly, he saw two pinpoints of pale blue light, somewhere near the top of the shadow.

'Maad!' gasped Hope in shock as he stumbled backwards. 'But how did he......' He didn't finish the sentence.

He suddenly had a clear vision of that morning on top of the last mountain. In all the confusion and excitement at the end of the monkeys liberation, they had forgotten about Maad, who had been laid out unconscious on the ground. He could easily have slipped away unnoticed while Hope and Pu-pa were listening to the old monkey's story. Afterwards, they had been caught up in all the emotion.

Hope turned and charged back toward the clearing. He didn't stop until he had reached it, which he did very swiftly, bursting through the trees. By this time, all five of the pig family were standing in the clearing. They were wondering where Hope had gotten to. They got their answer presently.

When Hope burst into the clearing, the three little piglets squealed with fright and dived back into their hole so quickly their little curly tails stretched out momentarily before springing back and snapping against their bottoms as they disappeared one by one. Ma quickly followed after to make sure they were okay.

'What's wrong with them?' panted Hope, gasping for air after his mad dash through the jungle.

'Don't mind them,' said Pa. 'What on earth is wrong with you?'

Hope paused for a moment to catch his breath which was doing its best to get away from him as quickly as it could. Hope made a mental note to himself to do more exercise and to cut down on the bananas. It was no good having a king who couldn't keep up with whatever he needed to keep up with; or to get away from whatever he might need to get away from.

After getting most of his breath back, and letting the rest go wherever it was so determined to go, Hope filled Pa in as quickly as possible on what had happened on the last mountain top. About the monkeys, about Temi, about Queen Freasell and, most of all, about Maad.

Pa's face turned very serious with concern as he listened to Hope's story, and when Hope finished by telling how he thought Maad had come to this mountain, Pa's eyes opened wide. He glanced to the hole that hid Ma and the boys. He turned back to Hope with a look of fierce determination in his eyes.

'We must leave. Now!!' he almost whispered, almost shouted. 'Our friend may be the only one who can help us in this. Let's just hope he's in a good mood.'

Pa disappeared down the hole. Hope could hear a very worried exchange between Ma and Pa. Ma was crying, and she obviously didn't want Pa to leave them.

Pa re-emerged from the hole. 'Right,' he said, storming past Hope without even looking at him. 'Follow me.'

Hope fell in behind Pa and they marched away from the clearing. It was early morning and the sun had just revealed itself from behind the far mountain. Hope watched it through the gaps in the trees. He had set off two mornings previous, with a simple goal; to find out from where the sun rose. Now he was further away from his home than he ever imagined he would be, and yet, no closer to his goal. But that feeling that had filled him as he had charged down that first mountain remained with him through it all, as strong as ever. He had felt from the beginning that he was doing something he simply had to do.

They continued their journey in silence, each lost in their own thoughts. The way up this part of the mountain was much easier than Hope had expected after what he had been through the day before. This was largely due to the fact that Pa knew exactly where he was going, and the only trouble Hope had was keeping up.

The sun had continued to climb the morning sky and the jungle was wide awake now. All the birds were stretching their wings in the treetops and singing their appreciation of the new day.

A little ways on, Hope was stunned to see the remains of some elephant dung on the side of the path, and he stopped, in shock. This meant that there were elephants nearby. Hope's heart leapt. He was just about to bring Pa's attention to this when a dung beetle, who was busy rolling away one large piece of dung, caught his eye. It had stopped rolling its ball and was propped against it, one leg crossed over the other looking up expectantly at Hope. Hope felt he should say something but was unsure as to what.

'Er, good morning,' he tried.

'Never mind good morning,' barked back the dung beetle in a surprisingly strong and hoarse voice. 'Have you got anything for me or not?'

'Well, um, I'm not really sure, but I would have to say……not.'

'Really,' replied the dung beetle impatiently. 'Well then what the heck are you looking at, huh?'

Hope was taken aback. 'I just……' he stammered.

'You just what? You think it's funny to look down here and see a little dung beetle cleaning up your mess, do you? You just wander around, dropping dung wherever you see fit; but it's no problem, our little friend the dung beetle will clean it up, hey. Well one day fella, I promise you, the tables will be turned. You think we take all this dung back for food or shelter, don't you?'

'Well I never really thought………' started Hope, but there was no stopping the dung beetle now. He was on a roll, so to speak.

'Well we don't, you know. We've been storing it up in a secret location for generations. We've got tons of the stuff, and when we can figure out the best way to use it, we're going to take over the world, and you'll all regret leaving your mess everywhere for us to clean up, mark my words. But I've said too much already. Go on, get out of here; but watch your back, because one day, when you're least expecting it…….BAM!'

The dung beetle made a violent motion with its tiny little legs, and looked menacingly up at Hope. Hope stared at the ground to see if it had anything to say about it and, finding it as lost for words as he, quickly took off to catch up to Pa, leaving the strange scene behind him, which is exactly where he preferred it to stay.

He fell in once more behind Pa. They were within sight of the mountain's peak now, and Hope wondered if that was maybe where they were meeting this friend. He could have saved that thought if he had waited just a little, because at that moment Pa came to an abrupt stop.

'Right,' he said to Hope. 'This is it. You wait here; I'll go and see if he will come to speak with you. I can't guarantee it, but after this morning, I think he will. I'll explain to him quickly what you told me earlier; although we have all heard whispers of such things before, and I fear we have ignored them for too long.' Pa looked solemnly to the ground and then, remembering his purpose, he disappeared into the jungle, leaving Hope alone to marvel at the situation. He thought of the fantastic tales he had already collected, and he wondered if anyone at home would even believe him when he told them. He thought of all the adventures still to come before he found the giant sun throwing elephant; the most fantastic tale of all.

He looked up. The sun was climbing high in the sky, but there was still many hours left for Hope to reach the top before tomorrow's sunrise, and the top was only a short march away.

'Things really have a way of working themselves

out so long as you don't go sticking your nose in and disturbing them too much,' he said to himself.

Hope was awoken from the bed of self-satisfaction he had made for himself when Pa suddenly reappeared. He scampered over to Hope. 'He's here,' he whispered in what Hope thought was an overly dramatic way. He didn't think so for long.

Hope watched the shadows of the jungle as they gathered themselves together in the centre of his vision. They poured over each other, dragging themselves up the tree trunks, forming and reforming into one large mass that stepped out from amongst the trees and into the light. The sun struck the shadows mass, revealing its true form.

Hope drew a breath, forgot what the next step was, and held it.

From out of the darkness stepped the most magnificent elephant Hope had ever seen.

The great bull stood more than twice as tall as Hope and seemed almost as wide as he was tall. His skin was stretched tight over his massive frame and with every movement he made a ripple passed over his body as his muscles jostled each other for position. He had a high domed forehead, flanked either side by ears so big they could have enveloped Hope in a flap. The centre of his forehead bore a large protrusion that could just as easily have crushed Hope on the spot as it could send out the long vibrations that elephants use to talk to each other over great distances. Set just below this on either side were the fiercest eyes that Hope had ever fallen under. Meeting their gaze, Hope's eyes began to water, his eyelids twitched, but he could not look away. He

117

couldn't even blink.

The elephant's most distinguishing feature however, lay below his eyes, on his left side next to his tightly drawn mouth. About two foot long and as thick as a small tree trunk was a tusk of the purest white ivory. It must have been longer once, as it ended jaggedly where it had broken in two. On the right side there was only an empty cavity.

The bull strode toward Hope with purpose and presence, and anything that wasn't already aware of him suddenly became aware of nothing else. He didn't stop until they were face to face, his forehead only centimetres away from Hope and his tusk pressed against the right side of Hope's face, resting on his shoulder ever so slightly. Even with that merest of pressure, Hope could feel the immense power coiled up behind it, ready to unleash whenever it was called upon.

'Hope,' said Pa, trying not to sound too concerned, 'meet Boon Khum.'

Hope tried to say something, but failed. He tried to smile, but his mouth was having none of it. He considered bowing, or reaching his trunk to Boon Khum's mouth in a traditional elephant greeting, but he decided the appropriate response was to stand perfectly still, hold his mouth open wide and his eyes even wider, and try not to crumble into a thousand tiny pieces on the spot.

This, he just about managed.

'So,' said Boon Khum in a voice that rippled with as much muscle as the rest of him, 'I hear you have been telling people that you are the new King of the jungle. Is that true?' He ever so slightly, but noticeably, increased the pressure on his tusk and closed the gap between their foreheads.

Hope, to his own surprise, stood his ground, although he wasn't sure that's what he had intended to do. It wasn't going exactly the way he had imagined.

'Uh….no..I mean….. yes, but….eh…well……not exactly,' stammered Hope.

Boon Khum's eyes narrowed, concentrating their gaze through the smaller space.

'Well, you see,' started Hope, taking the hint, 'I never said that I *am* the king, just that I will be. Soon. At least, that's what I've been told, though I am open to suggestion. I mean if you'd rather I…'

'This is not fun and games, little one,' interrupted Boon Khum severely. 'You are a long way from home, and from what Pa has told me, trouble has followed you here. I came here to get away from trouble, so think very carefully about how you answer the next question.

'Why have you come here?'

Very carefully, Hope replied.

'Well, sir, I feel a little silly saying it, but I wanted to get to the top of this mountain to see the giant sun throwing elephant who throws the sun from one side of the land to the other every morning, but you see, I'm not even sure any more if….' Hope's voice trailed off and fell flat and lifeless on the ground.

Boon Khum had taken a step back and was staring in disbelief at Hope. 'Who told you about the giant sun throwing elephant?' he demanded in a whisper.

'Ah, well, no one really,' said Hope shyly. 'I just

kind of imagined it actually, which is why I'm not really sure any more if....' Again, Hope didn't manage to finish the sentence as Boon Khum interrupted him.

'Then it's true,' he said quietly, almost to himself, and then much louder, to everyone; 'IT'S TRUE!!'

Boon Khum looked as if he might burst out laughing, or possibly into tears. He moved closer to Hope again, only this time there was nothing threatening about him at all. He reached his trunk out and laid the end over Hope's head.

'It's true,' he said once more, to Hope, in a calm but firm voice. 'You don't know how long I have waited for this day. After what happened I thought this day would never come again, that I would live out my days alone, here. I thought the days of the king were over, that the jungle would descend more and more into disorder, eventually turning on and devouring itself. I had given myself up to this idea and yet, here I am, face to face with the new king and suddenly, there is......hope.'

Hope was a little confused.

'I don't understand,' he said. 'Why do you seem so certain that I am the new king?'

'It is only the one who will be king who goes in search of the giant sun throwing elephant,' replied Boon Khum. 'There are very few who have even heard its name spoken, but only one in every generation who will ever see it; and they always return as king. If they return at all.'

'But it can't be.' Hope was confused, and chose to ignore the last remark. 'A few mornings ago, I left my family in the valley because I wanted to climb a mountain. It was only on the way up that I wondered where the sun came from every day, and while I was wondering, I imagined that a giant elephant might throw the sun into the sky every morning. Nobody had ever mentioned it to me before. None of them even know where I went to, and they're probably searching for me right now.

'The giant sun throwing elephant is something I dreamt up.'

Boon Khum slid his trunk from Hope's head and let it rest between his front legs.

'No,' he said solemnly. 'You did not dream it up. It has been dreamt up by every past, present and future king. At the same age, every king to be sets out on a journey to find it, thinking that it is something they have conjured in their minds, thinking that it is a means of escaping their responsibility; their destiny. To have one last great adventure before their freedom is taken from them, not realising that only through this journey is their destiny fulfilled and their freedom found.

'Everyone in your family knew that you would disappear that morning. If they had been searching for you, I guarantee they would have found you long ago. They know that as the new king, you must undertake this journey, although they do not know the goal. Only the king and his finest warrior, who always accompanies the king on the quest, know what they are searching for.

'So you see, when I heard that you were claiming to be the new king, I was suspicious because you are travelling alone; without a warrior. But now I understand.'

'You do?' asked Hope in surprise. He looked at Pa beside him, who was listening with great interest to what Boon Khum was saying, and then back. 'I'm not sure I do.'

'*I* will go with you,' stated Boon Khum without the slightest hint of doubt in his voice. 'I have made this journey once before, but never completed it. I am blessed to have been given this opportunity to attempt it once more.'

'You mean?' started Hope, his voice shaking in anticipation of the answer to his coming question. 'You are the king who disappeared: whose return everyone has been waiting?'

'NO,' replied Boon Khum sternly. 'You are the king who will return. I will help as I should have helped one before.'

'Then,' Hope's anticipation was no less as he put the pieces together in his head, 'you must be the warrior. The one who accompanied the last king on this journey, the great tusker whom everyone talks about. Or tries not to talk about, I should say.'

'Not exactly,' replied Boon Khum sadly. 'I served the previous king, it is true. We were very close, but I did not take this expedition with him. He was older than I, and I was not even born when he undertook it. When I set off on the search, I went alone. It was a mistake, inspired by an even greater mistake I had made before that, but was too proud to admit. Now I remain here, with no pride and only the memory of my mistakes to keep me company.

'I have never spoken of my story to anyone before, but if I am to accompany you, the future king, then perhaps before we go any further, you should know of the events that have led to us being here now.'

'I should very much like to,' said Hope.

'As should I,' added Pa, and they both settled down to hear Boon Khum's story, forgetting for the moment the danger that had sent them there in such a hurry.

The sun continued to climb in the sky and the trees stretched their limbs towards it, bathing in the light it so generously poured on them every day.

They didn't listen to Boon Khum's tale. They knew it all too well already.

Chapter Eight
Boon Khum's story

'As a young calf, all I wanted to be when I grew up was a great elephant warrior, just like my father. He had served the king at that time for many years. When the king had set off, just before his tenth birthday, in search of the giant sun throwing elephant, it was my father who accompanied him; watched over and protected him.

'My father lived to a great age, but he had already been a mature bull when the king had been a little boy, so when he passed on, the king was left without a warrior, and many years still ahead of him.

'I was chosen to replace my father. By that time, I had outgrown him in size, in strength, and my tusks were larger than any known in the land. But I could never outgrow his reputation.

'When he left us, the entire jungle came together to celebrate: not to celebrate his death, you understand, but to celebrate his life. He had been famous throughout the land as the strongest, fiercest warrior in memory, and yet, in his many years serving the king, he had not once thrown his trunk in anger, or used his tusks for other than foraging or gentle sparring with the other bulls. It was his gentleness, compassion, fearlessness and loyalty that was celebrated; for this is what it is to be an elephant warrior. In his lifetime, the land had known only peace and harmony, and I meant to continue in his footsteps; as large as they were.

'And for a long time I did. The king and I became firm friends. He was a great king, and all the elephants loved and respected him, as did I. He told me many stories of adventures he had undertaken with my father, even the story of their first journey together; their search for the giant sun throwing elephant. I was fascinated by the story, though the king would never say if he had seen it or not, and I felt a sense of pride that he would entrust me with this secret that was usually only known by a privileged few.

'In fact, pride was the feeling that filled me the most at that time. I felt pride when elephants spoke of how I reminded them of my father; I felt pride when they admired my tusks; I felt pride as I walked side by side with the king through the jungle. Soon I was bursting with it.

'It was to be my downfall.

'I started to believe it when I heard people speak of how I was the greatest ever elephant warrior. I would display my strength for any who wished to watch. I would throw massive boulders into the air with my trunk, and smash them to pieces with my tusks before they hit the ground, or I would lay on the ground and allow as many young elephants as wanted to climb on top of me, then I would leap up with a roar, sending them all flying through the air. More and more came to watch, and my displays became more spectacular. One day, in front of an enormous crowd, I destroyed a large area of forest in one furious act, flattening and uprooting trees, tossing them over my head or splitting

125

them with my tusks.

'There were some in the crowd who turned and walked away when they saw what I was doing, but the others roared their appreciation. I was so filled with my pride that I became it. I *was* pride; there was room for nothing else.

'The following day, I was summoned by the king. I imagined that he might want to commend me on my rousing display, but it was not that at all. He was angry. It was the first and last time that I saw him that way. He told me that an elephant with such an enormous gift of strength and might should only display it if absolutely necessary, and if it were never necessary in its lifetime, then it was a good and fortunate one.

'He said that to possess these qualities was to possess the potential for great violence and destruction, and these were not things to be boastful and proud of. The elephant, he said, should display gentleness, forgiveness and tolerance for all, as these were the qualities that had placed them as the holders of balance in the jungle, not their power.

'Before he sent me away, he said one more thing: "You're father would be disappointed."

'It was these final words that struck home. My pride had been severely wounded, but instead of allowing it to die, I held on to it. I reopened the wound, kept it fresh by replaying those words in my mind, again and again and again.

'Life returned to normal and I no longer performed any feats for the disappointed crowds. I went about my business as I had done before, and in appearance, nothing had changed. But a seed had been planted, and over the years I nourished and tended to it, and it grew inside me.

'Many years passed, and still the land remained at peace. I had taken to wandering far and wide in search of adventure. The king was growing old, and so on most of those long journeys, I went alone.

'It was on one of these travels that I first heard of the monkeys. I heard that they were trapping all the animals in their corner of the jungle, and that they had devised many devious ways of doing so. They were able to trap animals much larger and stronger than themselves, and they were spreading farther and wider in their search for prey.

'I was greatly concerned by what I heard, and I rushed home to speak with the king. I told him all that I had heard, and he too grew concerned. It was the first real trouble that we had faced and, although it was still far away, eventually it might spread across the entire land. By that time it may have grown beyond our power to stop: at least, that's how I felt, and I said this to the king.

'I suggested that we gather all the warriors in the area and strike at them immediately. They would never expect it, and with the strength of so many elephants we could have dispensed with as many monkeys as they could have possibly thrown at us.

'He disagreed.

'In fact, he was most upset I had even suggested it. He said he had never heard of elephants doing such a thing, and he was certainly not going to be the first. We argued for a long time, but he insisted that if we took the time to become aware of all the facts, and could

127

look at them from every perspective, then we could surely find a solution involving no violence. I was furious at his refusal to take immediate action, and the more incensed I became, the more placid he fell. Which of course only ignited my anger further.

'When I left him that night I had already decided what I was going to do. I was convinced that the king was a coward, and it was his fear that prevented him from doing what I felt was necessary. The truth is that I was the one who was afraid, although I never would have admitted that to myself at the time.

'I went in the night and gathered all the warriors from the surrounding area. I told them of all that had happened, and of the king's refusal to take action. I gave a stirring speech, presenting both sides of the argument, though smearing the king's point of view with derision and ridicule, while flourishing my own with finely illustrated points and delivered with great gusto. It was a piece of cunning worthy of the monkeys themselves, and the shame of it burns me to this day.

'But it worked. They all agreed to follow me, and we left immediately before anyone discovered our plan. Unfortunately, or fortunately as it turned out, someone overheard us, for soon after we left, we were confronted by the king himself.

'He did not order us to stop, or to go back. He didn't even ask where we were going. He simply regarded us silently for some time, as we did him. The elephants with me stared at the ground and hung their heads in shame; but not I. I held my head high, never taking my eyes from his.

'Slowly, one by one, the elephants behind me

turned and headed back from where we had come, without a word being spoken. I must admit that I felt admiration for the king who could command such respect without ever asking for it. Still I would not back down. I was more determined than ever. We remained silent for a while longer until finally he spoke.

' "Boon Khum," he said, "I will not stop you from doing what it is you feel you must do, but you should know this. If you pass me now, then my time as king will end at that very moment, for if I do not have the respect and loyalty of all around me, then I am not worthy. I will disappear into the night and you shall not hear from me again. I will accept your decision, however you decide. I only want you to be aware of the consequences of your actions."

'I considered what he said, but it only reinforced in me the idea that he was a coward, and it was up to me to defend all the elephants from the potential threat.

'I strode past him.

'I was only a few steps past when I overwhelmingly realised that I had made the wrong choice. I turned back, but he was already gone. I searched the whole area, but it was as if he had vanished.

'I raced back to the others to see if he had turned up there, but they had not seen or heard from him. When they heard what had happened, they all turned their backs on me. At that moment, it was as if I too had vanished.

'I had the idea that if I could find the giant sun throwing elephant, then perhaps I could return as king and set right the wrong I had inflicted. I left that night, and have never returned. I heard rumours and whispers in the jungle that the elephants were without a king and had divided in their confusion. Some had blamed me for what had happened, some felt the king had abandoned them, but I knew at whose feet the blame lay.

'I wandered aimlessly for years, like a ghost in the shadows, tormented by the thoughts that gripped my mind. I never saw or even heard mention of any sign of the king. Perhaps he too had become as a ghost.

'I forgot all about the monkeys, though in my travels I still heard mention of them, and soon enough I would come across them.

'I came one night to a mountain. It was a beautiful and friendly mountain, but there was a dark shadow creeping across its peak and it drew me towards it. I climbed the mountain that very night, and near the top I grew tired and decided to rest. I came to a clearing near a river and there, laid out in front of me as if I was expected royalty, was a stack of lush green grass, just waiting for me. In years past I would never have trusted such a thing, but by that time I had worn away all my sharpest instincts with the abrasiveness of my guilt.

'I ate the grass greedily, but something had been mixed with it, and I caught its scent too late. I began to feel sleepy and my legs gave way under me. I slumped to the ground, unable to move, but my mind remained awake, though only just. Enough however, for me to hear the sound of the giggling gaggle of monkeys that swarmed over me, clambering from my trunk to my tail, somersaulting from my back and hiding under my ears, taking great pleasure in their games.

'Through my half open eye, I saw one appear in front of me, different from the others. His fur was fairer, and I will never forget his steel blue eyes that stared straight through me. He seemed to acknowledge that I was watching him, and a smile spread across his face.

'He came towards me. It was then that I noticed that he carried something in his hand. It was a rock. A very long and sharp rock. I had never seen stone like this before, but I know now that those monkeys devised many clever ways of carrying out their cunning plans.

'He came right up to my face and reached down with the rock towards my tusk. I suddenly realised what he was doing and I tried to get up. I tried to roar, to do anything to stop him, but I couldn't move. I could only watch. And feel.

'He cut into my tusk with the rock and searing pain shot through me. He cut through the nerves and the surrounding flesh. The pain was indescribable, but it was nothing compared to the fury that welled up inside of me.

'And all the time he cut into me, he stared directly into my eye with a satisfied grin on his face.

'When he finished, he stepped back and four other monkeys moved forward to lift my tusk up. They raised it above their heads like some obscene trophy, blood still dripping from one end, and they all hooted and hollered their triumph. All the time, that one monkey never took his eyes off mine. He seemed to take more pleasure in the fact that I had witnessed the whole act, than in the act itself.

'At that moment I felt the end of my trunk twitch. Feeling was returning to me. I should have waited until the effects of the poison had worn off completely, but my anger drove me. I surged to my feet. The monkeys scattered in all directions screaming like the cowards they really were, but I had eyes only for one.

'I lunged for him with my remaining tusk, but I was still dazed from the poison and he was quicker than me. He dodged my tusk, and instead I struck a large rock behind him with my full force. I had struck out with such anger and violence that when my tusks struck the rock, the rock split in two. So did my tusk.

'The monkeys disappeared into the shadows and I slumped once more to the ground. This time I fell into a deep sleep, unsure if I would ever wake from it: or even if I wanted to. I'm not sure for how long I lay like that, but when I awoke, it was light. The memory of what had happened came flooding back and with it, the pain in the cavity where my tusk had been. I dragged myself to my feet and noticed beside me the broken half of my surviving tusk. I picked it up and held it for a long time in my trunk, feeling its cool hardness, wondering all the time why those monkeys would want it so much. But it was impossible to comprehend.

'I raised the broken tusk over my head and brought it crashing down on the rock nearby. It smashed to a thousand tiny pieces, and I wept at what I had become.

'No longer a warrior, barely even an elephant, I took to wandering in the shadows once more, with my jagged stump a constant reminder of all that happened, and my memories as my only companion.

'Some weeks later I came to this mountain. I was skinny and weak from having barely eaten, and I fell into an ivy trap laid by the jungle that seemed to have taken offence to me. At one time I would have burst the ivy apart with one shake, or torn it in two with one swipe of my tusk, but I had neither the strength nor the tusks, and I settled in, almost welcoming the end. But it was not to be.

'Soon after, Pa here found me and tore the ivy from around me. I felt a kinship with him straight away, perhaps on account of his tusks, but also because he knew nothing of my story and simply accepted me for what I was: a fellow animal who needed help.

'He led me here, where there is plenty of fresh food and water, and where I could be alone to wrestle with my dark memories. He never asked too many questions and was always satisfied with my answers, even though I could see he wished to know more.

'I have recovered almost all of my strength now, and it would seem, with your arrival, that I shall perhaps have the chance to redeem myself, and help restore the balance that I upset all those years ago.'

Boon Khum finished his story there, and they all sat silently. It seemed as if a great weight had been lifted from him in the telling of his story. He breathed in deeply, as if there were a great big open space inside him now, and he filled it with the fresh air and pleasant smells of the jungle. He held his breath, allowing it to soak into his being as much as it could, and then he let it out again slowly with a contented sigh.

'Well,' he said with a new shimmer in his eyes, 'the

133

sun won't wait for us. Perhaps we should be on our way.'

'I'm ready,' said Hope, jumping to his feet. Boon Khum's story had been a painful one, but it had inspired him and filled him with confidence and purpose. For one thing at least, he knew now that his search for the giant sun throwing elephant was in fact something he was supposed to undertake, whether it existed or not was not so important.

'I would dearly love to accompany you both,' Pa spoke up, 'but I must be getting back to my family. What with this Maad character slinking about the place and all, I'd feel better knowing they were safe.'

Boon Khum stepped over to Pa. 'Thank you,' he said. 'Without your help, I doubt I would even be here now, let alone have this second chance that I have been blessed with. I will see you again.'

Hope came up beside Boon Khum. 'For the same reason I also thank you. Never again will I be afraid of pigs. I shall consider them only as a friend. Please say goodbye to Ma and the three little boys. I hope to meet them again when they are grown up and a little less……eh….small,' he finished, choosing to be polite.

'Goodbye and good luck,' said Pa, 'and don't forget the little pigs when you are ruling over this place. It's always good to have friends in high places.'

'Of course,' smiled Hope.

Pa turned and started back down the mountain.

Hope and Boon Khum turned and started the short climb to the top.

As they headed up the path, side by side, Boon Khum towering over little Hope, the bigger elephant looked at the smaller from the corner of his eye, his brow furrowed in confusion.

'Pigs?' he said. '*Really*??'

'What? Oh…no, it's not what you think. Really. It's just that, well, you know; I like to make others feel good about themselves, so, you know, when Pa found me, I thought he'd be terrified of a big elephant like myself, and so...ahem, just to put him at ease you understand, I, um, pretended I was afraid of him. And his lovely wife.

'See?'

'Ahh, yes, of course.' Boon Khum tried hard not to laugh.

'I mean really,' Hope continued, when he really should have stopped, 'an elephant afraid of pigs; it's just not possible, right?'

I think you already know how this conversation would have continued, so we'll just skip to the next chapter, when our two heroes arrive at the top of the mountain, shall we?

Chapter Nine
The reunion

Hope had travelled with so many different companions in the past few days, he had to wonder who he would pair up with next, but for the moment he was more than happy to be treading the same path as the great elephant warrior, Boon Khum, whom he had heard so much, and yet so little, about.

Not only was he in awe, and very humbled, to have someone of Boon Khum's stature perform such a duty for him; he also felt a great deal safer. And given what he had already faced, and also, given Pa's warning about travelling to the mountain's peak alone, that was no small thing to the little elephant Hope.

Reminded of Pa's warning, he asked Boon Khum if he knew what it referred to. Boon Khum had been walking in silence, his eyes filled with purpose and renewed determination, but a gentle smile on his face. The smile fled from Hope's question.

'Yes,' he replied solemnly, his eyes remaining fixed on the path ahead. 'It is a different jungle that you are inheriting Hope, than the one I knew all those years ago. There are dangers growing in every shadow, and in recent times, they have started to emerge from the darkness into the light, where we have no choice any more but to be faced by them.'

He grew silent again. Hope didn't press him any

further. He wasn't sure he wanted to know more, and he returned to enjoying the warmth of the midday sun that came filtered through the leaves and branches of the jungle canopy.

He had just managed to stop himself from wondering what the danger ahead might be, when Boon Khum spoke again.

'There have always been things in the jungle that prey on one another,' he said, 'it's the way of the jungle. The bird eats a worm, a snake kills and eats the bird, an eagle swoops down and carries the snake away in its talons, while later, a cat hunts and snares the eagle. This is the way of life. Life supporting life, and everyone accepts their part in it. But at the top of this mountain there are some who have begun to hunt and kill, just for the pleasure of it. Have you not noticed how few animals you have seen here. You may notice some scurrying in the shadows, but they will never come into the open unless they have no choice. Ma and Pa are two of the few who move with any freedom, but they know this mountain better than most, and even they stay only on the paths they know are safe, and only ever in the daytime.

'I have thought of coming up myself at night to see if there was anything I could do to remove the danger, but I am wary of taking any such action now, as you can understand.

'As it happens, I am glad now that I waited, as tonight we can face the danger together; if it dares to face us, right?'

'Right,' agreed Hope weakly. He had been looking forward to a good night's sleep, after maybe being

137

entertained by some of Boon Khum's warrior tales, and then be up in time to see the giant sun throwing elephant.

He'd had enough danger already to fill many stories, and he could gladly have gone one night without.

'Er,' he started, 'Do you know exactly what this danger might involve?'

'Oh, sure. Everyone knows,' answered Boon Khum matter of factly. 'It's tigers'

'Tigers,' repeated Hope to himself. An image flashed in his mind of the one tiger he had met in his short life: Queen Freassel. She had been the most beautiful and awesome animal he had ever seen, but she had also been the most fearsome. If they encountered a number of them at once, he wondered if even Boon Khum could hold them off. He looked up at the massive elephant.

Well, he thought, *if anyone could, it would be him*, and he turned his attention back to the path ahead of them, and the mountaintop which they were coming upon now.

Boon Khum, for his part, strode ahead with great eagerness in his marching steps, a smile across his face bigger than any he had worn in a long time. Above them clouds had started to form, darkening the sky ominously.

They climbed over the final ridge and onto the wide, flat plateau that was the mountaintop. It was an area large enough for many elephants to share, but for now, it seemed, it was only the two of them.

Some large birds of prey circled them overhead, but

from what Hope could see they would find nothing to prey on there. Apart from the tall grass and the few trees bending in the wind, there was no movement at all. The birds seemed to realise this soon enough and they flew off in search of better hunting grounds.

The grass was overgrown, apart from a small number of clear cut paths which led from the centre of the plateau, out and down each side of the mountain. Following one of these paths the elephants came to the centre, where a large patch of grass had been worn almost completely away. In the centre of this clearing was a large tree, and scattered around this tree was a sight that made Hope and Boon Khum stop dead in their tracks.

Hope swayed in the wind along with the grass as he fought against the wave of nausea that swept over him, his legs keeping him upright only out of sheer habit, while Boon Khum stiffened visibly, taking one step forward and one to the side, placing himself between Hope and the gruesome scene that confronted them.

Spreading from the tree out to the edge of the circle where Hope and Boon Khum now stood, was a collection of every skull, skeleton and body of almost every animal known to the elephants. Some looked like they had been stripped to the bone, while some looked as though they had barely been touched: most gruesome of all were those who had only random pieces of flesh removed, or odd bits remaining. Some were half buried in the ground while the rest sat above, where they had been dumped, stacked one on top of the other where space seemed to have run short.

Dotted amongst this makeshift and unfinished

burial ground, curled up asleep with contented bellies and grossly bloated grins across their purring mouths, were the tigers. At a quick count, there must have been at least twenty of them.

'That's strange,' whispered Boon Khum to no one in particular. 'Tigers normally live solitary lives, unless they are young. I've never seen so many in one small place. Or so much carnage and waste.'

'What should we do?' Hope whispered back, gulping hard.

'Well,' said Boon Khum thoughtfully, 'tigers are more active at night, when they go hunting. If we want to confront them, it would be best to take them by surprise now while they are dulled by their full stomachs: but this many tigers, even slowed down.....' Boon Khum failed to finish the sentence, but Hope guessed what he meant. He agreed.

Boon Khum continued. 'Maybe it would be best to slip past them while they sleep, and we can watch the sunrise from halfway down the other side.'

Hope liked the sound of that idea and was about to tell Boon Khum so, when a voice interrupted from behind. It was a voice that reached Hope, not through the normal channel, being his ears, but rather it entered at the base of his spine and shot up to his brain, leaving a trail of cool fire and erect hair along his back.

'Now, I ask you, what fun would that be?' the voice said.

Hope and Boon Khum spun around to face the voice, Boon Khum instinctively pulling Hope back behind his front legs with his trunk.

Standing in front of them at the edge of the ridge

was Maad, leering at them both with an obscene grin, his blue eyes locked on Hope.

'You,' breathed Boon Khum in disbelief. His trunk slid away from Hope, its duty forgotten at that moment. His trunk curled up threateningly under his chin, his ears slowly spread themselves wide at the side of his head, making him seem even bigger, if that were possible. His muscles rippled uncontrollably across his shoulders, and he was leaning forward as if he was in a terrible struggle within himself.

'Yes. Me!' replied Maad, pulling his attention away from Hope with great effort, and focusing on Boon Khum. 'It's quite the reunion don't you think. I'm sure we have a lot to catch up on, but it might have to wait for another day. Today I'm only interested in one thing,' his voice and expression took on a serious and menacing tone, and his hand came up from his side to point at Hope. 'Him,' he finished, and in his hand, which was pointing aggressively at Hope, he held a long, sharp stone.

Boon Khum's eyes ignited in a blaze of fury. It was the same knife that had scarred him all those years ago, he was certain of it. His battle with himself ended at that moment. With a deafening roar, he charged at Maad. The air itself seemed to split in two, such was the ferocity with which Boon Khum cut through it.

Once again Hope was reminded of how incredibly powerful and awesome an elephant was when pushed to display it. The ground shook beneath his feet as Boon Khum pounded over it and, surprisingly, a wave of fear raced through him.

More surprising was the fact that as Boon Khum

bore down on him, as an avalanche crashes down on an unsuspecting tree below it, Maad did not make any movement to get out of the way. Instead, he reached into the long grass beside him with his free hand, and from its hiding place there, he raised a large squirming net woven of thick ivy and tied in a knot at its top. He held it in front of himself, and moved the sharpened stone dangerously close to the wriggling shapes tangled inside.

Boon Khum's eyes were drawn to the net. Through the gaps in the ivy he immediately recognised what was inside. His legs locked mid charge, and he skidded to a halt, coming to rest with his blunted tusk faintly brushing the golden hair of Maad's chest.

Maad's face retained its cool expression, but his hands trembled uncontrollably, betraying his true feelings. It was all he could do not to drop both the net and the stone, sealing his fate. Unfortunately, he managed to keep his grip on both and regain his composure.

'Well,' he said, taking a step back from Boon Khum, 'that was all a bit dramatic, wasn't it? But with all your huffing and puffing and flapping ears, you let your sentimentality stop you from doing what you have to do. That's why you elephants are in the position you're in now; and why it's time for a new ruler in this land. You had your chance and you blew it. You abandoned everyone once before, and you think you can go on some ridiculous search for some sun-catching elephant, or whatever you call it, and then just stroll back in and take over as if nothing has changed.

'*Everything* has changed; and elephants are not the

only ones with long memories.

'So here's what I suggest, although it's not really open to discussion. Hand over the little one to me,' he gestured at Hope, 'and he can take me to see this sun eating elephant. Then I shall return as king, and he, well, he will have to make up for all the trouble he has caused me, won't he.

'As for you; you can go back to hiding in the forest and forget about the idea, which I can already see forming behind your eyes, of seeking revenge against me.

'I mean, losing two kings in one lifetime will hardly do your popularity any good now, will it, so best we keep that as our little secret; what do you say?'

Boon Khum stared hard at Maad. 'You will have to kill me first,' he replied through his clenched jaw.

'As I said,' sneered Maad, 'we do what we have to do.'

The clouds overhead grew darker still, adding to the heaviness in the air.

Chapter Ten
The warrior

Maad dropped the net heavily on the ground beside him and the contents responded with a cry, a yelp and an oink respectively.

'PIGLETS,' cried Hope as he instantly recognised the voices inside. He took a few steps toward them, but Boon Khum held him back with his trunk. Maad took two more backward steps, waving his stone weapon to remind them why they hadn't simply crushed him already.

'What have you done with Ma and Pa?' Boon Khum demanded.

'Oh, good ol' Ma and Pa are just fine, don't you worry,' mocked Maad. 'I mean, what kind of a monster do you take me for? Though I did have to give poor dear Ma a bit of a bump on the head, as I'm sure she wouldn't have just allowed me to stroll away with these three,' he motioned at the net which was motionless now, listening anxiously to the conversation.

'So what happens now?' growled Boon Khum, 'because it seems to me that you haven't really thought this through.

'You want Hope to lead you to the giant sun throwing elephant, yet you must know that he would never do so willingly, and that I would never let you anywhere near him as long as I am still able to draw breath. You think you can hold three piglets for ransom, and suddenly the world is yours to do your bidding? And I thought you monkeys were clever.'

Maad seemed stung by that last remark, but he retained his cool exterior and superior air.

'You are mistaken, my tuskless friend,' he replied, and Boon Khum was stung in return. 'These cute little guys are not my ransom.' Maad was obviously enjoying the fact that they had reached this point in the proceedings. 'They are a payment.'

'Payment?' questioned Boon Khum, not following. 'For whom?'

Maad opened his mouth to reply, but it was Hope's voice that was heard. 'For them.'

Boon Khum turned to see whom exactly Hope was referring to, although he had already guessed.

The tigers, which seemed to them now to number much more than twenty, had silently raised themselves from their sleep and completely surrounded the two elephants. Some were barely visible in the long grass, and indeed there was very likely many more who were completely hidden there.

'Indeed,' snapped Maad at Hope, '*for them;* but don't you ever steal my big moment like that again, you understand? I mean, this whole discussion had been building to that moment, where I say "for them", and you both turn around and are shocked and terrified to find that you are surrounded by tigers. Instead, you jump in, as if it was *your* plan all along, and I'm left standing here like a fool, as if I had nothing to do with the whole thing.'

145

Boon Khum and Hope watched in confusion as Maad ranted and raved, waving his stone in the air. Even the tigers seemed to have lost their focus and were staring at him. Maad noticed this and pulled himself back together. He smiled at the two elephants as if he were their closest friend.

'Let me fill you in on some of the details,' he said in his friendliest voice.

'That morning, after you and that idiotic friend of yours ruined everything I had built up over the years, I slipped away unnoticed while you were all too busy patting yourselves on the back for a job well done. For the first time in my life, through some instinct I had long forgotten, I climbed up into the treetops. From there I watched what was happening.

'Initially, I intended to return inside the walls once you had left, but when I saw that one of you, the big oaf, was remaining behind, I had a better idea. I followed you, little Hope, seeking my revenge. When you took that bamboo cage to the other mountain, you unknowingly saved yourself, for I would have pounced on you there and then. But I had to be patient and as it turns out patience does, surprisingly, bring its own reward. I was able to learn a great deal by following you and listening.

'I swung across that entire length of vine to the other mountain, but by the time I got there you had long gone. But an elephant climbing up and over rocks leaves an obvious trail, and I followed you.

'When I got to the top, again you were already gone, but in your struggle with the jungle there you had left an even easier trail to follow. I laughed at how careless you were, but then you thought I was locked away safe and sound on the other mountain, didn't you?

'I followed your trail to that ivy trap and found you thrashing about pathetically inside. You never noticed me because you were too busy worrying about yourself. I climbed up into an overhanging tree, deciding on the best way to enact my revenge, waiting for the right moment. Imagine my surprise when you went and fell asleep, like a baby chick in its nest. I couldn't believe it. It was too simple.

'I crawled along one of the branches that held up that net that covered you, and I climbed down the ivy. I was right over you. I could have reached out and touched you. I raised my stone over your head, and just as my moment was at hand, that blasted pig makes a racket in the bushes, you wake up, and I have to disappear back into the treetops to wait again for my vengeance. You never knew how close you were.

'I watched those pigs free you and lead you away, and again I followed. And again, I was glad I had waited. I learnt some interesting things that night. It was the first time I heard you mention that fire breathing elephant, and I overheard from Pa of this friend of his. Most interesting to me at the time, however, was talk of the danger that prowled this mountain at night. I hatched a cunning plan. Of course, I could have taken care of you that night as you slept so peacefully under the stars, but I wanted to find out more about your precious sun juggling elephant.

'While you slept, I made my way here, already guessing at what I might find. I was right. I was set upon by two of these oversized pussycats,' he motioned to the tigers, who shot him a deathly glance in return, 'sorry; magnificent beasts,' he corrected, offering them a sickly sweet smile in reconciliation. 'I quickly explained to them how their great Queen and I had struck up a deal in her time as our guest.'

Hope's eyes spread in disbelief at the reference to Queen Freassel, remembering how he had freed her from her cage. Maad took note of Hope's expression.

'Oh my dear lad,' he laughed at Hope. 'Did you think that you had set her free? I'm afraid not. You see, she was only kept in that cage to keep watch over dear old Temi. Not to hurt him of course, but to stop him from causing us any more trouble. He just couldn't keep his grip on reality, poor old fellow. Too much time alone in the jungle I guess. He had all sorts of crazy ideas about things that had happened, or were going to happen. The problem was, some of my monkeys started to wonder if what he was saying were true. I had to put a stop to it, you understand.

'But old Queenie and I, best of friends I assure you, and don't let anyone tell you otherwise. She came willingly to meet with us, ask anyone here, and we negotiated a deal, as I explained to those two tigers that night, just in time I might add, from the way they were eyeing me up and down.

'Thing is, the Queen and I are going to rule this land together. With my cleverness and her ruthlessness, we will be unstoppable. Our original plan had been to spread my existing kingdom out and over the jungle, but that would take a long time, and there would be opposition. Particularly, we realised, now that you were

148

travelling around telling anyone who would listen, that you were the 'new king' and all that. So these tigers agreed to help me to take care of that little problem, in return for some payment. A gesture of trust, if you will.

'So I came back down to get their payment, and that's when I almost bumped into you, out for a morning stroll. I had to clamber quickly out on that vine to avoid being seen, but you saw me anyway, didn't you, and away you raced on your stubby little legs to raise the alarm. I followed of course, and arrived just in time to see you and that pig leaving.

'Curious as always, I trailed you both. Imagine my surprise when I discovered who this mystery friend was.' He turned to Boon Khum. 'And that story you told; damn near broke my heart, I swear, I almost felt guilty.

'But even more interesting was what you had to say about the big sun throwing whatsit. I had a new plan. I'd get you to lead me there so I, and not you, could return as king; easy as that. I could enclose the world inside a giant wall, and there would be nothing outside my kingdom to threaten my rule.

'Mine and the Queen's, of course,' he quickly added for the benefit of the tigers, who were listening with their full attention.

He continued. 'So I raced back down to get what I needed,' he lifted the net to show what he meant, 'and raced back here, just in time to catch the two of you before you departed and ruined such a lovely plan.'

He finished with a self-satisfied sigh and searched the faces trained on him for any sign of congratulations. Finding none, he turned to Hope once more.

'Well,' he said, 'I guess it's time to pay up,' and he flung the net holding the three little pigs high into the air over Hope's head to the waiting tigers behind, already licking their lips in anticipation. What happened next is open to debate; because it happened so fast no one saw it clearly.

This is how Hope remembered it.

The piglets in their ivy sack sailed over Hope's head, well out of his reach, and he watched helplessly as the tigers readied themselves to receive their gift. Beside him, in a split second manoeuvre, Boon Khum somehow lifted himself onto his hind legs, casting a shadow over Maad and maybe half the tigers. Stretching every muscle in his body, he reached out with his trunk and, with the very tip, he managed to grab one corner of ivy and pluck the piglets from mid-air.

Coming back down on all four feet with a mighty thud that shook the mountain to its very core, he laid the sack gently down and, still in the one movement, he whipped his trunk around in an arc, sending the confused tigers leaping backwards, hissing their displeasure. They narrowly avoided Boon Khum's trunk (or Boon Khum's trunk narrowly avoided them, it wasn't quite clear). Either way, the tigers backed away, unsure what to do next.

Boon Khum had no such dilemma.

He turned toward Maad and, without hesitation, he charged once more at the monkey, with even more fury than before.

Maad, having nothing left to stop the runaway

elephant, did what every self-respecting coward would have done: he screamed in terror and dashed to the nearest tree, scrambling up with amazing speed. He managed to get himself to a branch out of Boon Khum's reach just as the warrior reached the tree. Instead of slowing down to avoid crashing into it, Boon Khum lowered his head and sped up.

He crashed head-first into the tree trunk and there was a terrible sound of wood splitting and roots being torn from their peaceful home. It was a thick tree, and so managed to keep itself from toppling completely, but it did lean precariously to one side, away from Boon Khum's massive head.

In the violent collision, Maad was shaken from the safety of the treetop. He plummeted towards the ground and the waiting Boon Khum. At the last moment he reached out an arm and managed to grab a hold of the last branch between him and the ground.

Boon Khum, noticing, acted swiftly. He swung his trunk at the monkey, now well within his grasp, but Maad managed to swing himself up and out of the way to the next rung as Boon Khum's trunk smashed through the vacated limb, leaving only emptied air.

Boon Khum's trunk had only just missed Maad, and he immediately swung it at the next branch up, and the figure dangling from it. This time he felt his trunk brush against Maad's feet, but once more the desperate monkey avoided being struck and clambered to another, higher branch. And once more the branch shattered beneath his feet as Boon Khum's trunk passed effortlessly through it.

From his regained position of safety, Maad started

to bounce up and down on the branch, screaming at the top of his lungs. 'Kill them! Kill them now and their flesh is yours to feast on. The piglets too. Kill them now, before we lose *everything*.'

Hope, with the piglets now huddled trembling beneath him, had watched these events, motionless. The tigers had too, but now they started to move. Hope didn't.

Boon Khum had stepped back and was about to ram the tree a second time, which surely would have finished it off, when he heard Hope cry out from behind. He whipped around to see Hope and the piglets surrounded by at least ten tigers.

Roaring his intent, he charged straight for them. Two tigers, one on either side, pounced from their hiding place in the tall grass directly at Boon Khum's face, their insanely long and sharp claws drawn and raised in attack. Boon Khum swung his head left, then right, and the tigers were sent tumbling back from where they came.

Four more dived at his feet, one at each leg, and sank their claws into his ankles. He let out a startled and furious trumpet, but his momentum continued without slowing and the tigers were shaken off, some being trampled, some kicked aside.

Boon Khum bore down on the tigers around Hope and, in a display of good sense, the tigers scattered before him. He came to a halt beside Hope, his breathing heavy and laboured.

'I'm not in as good shape as I once was,' he said between gulps of air. 'Are you okay?'

'Yeah,' answered Hope, but his voice was shaking,

'but I think these guys are about to shake themselves into a thousand pieces.'

The piglets pressed under Hope's belly were indeed trembling violently, pressed so close together they looked more like one pig with three heads.

'Keep them with you,' Boon Khum said, his breathing back to normal. 'We can't let them separate us, or we're finished.' He had his back pressed against Hope so that he was facing the danger, and in this way he circled slowly, always keeping Hope and the piglets at the centre.

The tigers had scattered, but now they were regrouping. They completely encircled the elephants and piglets, and warily but steadily they were closing in.

Boon Khum was watching them closely, trying to decide what to do next, but there seemed only one option. To wait.

Up in his tree Maad watched on with delight, swinging from branch to branch and occasionally letting out deranged squeals of laughter. Presently he was suspended upside down by his tail and giggling maniacally to himself.

Boon Khum and Hope, with the piglets never straying from under him, had edged their way back to the tree in the centre, trying to ignore the sound of cracking bone underfoot. The tigers followed, all the while tightening the circle they had formed around their prey. They were in striking distance now. They crouched low to the ground, their tails stretched up behind, rhythmically swishing from side to side.

Boon Khum readied himself. He drew himself to

his full height, threw his head back, the trunk curled up, its end pointed at the heavy black sky above. He drew a deep breath, and when he let it out again, it came accompanied by the loudest, longest, sharpest trumpet blast that Hope, or anyone there for that matter, had ever heard. Every other sound in the jungle made way for it, and every available space was filled by it. Hope's ears tingled, and inside him, a strange sensation stirred. It started in the soles of his feet and vibrated and grew there for a moment before it spiralled up his legs, filling his stomach with restless butterflies. It shot up his spine, bypassed his brain which played no part in this, and exploded from his trunk in a mighty blast that collided with Boon Khum's, pushing it farther, wider and higher than it could have gone alone.

The tigers shrank back from the sound, the hair on their arched backs standing erect. They bared their teeth and hissed, but their eyes had lost some of their confidence.

Maad stopped his giggling and swung himself up to a more respectful sitting position, and his eyes too had lost their certainty and were already searching out escape routes should things turn against him.

The trumpet call faded along with the elephant's breath, but even before it ended, the sky above, laden with black and bloated clouds had responded.

It started with a deep low rumble that slowly increased in intensity and volume until the air all around throbbed along with it. When it reached its crescendo, it finished with a violent crack that split the sky open, sending massive droplets of rain crashing down on everyone.

'Eh - this is not good,' said Maad to himself.

The tigers hissed now at the treacherous sky, but again they turned and crept toward the elephants, their fur soaked, but their determination only slightly dampened. The rain was heavy and was already pooling on the flat mountaintop. Boon Khum proceeded to slap those pools in front of him, mixing the water with the earth beneath, scooping up the resultant mud in his trunk. He started to spray himself from head to toe, and when Hope saw this he started to do the same, and soon there wasn't an inch of their skin that wasn't thickly covered in oozing mud. The piglets too were covered in the process, and they didn't mind one bit.

Already completely covered, Boon Khum drew one more trunk full, and with this he sent a spray of thick, wet clay into the faces of the tigers approaching him. The tigers disliked the mud even more than the rain that continued to batter them from above and some dropped to the ground, pawing at their eyes that had filled with it. The rest of the tigers took this as the signal to move in.

As you would expect, it was the tigers behind that pounced first, but Boon Khum anticipated this and swung around the tree to position himself between them and Hope. He was just in time, as some of them werė already leaping through the air, their eyes locked on the young elephant. They were surprised then, when they found instead the great brown wall of slime that was Boon Khum blocking their path. They collided hard with him as he moved into position, and bounced

155

off in a sudden and unexpected change of direction.

Before they even hit the ground a second wave of tigers launched themselves. Boon Khum managed to swat two of them clean out of the air with his trunk, but five more reached him. They dug their claws into his side, but the slippery mud made it difficult for them to get a hold, and all but one fell bewildered to the ground at his feet. One had managed to get a grip, and its claws sank deep into Boon Khum's shoulder, while it stretched its jaws towards his neck.

Boon Khum drew a sharp intake of breath against the pain that shot through him. He reached down his side with his trunk, grabbed hold of the tigers tail, and pulled so hard that if the tiger hadn't let go there and then, he would most definitely have been parted from his tail forever. However, the tiger did let go and was flung far away, but not before opening a gaping wound across Boon Khum's shoulder.

The four tigers that had landed at his feet were now receiving a sound thrashing from Hope, who had backed up to them and was kicking them all over with his hind feet, while the little piglets, their legs a blur, sent a constant spray of mud into their faces, blinding them. Confused and in pain, the tigers scrambled to their feet and disappeared into the long grass.

But still more came!

From the grass, at least fifteen more tigers emerged and stalked towards Boon Khum. This time Boon Khum did not wait.

Before they had time to pounce, he charged directly into the middle of all of them. Surprised, the tigers hesitated, and Boon Khum commenced his onslaught.

156

His trunk flailed about him in a frenzy sending tigers yelping through the air. He kicked out with his feet and they met the tigers with a dull thud that left them sprawled in a heap. One managed to leap at his face, its claws digging into his ears on either side. Boon Khum bellowed and threw his head back sharply, catapulting the tiger straight up at the sky, and before it came back down, which might have been bad enough for the tiger in question, Boon Khum plucked him from the air and flung him over the side of the mountaintop.

Yet another was trying to creep unnoticed towards Boon Khum's soft underbelly while he was distracted, but he was noticed, and Boon Khum turned sharply, lowered his head, and with his remaining tusk, he flipped the tiger into the air and swatted him away with his trunk, as he would an annoying insect.

While this was happening, Hope had watched on in awe and admiration, his back to the tree. Unseen to him, a lone tiger had crept up behind and stealthily climbed the tree trunk, slinking its way out onto a bough overhanging Hope and the three piglets beside him. The tiger waited until Hope was directly below - and then launched.

It fell square on Hope's back, and though the mud caused its claws to slip down Hope's sides, the tiger remained balanced on top and, before Hope could react, dug its claws in. Hope screamed.

Boon Khum whipped around at the sound. Before he even saw what was happening he had started racing back to Hope. Hope was trying to shake the tiger from his back, but its grip was too strong and its claws sank deeper into Hope's hide.

Hope cried out in agony. He fell to his knees under the weight of the attack. It was the moment the tiger had been waiting for, and now that Hope had stopped thrashing about, it stretched its jaws wide over Hope's neck. Its massive, dripping fangs yawned over the little elephant, their needle points pushing through his thick skin. He felt himself go faint as the blood drained from his head, but he kept himself conscious long enough to see Boon Khum's trunk sail over him, and he felt the tiger release its grip as it slammed against the tree and slumped to the ground. After that, everything turned to darkness.

Boon Khum grabbed hold of Hope in his trunk before he fell, and lay him gently to the ground. The piglets had fled out of harms way when Hope had fallen. Now they huddled again under his prone chin.

The remaining tigers had observed this, and sensed their opportunity. With his back to them, and distracted by Hope, Boon Khum had left himself vulnerable. All of the tigers still conscious and able to walk, launched one last wave against the great warrior, and still there were many of them.

One by one they leapt, claws drawn, at Boon Khum's rear. Most of the mud had by now washed off in the rain, and they were able to get a clean hold on him. In a flash, four tigers had attached themselves to him. He roared in pain and anger, kicking out with his hind legs, but the tigers were higher up, and they sunk their claws in, as deep as they were long.

Boon Khum didn't want to turn around for fear of leaving Hope exposed, and more tigers joined their friends, always from the safety of his rear. Soon his entire hind-quarters and broad back were crawling with them. He tried shaking them off, and a few did lose their grip, but the others only sank their claws still deeper.

The weight pushed down on the exhausted elephant and he sank to his knees, his head slumping forwards, his trunk still draped protectively over Hope's prone body.

Two of the tigers moved along his back, closer to his thick neck, positioning themselves on either side with their fangs bared. Every able bodied tiger had joined the fray. Boon Khum's sunken frame was swarming with them. From his vantage point in the trees, Maad could no longer see any sign of either elephant. He grinned evilly and clapped his hands in his blood-lust.

The tiger's fangs sank deep into Boon Khum's neck. The fallen warrior closed his eyes tight against the pain, but he did not make a sound. He felt his spirit fade, and with it, the pain.

The tigers continued to tear at him with their claws and exaggerated teeth, but he barely noticed them now. In their place, a wonderful feeling of calm spread through him, and his body relaxed. The sounds of the wind and the rain and the bloodthirsty tigers vanished. He only heard the sound of his own heart, beating hard in his chest. As he listened, the sound slowed steadily. A heavy blanket of sleep fell over him.

He opened his eyes one last time to look down on Hope, who he still held protectively under his trunk, and he saw that Hope had awoken and was looking back up at him. In Hope's eyes Boon Khum saw reflected back at him all his pain and anguish that had tormented him all those years. There was such a look of despair in Hope's eyes as the little elephant realised what was happening, and the fate that awaited him.

Staring deep into Hope's eyes, and recognising all the past events that had led them to this moment, sent a bolt of lightning through Boon Khum's body. He felt his muscles twitch back to life. Keeping his eyes locked on Hope's, he continued to listen to his heart beat its rhythm against his chest. The rhythm quickened!

The sound of the howling wind and lashing rain came roaring back to his ears, and with it the searing pain returned. It was the pain that he had been waiting for. His eyes ignited in a blaze of fury, and when Hope saw that fire return, a smile crept knowingly across his lips.

Boon Khum braced his feet against the mud to steady himself, took a deep breath and then, as he had done all those years ago in play with the young elephants, he surged to his feet in one powerful movement, letting a mighty roar loose against the heavens. His body seemed to expand outside of itself. The air of the mountaintop was suddenly filled with bewildered and terrified tigers as they were cast aside in every direction, their grip failing as if they had been trying to grip the surface of smooth rock and not rough elephant hide.

Maad froze mid-clap in his treetop, his mouth frozen in disbelief.

Boon Khum prepared to face once more whatever might come. His body heaved with the effort of keeping upright, and the rain washed the thick mixture of blood and mud down his body where it pooled around his feet. He looked for all the world like a broken and beaten elephant, but his eyes still blazed with a fury that threatened to ignite the world around him.

Most of the tigers had remained where they had fallen, but a few had raised themselves to their feet and were hesitantly moving towards Boon Khum, hoping that he had spent all that he had left to spend.

Maad sensed this too and resumed his manic bouncing on the tree branch, screaming, 'Kill him! Kill him!'

Hope had raised himself to his feet beside Boon Khum, ready for this final confrontation. The piglets had once more taken up a position under his belly, peering out from behind his front legs.

The few remaining tigers moved in, ready to finish what they had started, and they almost certainly would have done so. I say, "almost certainly," because at that moment a thundering roar burst from the trees, flattening against the ground those tigers still standing. And there they remained, cowering at the sound they knew so well.

Through his rain, mud and blood filled eyes, Boon Khum could barely make out the hazy, pale figure that had emerged into the clearing.

Hope's vision was clearer, and he recognised the figure instantly.

'Queen Freassel,' he whispered to himself.

Chapter Eleven
Queen Freassel's story

Queen Freassel strode onto the bloody scene that was the mountaintop. Hope was once more struck dumb by the powerful presence the Queen carried with her wherever she went. Beside him Boon Khum, sensing that the immediate danger had passed, relaxed slightly and the fire in his eyes dimmed as he too gazed upon the Queen. As she approached him, his head, of its own accord, bowed slightly to pay the respect that her presence demanded.

The rain and wind had retreated from her, and the silence that settled on the mountain was complete. All the other tigers were crouched low and the only movement they made was to crawl out of her way if they found themselves on her intended path. She never once had to step over or around any of them, let alone look down to check that she didn't.

She made her way directly to the centre tree where Boon Khum and Hope – and let's not forget the three traumatised little piglets – awaited her. She kept her eyes locked on Hope's. He held her gaze for as long as he could, but as she drew closer he was forced to look away, and he focused instead on her massive paws as they padded towards him.

Coming up to him now, he heard her speak for the first time as she addressed him. Her voice growled like a turbulent river fighting its way over a gravelly bed, all the while threatening to become a raging sea if called to.

'So; my rescuer has become my rescued. Balance is restored,' she said, 'but once again, in our distraction, the one responsible has slipped away to swing from the scales as his desires demand.'

Realising what she meant, Hope and Boon Khum looked up to where Maad had been revelling in their imminent demise only moments ago. Now there was only an empty branch.

'Do not concern yourselves,' said Queen Freassel before they could even consider taking off in pursuit. 'His wounded pride and seething vengeance have attached themselves wholly and completely to you now. He has nothing left but his desire for revenge. You will meet him again, I assure you.

'As for you and I, I consider my debt repaid in full as of this moment.'

Hope was confused, but he nodded anyway. He had never considered that there was any debt to be repaid, but thinking about it, he was glad that the Queen had.

Turning now to Boon Khum, she addressed him. 'Mighty warrior, your display here today has taught me an invaluable lesson and I am now indebted to you; a debt I feel I may never repay in full.'

Both the elephants were confused now. Boon Khum respectfully replied to the Queen. 'Your Majesty,' he said, 'please forgive my ignorance, but I cannot imagine for what you might be held in my debt. In fact, I would say that it would be the other …….'

'Look!' she interrupted him, and she indicated that

she meant for him to look about him. He did so, and what he saw was that the tigers, who only moments earlier had been tearing at him like savage beasts, were now pulling themselves to their feet and falling in behind their Queen. Some were limping, some were licking their wounds as they walked, and others had to drag themselves back to the mountaintop, having been unceremoniously dumped over the side by Boon Khum in the melee.

'You fought against every tiger on this mountain to protect the thing most dear to you. You fought ferociously, until you were ready to draw your last breath; and when you drew it, you held onto it long enough to ensure you fulfilled your duty.

'This mountain is painted now in your blood, and you stand before me only through a spirit that refused to be broken.

'I have never looked upon such a display of strength and ferocity, and yet, look!!' she once again indicated the wounded tigers around her. 'There is not one of my tigers who is not now back on their feet.'

Boon Khum bowed his head and held his eyes respectfully at the Queen's feet. 'It was never my intention to kill,' he remarked humbly, 'only to protect.'

'Yes,' Queen Freassel purred in response, 'indeed it was so, and it is for this that I am now in your debt, for it is apparent to me now that our intentions over time have become only to kill, when our actions should always have been to protect the balance that has become so one sided in these past years.

'If you will allow me, I would like to start from the

beginning so that you might better understand.'

Hope and Boon Khum gladly gave their consent, thankful to have the opportunity to rest their weary bodies.

'The beginning,' started Queen Freassel, 'is a long time before I came to be born into this jungle, but the beginning and I are forever connected, as you shall see.'

The Queen settled down to tell her story, her thick long tail flicking from side to side, keeping all attention on her. Her tigers, apparently also hearing the story for the first time, lay themselves all around her, some even curling up next to the elephants, recent tensions already drifting into past memories. The piglets curled up under Hope and shut their eyes, but they kept their ears open.

The sun was setting behind them, but Hope didn't notice: all his attention was given completely to the Queen.

She continued. 'At that time tigers were still solitary animals. We hunted alone as we had always done. It was only as cubs that we played and hunted together under the protective and loving care of our mothers.

'We were spread thin across the land and a mountain such as this may only have been home to four or five of us. That way we all had our territories, and food was plentiful for all. Everyone was content and the jungle remained in balance.

'That all changed forever one night when a fierce wind blew across the land. No one and no place was untouched. It was a wind like none of us had experienced before. Trees were uprooted, or at the very least had their branches torn from their trunks, and all their occupants were scattered to the jungle floor. The tigers fled to their caves for shelter and security. There, they waited until the wind had passed; then they waited some more before they finally ventured out.

'The world had been turned upside down and everything lay in confusion. The tigers were cautious at first, unsure if the danger had passed completely, but when it became clear that it had, they realised that the ill wind had in fact been a boon for them.

'At least, that's how they saw it.

'The jungle was filled now with animals unused to surviving on the ground. Deprived of the safety of the treetops they were easy prey for tigers whose hunting prowess is unmatched. We soon forgot about the devastating wind that had thrown this bounty at our feet, and simply set about collecting it.

'We became fat and lazy, no longer needing to exercise our talents to their fullest, as the prey was simply waiting for us to snatch it up as our needs arose. Territories soon blended one into the other, then disappeared altogether, as there was no longer any need to guard what was yours and mine. There was more than enough for everyone, and we prospered.

'There was little for us to do but laze around in the sunshine and wait for our meals to almost present themselves to us. We started to live in groups because, without the necessity of hunting, we became bored in our solitary lives. With so many of us living together we produced many offspring; more than we had ever produced before, and our numbers swelled. But still we had enough to care for our needs and life seemed better than ever. We thanked the wind that had blessed the tigers, but there was one tiger who was able to look past our immediate good fortune and see the bleak future we were stumbling blindly towards. She was a white tiger, just like me, and she had never been able to produce offspring, and as a result she had remained isolated from the others. She lived with them, but apart, and she had observed all that had happened intently.

'She was my mother.

'She didn't agree with everyone's view of the wind as a great blessing; though she didn't hold that it was an ill wind either. She decided that she must find out.

'In the night she left the mountain that had been her home since she was a cub and set off in the direction that the wind had blown from. She knew that the way she had chosen was a treacherous one, but she could no longer watch the tigers revel in their gluttony and apathy, oblivious to where it was leading them.

'She determined to help them in any way she could and, for reasons unknown to me, she felt that finding the source of the wind was the only way, and so she said farewell to her home of many years, not knowing if she would ever return.

'Soon after leaving the mountain she came upon a great expanse of desert. The sand stretched in every direction for as far as she could see, and the sun beat down on it with unforgiving intensity. It was not an environment in any way friendly to life, but my mother had decided on her course of action, and she refused to turn back. And so she entered a land that no tiger had

167

entered before.

'She wandered the desert, tormented by thirst and hunger and the unrelenting sun. Exactly how long she was there she could not remember, but she never managed to cross the endless sand. She closed her eyes to sleep one night, sure that she would never open them again.

'But she did.

'When she awoke she was laying amongst cool grass under the shade of enormous and beautiful trees. Food was laid out in front of her and a fresh mountain stream trickled beside her. She had no idea how she had arrived there, but she didn't question it. She ate and drank her fill and fell back into a deep and satisfying sleep.

'When she awoke, she set off to explore this new mountain. Not knowing where she was, or in which direction she had travelled, she gave up on looking for the source of the wind.

'It was then that she found it.

'I, of course, at this time had not been born yet. I am relaying only what my mother told me when I was young, and I always felt that there were many parts of her story that she always kept for herself. She only told me what I needed to know.

'She never told me what had been the source of that wind, but she was certain that she had found what she had been searching for. In fact, she found more than that, and knew that she had been right to leave the tigers, even though it took her on a hazardous journey that almost cost her her life.

'The one lesson she always instilled in me as a cub,

was to always follow what you know in your heart to be right.

'As I mentioned before, my mother had never given birth and had become resigned to the fact that she never would, but at that time when she remained with the source, she was told that she would give birth to a daughter. It would be white like her, and one day it would help the tigers to return to their natural lives. That was her reward for the efforts she had taken to help her friends.

'She left that place confused, but also with a sense of excitement and contentment. Not knowing which way was home, or what exactly was going to happen next, she stayed on the mountain. Food and water were abundant, and her life was comfortable; but she didn't give birth. Many years passed. How many, she did not know, because on that mountain it seemed almost as if time stood still. She waited and waited, but nothing; until one day her stomach started to swell. It grew bigger and bigger until she felt she must burst if she didn't give birth soon.

'One night she fell asleep and when she woke, she immediately recognised her surroundings as the mountain she had left so long ago. Bewildered, but accepting things for what they were, she set off for the mountaintop where she had left her companions

'Making her way up the mountain, she noticed that things were different. The jungle seemed darker, and the little wildlife that was there kept to the shadows. Her discomfort grew as she climbed the steep slope and before the summit she went into labour. Under the full moon she gave birth to the daughter that had been foretold. That daughter was me.

'Carrying me the rest of the way, she came to the mountaintop and found the tigers that lived there, but it was not the homecoming that she had expected. She was immediately surrounded and questioned threateningly. The tigers were suspicious and edgy, and my mother soon realised that she didn't recognise any of them. She asked after some of her old friends, but no one had heard of any of them, until one very old tiger was called forward. She recognised one of the names as that of her great grand mother, but said of course that it couldn't be the same tiger. My mother felt differently. It seemed as if she had been absent for generations, and yet she had hardly aged at all.

'She told them her story and, as she expected, they were disbelieving, but enough of her story matched with the stories that the old tiger had heard at the paws of her ancestors, and some of them began to wonder if it were true. They decided at least to accept her into the fold, and that is where I grew up.

'As it turned out, I didn't have very long with my mother. Time seemed to catch up with her very quickly now that she was back on the mountain, and she passed away in her sleep while I was still young. I found her in the morning with a peaceful smile on her face and, sad though I was, it seemed perfectly natural for it to happen that way.

'Accepted, though still regarded with suspicion, I grew up as a loner. The others still hunted in groups and killed everything they could find. Often they killed more than they could possibly eat, and the wasted food rotted in the hot sun. They took great pleasure in the simple act of killing, and it seemed to matter not whether they were hungry. Against such numbers the animals stood little chance, but soon they started to become scarce and rarely came into the open.

'Being an outsider, I hunted alone. I went as far away as possible from their hunting grounds and sometimes I hunted for days before I managed to fill my stomach. But I became stronger because of it. My senses were sharp and I knew the jungle inside and out. The others grew fat and dull, and when the food became scarce, they came to me. They didn't know how to help themselves, so I became their appointed leader.

'I wasn't at all sure what to do. I could teach them how to hunt, but there simply wasn't enough food to sustain us all, and yet they refused to separate. They had grown too comfortable in the easy life that they had lived for so long. So I looked for another, quicker solution.

'I soon found one; or so I thought. Rumours had reached us of a group of monkeys who lived on a nearby mountain. They were collecting up all the wildlife on their mountain, and using them for their own amusement.

'I had an idea and set off to find these monkeys. They weren't difficult to locate, as their reign of terror had spread throughout the jungle. I simply followed the direction that the animals were fleeing.

'I came upon a group of them on a trapping expedition. They seemed to consider trying to trap me but thought better of it. They moved off, but I stopped them. I told them that I would like to speak with their leader; that I had a proposition for him. They told me to wait where I was, and disappeared up the mountain. I waited patiently, but it seemed as if they didn't mean to return. I was about to leave, feeling disappointed, when I was hailed from behind. I turned, and that was the first time I laid eyes on our friend Maad.

'Immediately, I disliked him. There was something very unnatural about him. His eyes, his fur; his way of walking, of talking, but I was thinking of my companions who were relying on me. And also of my mother who had always told me that I was destined to help the tigers.

'I offered my proposal. I was, in all humility, an accomplished hunter. I could track better than any monkey could possibly hope to. With my hunting and their trapping skills, we could collect many more animals in a single raid. I would take enough to feed my tigers, and they could do what they liked with the rest

'I am not proud of it, but at the time I was only thinking of my hungry clan. Maad accepted, so long as I could prove my worth. I sensed there was a threat hidden in his words, but I wasn't afraid of him. I sensed that he, in fact, was filled with fear himself and despite his bravado, he was at heart a great coward.

'I set out to prove my worth regardless; and prove myself I did. That same day I managed to round up maybe a hundred or more pigs and chase them into a trap set by the monkeys. Ironically, it was almost spoiled by an elephant and her baby who got tangled in the stampede, but we succeeded in the end.

'Maad was impressed and agreed to my terms. A

cage was built to transport our tiger share to our mountain. Every morning I travelled to the monkey's mountain to help them collect their specimens, and every evening I brought the spoils back to feed my family. My hunting prowess grew to ever greater heights, while the rest grew fatter and lazier. They didn't even have to kill their own food any more. They started to complain of this. They missed killing, they told me. They didn't miss hunting, as they had never really known it anyway, and were too lazy to learn; but they had enjoyed killing.

'I spoke again to Maad and, wanting to maintain my services, he agreed to move parts of his menagerie to our mountain when he had grown bored of them. I had been so successful, it seemed he was running out of room anyway. He was happy to start moving the old out as the new arrived. So, occasionally, he would send over a cage full of animals, in addition to what I brought back with me, and release them on our mountain. Of course, I had to chase these poor creatures to the top where the others waited to slaughter them.

'So focused was I on what I was doing to supposedly help my kind, I failed to see how we were all descending deeper into the pit I had initially intended to drag us from. Sometimes I even joined my companions in their pleasure killing.

'We continued like this for some time but again, in time, food became harder to find. Maad sent word that he wanted to meet with me to discuss this problem and the following morning I went to see him. However, he wasn't at all interested in discussing anything with me.

173

As soon as I stepped on to their mountain they sprung their trap. I was set upon by maybe two dozen monkeys or more, each carrying a length of vine which they expertly and speedily tied me up in. By the time I realised what was happening and started to fight back, I was already restrained. Their agility and skill in trapping surprised me, I must admit, and I had let my guard down in the belief that I had become indispensable to them. It appeared that they had intended to ensnare me all along, and had only waited until I was of little use to them, or they had grown bored of me.

'I was dragged up to their little kingdom, which you already know so well. I fought inside my restraints the whole way and made their task as difficult as I could. For my troubles I received many beatings, and was stabbed repeatedly through the vines with sharpened bamboo, but I meant to make them work for their prize, and I never stopped struggling. By the time we reached the top the sun had already fallen, but my eyes are sharper in the darkness than the light, and so I saw clearly what the monkeys had been doing with all those animals whose capture I had enabled.

'The horror of it put an end to my struggle as it dawned on me what I had been doing for all those years. The shame of it burned me from the inside out, and I felt as if I might burst into flames at any moment.

'I was dragged to the cage and I resumed struggling. Not for my freedom, but because I wanted to exact my revenge on the one who I felt had made me into what I had become, though I knew in my heart that I had moulded myself, and if there was any blame to be

174

cast; it was to be cast at me.

'I was released into the cage and the cage was raised above the ground. There was a monkey inside the cage; an old and frail looking monkey. My instinct was to tear him to pieces for what his kind had done to me, but something in his eyes told me that he was different. Instead, I offered my name, and received his in return. Temi. After that we never spoke. I wish now that we had, for I feel he may have many things to tell me that I could have learned from. Instead I spent the next days pacing back and forth, waiting for my moment. I ate and drank nothing; instead I fed on my vengeance and quenched my thirst on my hate. I was oblivious to everything around me and was only jerked into the here and now only when I heard *his* voice.

'He never once came to speak with me, like the true coward that he is, but whenever I heard his voice beneath me it took all of the strength of that bamboo cage to contain me. I could feel his fear below when I threw myself at the walls and roared. The fear that I could smell seeping from his every pore was the only pleasure I took from that time.

'Within a few days, however, my moment arrived. It was when you, little Hope, and your friend set me free. At that moment, all of my pent up hatred and desire for revenge welled up inside me. I was bursting with it. It poured all around me. But then I saw Maad and your friend standing over him. All of those dark emotions exploded from me in a roar that shook even myself. Maad fainted, as you must remember, but then I was struck by something. Despite all that he had seen, your friend had not crushed that monkey into the

175

ground as I would have done. And you had not concerned yourself with him at all, but had set about freeing all the captive animals; the animals I had forgotten all about in my blood-lust. I remembered my mother's words all those years ago, and I looked deep inside myself and did what I knew what was right.

'I fled before I did something that I would regret. I had already done enough of that.

'I slowly made my way back here, not knowing to do next, or even if I should return here at all. After wandering for some time, I knew I had to come back. I had to somehow mend the error of our ways. Imagine my surprise when I arrived and found the scene that confronted me. My tigers locked in a bitter battle with two elephants; one of whom was responsible for my freedom.

'I was torn between my duties as the tigers Queen and my debt to the one who had saved me; and so many others. That's when I heard that voice calling from the trees. It sent a shiver down my spine and again I wrestled with my feelings. I could have taken him from that treetop, even before he felt my presence, but I realised at the same time that my tigers must have been fighting for him. Knowing his cunning, I figured he must have somehow tricked them into believing we were still on the same side, and it was *you* who were the enemy.

'I left him, and did what I should have done a long time ago. I stopped my tigers from committing another senseless and unnecessary killing.

'And so Maad lives to fight another day and I'm sure our troubles with him are far from over. More important however is that I, and hopefully all my companions here, have learnt something valuable, and this is the beginning of a change in us: a change which may become our means of survival.

'And your display, great warrior, was the final lesson I needed to learn to see clearly what this change would entail. No more shall we kill for pleasure. No more shall we gather in great numbers, spreading fear across the land. No more shall we wipe out life from large areas of land, throwing the jungle out of balance.

'From now on we shall be protectors. We shall protect our own survival by hunting only what we need to survive, and we shall protect the balance by ensuring, wherever we can, that all around us does the same.'

Queen Freassel's story ended there, and all the tigers around her held their heads low in shame, realising as they had listened what they had become.

There was silence for some time as the weight of the story sank in, and Hope wondered at how many of the events of the past days were woven together in a rich, but as yet unfinished tapestry. It was Boon Khum who broke the silence.

'Your Majesty,' he said. 'It has been truly an honour to meet you and to fight against your brave and loyal subjects. I would ask you one favour if you would allow.'

'Anything,' replied the Queen.

'My friend Hope is on a long and dangerous journey. I had planned on accompanying him, but I fear my wounds are too great and I will need time to recover. I know that Hope will not want to wait, and I feel anyway that he should venture from here once more on his own.

'What I ask is that first, these three piglets be immediately returned to their home. At the same time, Pa can be told that I shall return there tomorrow, and that I shall once more require his kindness and care.

'Tonight myself and Hope, who is also wounded but will recover quickly with his youth, shall rest on your mountaintop. In the morning, we shall go our separate ways, although I hope that we shall all meet again in the future.'

'As you wish,' purred Queen Freassel gracefully.

Hope was disappointed that Boon Khum would not be accompanying him any further, but he knew that what he said was the truth. The piglets were gathered up, and before they were sped away to their home and family, Hope touched each of them on the head with his trunk, promising that on his return he would come to tell them all of his adventures. He may even take them along on his next one, he told them.

They said their farewells. Hope turned to Boon Khum, who was already laid out under the great tree well on his way to the deep sleep that his body craved so much. He silently made his way next to him and lay down beside. The danger had passed, but still Hope felt a great security nestled up the massive warrior.

Soon he too drifted into sleep and dreamt of wondrous battles where he and Boon Khum fought valiantly against indistinct dark shapes in an unknown shadowy wilderness.

The moon sat over them, chasing away any

178

shadows that meant to creep to them as they slept.

The sun would rise soon and a new day would begin.

PART THREE

Chapter One
A new day

Hope awoke late the following morning. His weariness had finally caught up with him. Feeling safe in the company of the great warrior Boon Khum, he had allowed himself to sink into a deep and replenishing slumber. He had dreamt of many strange and wonderful things, and when he had awoken he had tried to grab hold of them to take with him into the day but, as always, he found that they wriggled from his grip like slippery fish and swam back to the depths of his mind from where they had come. He was left feeling slightly disappointed, as if he had glimpsed something important but realised too late that he should try to remember it.

In any case, he had to leave his dreams where they were for now and think about the new journey ahead. He rose from the spot under the tree where he had slept and found that he was alone on the mountaintop. Not only were Boon Khum and all of the tigers absent, but the mess of twisted and rotting carcasses had been cleared away. The grassy plateau retained no trace of its former life as a grotesque monument to the tigers killing spree. It was green and fresh in the late morning sun, its innocence and vitality once more allowed to shine through.

Hope stretched his rejuvenated muscles to attention

and bathed in the cool breeze that washed over him, gently stirring his senses to life.

He was ready. He was eager to set off on his next unknown adventure, but he could never leave without saying goodbye to Boon Khum.

He lightly grazed his way to the far side of the mountaintop that overlooked his destination. The long grass exploded with crickets and grasshoppers, hurriedly making way for Hope's grasping trunk. A red-striped, cream coloured snake slithered away to find a new spot to soak up the sunlight it needed to make it through the cool night. A flock of sparrows swooped in and out of an invisible slalom course in the sky, never losing their formation and never missing a note in their playful song.

Hope marvelled at how quickly the mountain had brought itself back to life. It was as if the moon had washed all of its stains away with its soft night light and now the sun was displaying its renewed glory, while everything that crept and crawled and jumped and flew over that mountain simply got on with living.

It was a new day!

Hope reached the edge of the mountain peak. The mouthful of grass he was hungrily eating suddenly lost all of its importance and his chewing jaw gradually slowed down as it lost interest, eventually deciding it was best to stop altogether.

The view that presented itself to Hope was not what he expected; but he had come to expect that. The mountain descended steeply down and away from the bottom, and the lush greenness spilt from the mountainside onto the wide open plain that stretched away to the horizon. But the carpet of green only spread so far before it was swallowed by an ocean of sand and rolling dunes that carried on as far as Hope could see. Once there, it merged with the searing blue and a shimmering haze blurred the line where the earth met the sky.

Hope's eyes watered as he gazed at the dancing line of the horizon, but he could not look away. If he stared long enough and hard enough he felt that what he expected to see might somehow reveal itself to him. But it didn't.

What he had expected to see, of course, was another mountain: the mountain that concealed behind it the giant sun throwing elephant that had been solidifying into reality ever since he thought he had dreamt it up. It was dissolving once more into the tiny particles of imagination that flickered inside Hope's mind, waiting to be bound together and set forth into the world.

Some years ago Hope had made an attempt to catch up to the horizon, but found that the horizon always managed to stay the same unreachable distance away and simply pushed the landscape at him to slow him down. He knew then that it was impossible to find out what was behind the horizon. If that was indeed where the sun throwing elephant resided, then he might as well start the long trek back to his valley.

'It *is* out there,' spoke a voice beside him in response to his unasked question. It was Boon Khum.

He had silently padded up while Hope had been caught up in this new insecurity. Boon Khum had sensed what his young companion had been contemplating and was fulfilling his last duty before sending Hope off on the last leg of his journey.

He knew that the next time he met Hope, if he met him again, Hope would be his king. He had to ensure that Hope fulfilled his destiny.

'It *is* out there,' he repeated, 'and the time has come for you to find it.'

'But there's nothing out there except endless sand,' said Hope despairingly. 'There's no mountain for the giant sun throwing elephant to hide behind, and I can never reach the horizon to look behind *it*. I know. I've tried.'

'Why do you say that there's no mountain?' asked Boon Khum.

Hope was confused. He paused to allow the question to settle in and make itself comfortable in his mind. He watched it to see if it hid any more meaning than he first thought, but seeing that it didn't, he gave the only reply he thought appropriate.

'Because I can't see one,' he said hesitantly, suddenly unsure of the obviousness of his response.

Boon Khum also paused, to allow Hope's answer the time it needed to make its point before it drifted away to the place that holds all the answers that have been rejected as unacceptable. Then he spoke, and when he did, it was with great authority.

'When you feel sad,' he said, 'can you see your sadness?'

'No,' said Hope.

'When you think of your family back home,' he continued, 'can you see those thoughts?'

'No.'

183

'When the wind blows through the leaves of the trees, you see the leaves fluttering against it; but do you see the wind?'

'No.'

Boon Khum was speaking very seriously and Hope was answering respectfully, but he was unsure where this was leading. The great warrior went on.

'Would you agree however that the wind in the trees, the thoughts in your head, and the sadness in your heart are all real, despite them remaining invisible to you?'

'Yes,' agreed Hope.

'Then why are you so sure that there is no mountain simply because you cannot see one?'

'Because,' started Hope, deciding to stay with the logical answers, 'every mountain I have climbed before, I have seen.'

Hope was satisfied with his response and was certain that the conversation would end with it. But Boon Khum wasn't finished yet.

'Have you ever been on *that* mountain?' he asked, referring to the invisible, imaginary or perhaps non-existent mountain that they had been talking about.

'Of course not,' said Hope, and waited for the next question.

But there were no more questions. Boon Khum turned away from the horizon to face Hope.

'It's time for you to leave,' he said suddenly and solemnly, though a satisfied and expectant smile toyed with the idea of spreading across his lips.

Hope was speechless. He wanted to say that he didn't want to leave, that he was afraid of the endless sand and relentless harshness of the awaiting desert, that he wanted to stay with Boon Khum until he recovered and they could make the journey together - and that he really would have preferred if he could see the mountain that he was supposed to climb, but he said nothing. He simply nodded slowly, glanced once more to the horizon, once more to the rising sun that seemed to burn brighter than ever as it sat on the precipice of baking sand that made up the horizon, and once more to the distance behind him that grew with every forward step he took. He turned to face Boon Khum.

'Will you say goodbye to the tigers for me?' he said sadly.

'Of course.'

Hope stretched his trunk up and placed the tip inside the mighty elephant warrior's mouth.

Boon Khum rested his trunk lightly on the little elephant's head, but he spoke strongly.

'We *will* meet again,' he said, 'You have given me life, when I had been wishing for death.

'Go now, and don't look back until you mean to return.'

Hope could find no words for the emotions that welled up inside him and so he said nothing more. He turned to face the unknown destination that awaited him and took his next step.

Chapter Two
The desert

Hope descended the mountain in very quick time. He found that once he stepped down from the mountain he became very eager to continue what he had started that morning which seemed now so long ago. He felt that he must be nearing the end of his quest; if indeed it had an ending and if, in fact, it was actually a quest.

Queen Freassel's story replayed itself in his mind as he marched down the mountainside. The desert that her mother had spoken of must surely be the same desert that he was now coming upon, he thought. And the mysterious mountain that she had found herself on may very well be the same mountain that he was hoping to find. What's more, the mysterious source of the wind, which had been mentioned in both Queen Freassel and Temi's stories, seemed as if it may somehow be connected to the giant sun throwing elephant. It certainly seemed, at least to Hope, to be just as intriguing and though it wasn't the goal of his present search, he would very much like to happen across it and add it to his growing list of tales to tell.

Midday had come and gone while Hope had been travelling down the path in the shade of the mountain trees. When he emerged onto the open plain at its base the sun had already expended most of its store of heat for the day and the cool evening approached.

Hope fairly ran out into the thinning green of the grass towards the looming dunes of barren sand that dominated the landscape ahead. He was filled with renewed energy, ready for whatever the day had planned for him.

As he strode to the desert he grazed on the grasses around him. He had been completely focused on the journey ahead when his attention was drawn suddenly to a sound behind. It was the sound of something cracking, but Hope had not seen anything on his way that might have accounted for it. His natural reaction was to swing around on the spot, his ears held defensively out. There was nothing that he saw that explained it. The flat grassland was clear all the way back to the mountain that he had come from. Out of the corner of his eye he noticed that one clump of long grass seemed to rustle a bit more than the light breeze called for, but he couldn't be sure that he hadn't imagined it. He considered going back to take a closer look, but he didn't like the idea of going backwards when there were much better reasons for going forward. And so he turned back in his original direction and continued on, though he kept his ears slightly tuned to what was going on behind.

He continued undisturbed until he came at last to the divide between grassland and desert, or as Hope saw it - friend and foe.

The grass had gradually thinned the closer Hope had come to the expanse of sand, and now, standing at the very edge of the desert, he saw how desolate the way ahead really was. There wasn't a single splash of colour that tainted the brown landscape that confronted him, and even the brown came in the barest minimum of shades. There really was nothing inviting whatsoever to a young elephant; except perhaps the opportunity to run up and tumble down the cushioned dunes, but Hope had become accustomed to extending his own invitations to himself regardless, and this would be no different.

However, he hesitated. The sun had almost set, and Hope wasn't overly excited about the prospect of his first experience of being in a desert coming in the night-time.

He decided that the smart thing to do was to spend as much time now stuffing his stomach with grass while he still could, and then camp just outside the desert's borderline, ready to take the plunge first thing in the morning. This is what he did.

He ate until his belly was so full, *it* decided it was time to lie down before the rest of him came to the same conclusion. He fell sound asleep under the nearly full moon and his loud snoring travelled uninterrupted across the wide open spaces of the grasslands and desert.

The desert sands heard, and shifted and jiggled in anticipation of Hope's imminent arrival.

They had been waiting a long time!

When Hope awoke the next morning he was struck by a very strange feeling; or, to put it another way, a very strange lack of feeling. I don't mean in the physical sense, like feeling numb, but more like a complete absence of any thought, any emotion or any memory. It was as if he were looking at the world for the first time. For a brief moment he was completely empty of everything, but then a sneaking remembrance crept into his mind and he was suddenly reminded that he was a little elephant, that his name was Hope, and that he was on a search for a giant sun throwing elephant. All of the finer points of his life followed smoothly into position and once more he was reconstructed as the future elephant king, Hope.

What he wondered though, was when had he been de-constructed, and where had his identity been for that period of time?

No answers seemed immediately forthcoming and so Hope allowed the questions to sit where they were, just in case a response happened to pass by. In the meantime, he decided that now that he was himself again, he might as well continue with what his self had started. He rose to his feet and stretched every muscle that he could in every direction that he knew.

'Right,' he said to no one in particular, 'there's no time like the present.'

He suddenly had a flash of Pu-pa in his mind. He imagined what Pu-pa might have said in response. Something like; 'Well, you know, it would be more correct to say there's no time *except* the present, because how can we be sure that yesterday even happened, or that tomorrow will ever come. I mean, I remember very clearly crashing through the side of a mountain and bursting out the other side but no one I ever spoke to remembers me doing it. The tunnel is still there for everyone to see, but they say that it has always been there. The point is; either my memory is wrong, or theirs is. Or perhaps we're both wrong; or even both right! Either way, we obviously can't always be sure of our memories, which means we can't always be sure of yesterday. As for tomorrow, well, let me tell you about tomorrow ....'

Hope stopped there. He was laughing to himself but he was a little concerned at how well he had been able to imitate thinking like Pu-pa. All the same, he missed him and hoped that he would see him again soon. He shook himself to bring himself back from yesterday to the present, and the desert that was to become his, hopefully, temporary home.

He spent a little more time collecting one last meal and, when he was satisfied, but not so full that he would want to lay right back down, he took his first steps onto the sand.

The sun was not long risen and it balanced itself just above the wavy lines of the horizon. Its light had only just settled on the uppermost grains of sand, which still held the coolness of the night before. It was Hope's first experience of walking on sand and he had to admit that it was a rather pleasant one. It was soft and cool underfoot, and he particularly enjoyed the way it moulded itself around his feet, politely taking on their shape rather than the other way around, as was the case with most other surfaces he had walked on.

He also discovered that if he twisted his foot a certain way as he walked, the sand squeaked at him. It wasn't unlike the sound that he himself made when he was a little overexcited; or maybe when he was in trouble and tried to show whoever he was in trouble with that he was really only a little elephant. (He found that this didn't work quite so well now as when he was younger, smaller and, well ….cuter.)

He imagined that maybe the sand was trying to tell him something, and so he concentrated hard on listening to the squeaking sand as he walked over it. Of course he never figured out what the sand was trying to say, but it did pass the time, and before he knew it Hope was deep into the desert's interior, surrounded by sleeping dunes.

If he had figured out what the sand was trying to say, he may very well have the decided that the desert wasn't for him after all. What the sand had been trying to say was, in fact, something like: 'Come in little one. Come to our centre, to our heart, to our mouth. Come amongst our stirring dunes, to be covered, to be tasted, to be swallowed.'

Hope didn't hear any of this. He simply heard the squeak, squeak, squeak of the sand beneath his feet, and he delighted in creating it.

As for the sand dunes that rolled out from him in all directions, he certainly didn't see them as any threat. He saw them as his newest source of amusement and he tried to decide which one he would charge up and tumble down first. He checked around himself to get his bearings on the mountain behind and chose the dune which lay in the direction in which he wanted to continue.

The sun was high in the sky and the heat was overbearing. Hope had managed to keep his mind on other things and so hadn't been overly bothered by it, but his mouth was starting to dry out. *Perhaps*, he thought to himself, *there will be some water on the other side of these dunes.*

He reasoned that running up and tumbling down the dunes would serve two purposes. One; to get to the water quicker, and two; to have fun and amuse himself. He found his reasoning to his liking and decided to pursue it.

He charged at the dune, which was only about fifteen to twenty steps high, and launched himself up its sandy slope. He was about three quarters of the way to the top when he realised that fifteen to twenty steps up the side of a sand dune actually felt like ten times that number if he had been running up a familiar grassy hill.

The sand gave way under each step so that his muscles had to work that much harder to keep gaining ground. The heat of the sun, which he had done so well to keep at bay until then, suddenly ignited across his skin. With his muscles burning from exertion, and his thick hide scorching in the midday sun, he felt that he was being burnt from the inside out and the outside in. As for his dry mouth; well, if you were to politely ask a stone for any water it might have to spare, you might have received more than you could have scraped from Hope's tongue at that moment.

By the time he reached the top of the dune, the option of stopping or tumbling down the other side was no longer open to him. Something other than his brain decided that it would be best to collapse in an undignified heap at the top and slide down, head first and barely conscious.

Hope obediently obeyed.

His head ploughed up quite a mound of sand, which stopped at the bottom slightly quicker than Hope did, resulting in his head becoming half buried in the mini dune he had created. The other result of this was that his mouth was filled with sand which, not surprisingly, didn't help very much with the whole dryness problem.

He remained in that position for a time, trying to decide if he should give in to the wave of exhaustion that had crashed down on top of him, or should he surge up to its crest and ride the wave to the shore, the way Boon Khum would have.

The thought of Boon Khum's heroics back on the mountaintop was enough to convince him that the second option was best. He extracted his head from the sand and pulled himself back to his feet.

Standing up, he saw that his descent down the sand dune, though much quicker and easier, had been a lot longer than his ascent. He was in the bottom of a deep basin, surrounded on all sides by tall dunes. The mounds of sand obstructed his view of any of the landscape, even the mountain that he had left just the previous morning. The only direction worth looking was up, and the only thing up there was the clear blue sky with the fiery ball of the sun suspended exactly at its centre, its intense heat seeming to push Hope deeper and deeper into the pit of sand.

Being cooked alive in a giant bowl formed from mountains of sand had not been on Hope's list of things to do that day. The only way he could see to prevent that from happening was to get himself up and over the facing dune, which was at least three times the height of the one he had just climbed: and he had *only just* managed to climb that one.

At least, he thought, he knew which direction to

take, as he could still see the trail that his less than elegant slide had left behind him. If he took it slow and steady then he felt that he could do it, and there was always the possibility of finding water on the other side, as he had imagined.

'Right,' he said aloud to himself. 'I can do this.'

The surrounding sand heard this, and as if it suddenly remembering something it was supposed to do, it replied, 'Er, sorry, but there's one more thing. We almost forgot all about it, and boy would we have been embarrassed. Waiting all this time, and when our big moment comes, we almost forget the most important part, heh! Well; um, anyway…eh…here it is!'

Hope didn't hear any of this, but he did notice a wind that suddenly spiralled down into the pit, swirling around the bottom and lifting a fine layer of sand which flew into orbit around him. He stopped what he was about to do.

The wind grew stronger, and more and more sand was picked off the surrounding dunes, until they had completely disappeared and it seemed to Hope that the entire desert was now spinning around his head. Or, perhaps *it* was still, and he was spinning on the spot.

Either way, he was becoming very dizzy, and more than a little nervous. Released from the confines of the now dispersed dunes the wind revealed its full fury. Coming out of its spin, it suddenly blew out in the direction behind Hope. All of the sand that the wind carried was flung with great force at the little elephant. He bowed his head and shut his eyes against it, unable to do anything else. The grains of sand that blasted him stung his body. It felt as if his skin was being stripped

194

off.

The wind continued, and so did the onslaught of sand. The sun was blocked entirely by the airborne desert and Hope was plunged into total darkness. The only sound he could hear was the thundering wind and the sound of a tiny particle of sand bouncing off his head; multiplied by a billion or so.

The desert rearranged itself around Hope, sand dunes forming and being torn apart before they even had time to be noticed. It was a force of nature unlike any he had ever experienced before. The wind howled with a fury that terrified him. It changed direction once more and threw itself at his back. The strength of it almost lifted him off his feet, but he managed to brace himself and hold on. His eyes remained clenched shut, though it would have made no difference if he had opened them.

He was sure that he must be down to his last layer of skin, such was the ferocity and abrasiveness of the lashing sand, and if his mouth were not already glued shut from the dryness, he would surely have let out an agonised scream.

The wind shifted again, then decided that no specific direction was more to its liking. It swirled and swooped and raced back and forth. It shot up and then crashed down, all the while centring itself on Hope, and all the while creating and then destroying the landscape around him.

As a barrage of sand danced violently against his ear, the sound it created seemed to Hope to form a word.

'Here,' he heard the gravelly voice whisper.

He turned, shocked by the sudden voice and his eyes instinctively opened, but were immediately shut by the stinging sand. He tried to tune his ears once again to the white noise that filled his head.

'Quickly,' he heard an urgent voice scratch against his eardrums. Was someone trying to help him out of this onslaught? he wondered. But there was no one nearby, and yet the sound seemed almost to come from inside his own head. He listened intently, desperate for anything that might save him from his helplessness. What he heard next, however, set his heart racing and sent a shudder through his entire being.

Thousands of tiny voices seemed to merge together in one roaring whisper that raced around Hope's head, triumphantly declaring, 'Here! Here he is!! Quickly, quickly, before *she* comes. Bury him! Bury him quickly before *she* comes. The sun is almost gone.'

'Before she comes? Who is *she*?' said Hope's voice inside his head. 'The sun is almost gone!? Gone where?' screamed Hope to himself. 'How long have I been in here?' He had to get out, but how?

He couldn't move against the force of the wind, and he couldn't move with it because it never held the one direction for more than a moment. He couldn't open his eyes against the sand to see where he might go and his thirst was so great that he felt he might crumble into a pile of sand himself, joining his own torment. He was also extremely hungry, but his brain was much too busy panicking to even bother relaying the message that his stomach was sending.

The sand started to deposit itself at Hope's feet. He felt it gather and creep over his toenails, and up and around his ankles. It was climbing quickly, and before he realised what was happening, he was buried up to his knees.

He remembered those words; '*Bury him.*' The words shouted themselves reluctantly in his mind.

Panic gripped the little pachyderm and instinct jolted him into action. He wrenched his front feet from the swelling sand with great effort. The wind still thrashed him with unnecessary violence, though it was more intent now with throwing sand *around* Hope than *at* him.

Sand quickly filled the holes that his feet had vacated and he was able to use this to push against in an effort to release the sandy grip on his hind legs. But in the short time that this took, his back quarters had become entrenched right up to the top of his tail.

The sand was raining down on him in greater waves. He pushed with all his strength, letting out a mighty roar, not caring any more about the sand that filled his open mouth.

His back right leg and his tail worked themselves free, but his left foot remained captive. His tail worked furiously, flicking at the sand around the ensnared leg. His back right foot joined the other two and pushed against the sand that had deposited itself in the hole it had left behind itself. It worked!

He managed, with great effort, to pull the last leg free. His mouth was filled with sand, and it was starting to work its way down his throat, choking him. Tears streamed down his cheek from the exertion, but still the sand thundered down on him.

Having only just released his last leg from its hold,

Hope realised that the sand had taken possession of his front legs once more. He was already buried up to his chest. He kicked his back legs up and down constantly to prevent them from also becoming trapped again, but each time he lifted one up and placed it back down, the unrelenting storm of sand had raised the ground under them and he became tilted forwards; his back end raised higher than his front. This made it even more difficult to push himself back out.

He heard the voices again. 'Hurry, hurry! The moon is coming, and it will bring her with it. Cover him so she cannot see. Bury him! Bury him!!'

The sand had gotten hold of Hope's trunk and started to cover it as speedily as it could. Hope swung his head violently from side to side, keeping his trunk free for the moment, but the sand swarmed up to his neck. His back legs could go no higher and were disappearing under the forming dune.

Hope heard a piercing screech from high overhead. He had no idea what gave birth to the sound, but the sand increased the intensity of its resolve in response.

Unable now to move anything but his trunk, which he held high overhead, and his tail, which was now the highest point of his body, he could only watch as the sand surged over him. It filled and then swept over his mouth. Soon after, watching became no longer an option as his eyes were overtaken by the rising tide. He was still able to breathe through his trunk, but as the sand swept over his head, he knew that it too would soon be covered and filled. For possibly one last time, he let out a soaring trumpet blast that carried even through the dense wall of sand and burst out into the open sky far above.

Again Hope heard the screeching sound, though it was heavily muffled by the sand that packed his ears. He wondered what on earth it was, but knew it would ever remain a mystery to him as the sand climbed up his trunk, first covering, and then filling it.

Hope held his breath. There was nothing else he could do with it.

The sand continued its endeavours. All that remained visible of the disappearing elephant was the very tip of his tail, which stuck out of the sand like a tombstone. Soon it too would disappear.

'That's it, that's it!!' the voices vibrated through the sand in Hope's ears. 'Finish him! She's coming. She's coming!!'

Hope started to feel faint. He really wished he could find out who *she* was, but there was no hope of that now. He felt his tail disappear and he knew that he was completely submerged under the sand.

He couldn't hold his breath forever.

Chapter Three
Ishopa

Hope could vaguely hear the sound of the storm above him, but it grew fainter with every passing moment as the sand piled still higher and higher over him. He could feel its immense weight pushing down on him, trying to force that last breath from his stubborn lungs. It was the only thing Hope had taken down with him from above, and he was determined to hold onto it for as long as he could.

The sand was packed tight under the force of the growing mound above. He could feel it start to crush him, and the incredible stillness imposed on him felt more violent than even the raging storm that had battered him moments ago.

He was about to reluctantly expel that last store of air, which would have sealed his fate forever, when he felt a massive thump on the surface far above. With great difficulty, he drew the air back into his burning lungs. He had no idea what the thump might mean, but he wanted to find out: if he could hold out that long. It was certainly better than his second option.

The sand crammed against his body became agitated. It started to shift uncomfortably around him. He could hear a furious scratching above and it seemed as if the weight pressing on him was lessening slightly.

Then, unexpectedly, it was lessened greatly.

200

His lungs were about to burst. His veins were throbbing against the constraints of his skin and his head threatened to explode, ruining any slim chance he had for escape.

The sound of the furious wind was coming rushing back to Hope as the layers of sand between it and him were thinned by some unknown means. He felt his tail exposed to the air above. He felt the wind and sand whipping against it, and it was the most refreshing feeling he ever felt.

He was no longer able to contain his breath. It burst from his trunk, still buried deep underground, and he knew that he would naturally then draw in a huge breath to replace it. Of course, the only thing around for him to breathe in was sand, which would then fill his lungs and leave no room for any air. I don't want to say what would happen then, and really this is where our story should come to a sad and premature end.

Amazingly, it doesn't!

Right at that moment, something very large, very sharp and incredibly strong grabbed hold of Hope's tail and pulled with such force that he thought for a moment that he would finish with a lung full of sand *and* a departed tail. Despite the pain of having his tail pulled so viciously, he was extremely grateful for it as he was extracted from his sandy tomb in one powerful movement.

He burst from the ground just as he drew a huge intake of breath, and the air that filled him, though still peppered with the flying sand, was the most welcome visitor he had invited in for a long time.

Hope was dragged from the sandy depths to the

surface - and then continued up. He was lifted by his tail high into the air, into the eye of the storm, which had thrown itself into a frenzy, furious that its prey had been snatched from it. The wind howled its rage and the sand that had settled itself over Hope now launched itself back onto the swirling currents and rejoined the attack, this time with even more venom.

The spinning darkness obscured Hope's view of; well, everything actually. He could barely see himself, and so his attempts to see his rescuer were fruitless, and he could only allow himself to be carried to wherever he or she decided to take him.

The wind was fierce and Hope was blown helplessly in whatever direction it blew, dangling like a loose thread of a spider web. His skin was again exposed to the sheets of sand that lashed against him. He really wasn't sure how much more of this he could take. He found himself wishing, perhaps a little ungratefully, that whoever was taking him to wherever it was he was being taken would hurry up about it.

He felt his tail slipping from the hard grip that held it. He was dangling from the very tip, suspended pathetically in mid-air. The wind saw its opportunity and threw all it had left at Hope.

He was blown free and tumbled head over tail through the sky, unsure where the ground was in the darkness, but sure that he would find out soon enough. He heard once more the screeching sound cutting through the storm. It seemed to be heading towards him. The wind covered and pressed down on him in an effort to speed up his impending reunion with the ground, which was taking longer than Hope expected.

For this he was both grateful and anxious. Grateful, because he was not at all looking forward to it, but nervous because, the longer it took, the higher he had been, and therefore, the messier the reunion when it finally came.

It would surely have come very soon, but sooner than that, the screeching came tearing into Hope's ears as a massive black shadow descended on him with wings as wide as his vision could contain and glowing yellow eyes, bigger by far than Hope himself. It swooped over him, and talons that could have held a sleeping elephant on each finger wrapped themselves around his body.

Nothing could have loosened him from that grip.

Once again he was soaring upwards against all the protests of the defeated storm. The bird, even with its enormous wings, was buffeted in every direction and Hope could feel the massive strain it was under to try and escape the clutches of the wind and sand. And then - it did!

In an instant Hope, and the gigantic bird that held him, broke free from the storm and out into the still evening sky. Hope was higher than he had ever been, higher than any mountain could ever have taken him. The full moon was low against the horizon and a blanket of stars was just starting to make itself visible against the darkening backdrop of the sky. The air was cool and refreshing as it blew through the gaps in the bird's talons and soothed his sand-burnt skin.

They continued to climb higher, the bird's wings creating a fantastic whooshing sound each time they flapped down past Hope, nestled in his little cocoon.

Below him, Hope could see the storm retreating further and further from them. It gathered itself together directly below them, the sand spinning itself into a spiralling tornado. The more sand that it gathered into itself the higher it climbed, and its speed amazed Hope.

The bird seemed less than amazed, sensing that they were not out of danger yet. It increased its flapping and soared even higher. The twisting sand shot up frantically, every grain participating in this last grasp effort. It was gaining on them. Hope could hear its rasping, desperate breath as it propelled itself like a coiled spring, its sandy tendrils lunging at the feathered giant.

The bird saw this and brought its wing down against the surrounding air with such force that Hope was pressed flat against the bottom of his taloned cage as they surged up. The sand licked the bird's underbelly and some grains found their way through to where Hope was concealed, bouncing harmlessly against him.

The desert was defeated. It collapsed down on itself with a frustrated moan, dunes forming randomly where the sand fell. Hope watched from between giant bird fingers. He hoped never to set foot in that, or any desert ever again.

Finally free from the threat of being buried alive, Hope was now in the clutches, and seemingly relative safety, of the biggest bird, or animal for that matter, that he had ever seen, heard of, or even dreamed of imagining. They were soaring through the night sky and the stars above seemed as close as the ground far below. The full moon was slowly rising over the land, and it was towards it that they were now heading. But who exactly were "they"? Hope wondered. He knew of course who he was; but who was his mystery friend? Or was it a friend.

Certainly, it *had* pulled him from his certain demise, but was it only so he could serve its own needs later; and by needs, he meant hunger. But it had been a dangerous thing in the storm, even for a bird of its proportions. Why would it risk its life just for a snack; and why would it be hunting over the desert where there would normally be very little to hunt? Hope realised that he was asking himself a lot of questions that he could never answer, and that he would be better asking someone who could.

'Eh, excuse me,' he tried. 'Would you mind if I asked you who you are, and why you risked your life to pull me from the desert the way you did?'

Silence.

'For which I am extremely grateful, I must say,' he quickly added. There was no immediate response. Verbally, at least. Instead, Hope found himself hurled from the safety of the bird's clutches. He was once more floating through the pale black sky. From a certain vantage point, the silver halo of the moon was blemished by a rather comical silhouette of a young elephant; trunk, tail and all four legs splayed and flailing about.

For Hope though, it was anything but funny. Although from such a great height it wasn't immediately apparent, the ground had begun to eagerly rush up to meet him. It was just one more concern for

205

Hope, who was almost becoming numb to such things, but it was a concern that was short lived.

Swooping down from above and behind, the bird dived under him and, in a perfect display of aerobatic ability, caught Hope in the soft downy feathers of its neck. Hope landed so lightly and softly that he thought for a moment he was still free-falling.

Lifting his head out of the thick plumage, he was able to get a closer look at the bird that he was effectively now riding. He saw that the bird was in fact an owl. It was identical in every way to every owl he had seen before, except for its enormous size. I know I keep mentioning how big this owl was, but I would like to impress upon the reader that it wasn't simply big: it was **BIG!!!**

It seemed as if its wings might wrap themselves around a mountain, or its hooked beak might tear a great canyon into the landscape. Looking at its gentle, iridescent yellow eyes, with pupils the size of cave-mouths, Hope was given the impression that the owl was a lady. He was right, though he was too polite to ask.

Her feathers reflected the moon's glow as a pale silver light, with each feather tipped black, as if dipped quickly in ink. The owl spoke, responding to Hope's questions, which he had forgotten even asking. Her voice was sharp and flinty, punctuated by the click-clack of her beak.

'My name is Ishopa,' she said. 'I pulled you from the sand because that was not where you were meant to be. Where you are meant to be, is where I am taking you.'

'Do you mind if I ask you where exactly that is?' asked Hope.

'It's not *exactly* anywhere,' replied Ishopa, without the slightest trace of irony in her voice. 'But it is exactly where you are meant to be. Or rather; it will be once you are there.'

'How is it,' asked Hope, 'that you know exactly where it is that I am supposed to be, when I myself have no idea where I am, where I am going, or even that there is anywhere that I *should* be, other than where I find myself?'

'Precisely,' replied Ishopa.

Hope took the answer for what it was and turned his attention to the night sky. The earth below was too far away and too dim to hold any interest for him. It was the countless stars and the glowing moon set against the dark emptiness of space that demanded his attention.

At that height, Hope felt that he was closer to their domain than to his familiar home below, and it was a privilege to be allowed so close. The stars were sprinkled across the sky, reminding him somewhat of a desert of sand that had been scattered through space and illuminated by some unknown force. Perhaps, he mused, it was a fierce storm - like the one he had recently encountered - that had blown so hard, it had blown itself clear into space. The grains of sand, now separated from their millions of brothers and sisters, who had always been crowded one on top of the other, now found themselves with as much space as they wanted, and so they expanded and grew and expressed their new found freedom by shining brightly for everyone to see.

Now, they were stars.

That explains the stars, thought Hope, delighted with his idea. What about the moon?

The moon tonight was complete and full, in all its glory. Its brilliance outshone all of the stars put together. It commanded the sky around it.

If the sun is hurled into the sky by the giant sun throwing elephant, wondered Hope, *well then, what sends the moon on its nocturnal journey's over the land*? Maybe the sun and the moon are actually the same, he thought. They were certainly the same size. It could be that the sun is thrown so hard in the morning that it goes around the world twice in one day, but when it comes back the second time, its fire has burnt out. That didn't seem right, he decided. For one thing, on occasion, he had seen the moon in the daytime, right alongside the sun. He did remember having the idea once that the moon was carried by the giant moon carrying ……..

'Ishopa!' he exclaimed suddenly.

'Yes,' she answered, despite Hope not actually intending to address her.

'Eh,' started Hope, not sure how to put the question. He decided to simply put it in the manner that it had come to him. 'Are you the giant moon carrying owl?' he asked directly.

'Yes,' answered Ishopa with equal directness.

Hope's heart started racing. He hadn't even been looking and yet he had found someone almost as wonderful as the giant sun throwing elephant. So many questions raced through his mind that he didn't know which to ask. Looking back, the one he chose may have been slightly rude, but luckily Ishopa appeared not to take it that way and happily answered all his questions.

'What are you doing here then?' he asked. 'Why are you not carrying the moon?'

'One night every month,' replied the owl, 'the moon is full. When she is full, but *only* when she is full, she carries herself.'

It seemed that she meant to leave it at that, but Hope wasn't entirely satisfied with the response. He wanted to know more. He wanted to know all about the moon, all about Ishopa, and was it simply good fortune that he happened to be in the desert on the night of the full moon, when Ishopa might be there to rescue him?

He pressed her with all these questions. Ishopa was silent in response.

Hope wondered if she would answer at all, but he knew that this would likely be the only chance he would ever have to ask these questions, and he meant to use it.

The moon was rising higher above them, and below, Ishopa's shadow raced across the surface of the earth. They were travelling faster and further than Hope ever dared to imagine.

Chapter Four
The moon and the mountain

Hope had almost given up on expecting a response to his many questions, when out of the blue - or should we say black, as it was night time - Ishopa spoke. She answered all of his questions without addressing any of them specifically.

'The moon,' she started, 'is very shy and unsure of herself. The sun is the opposite. He is brash and daring, blazing in the daytime, showing off all of his glory everyday. He is always on time in the morning, racing over the mountains and lingering reluctantly on the far horizon each evening before he relents and disappears for the night. He is always full, and even when he is obscured by the clouds he will try to burst through them, evaporating them into mist.

'The moon is different. She prefers the cover of darkness. She feels that she pales in comparison to the fiery sun. It takes her a whole month to build up the confidence to display her fullness, and then it's only for one night before her confidence begins to wane once more.

'The stars around her whisper always of how beautiful, how magnificent she is, but she will only allow herself that one night to believe what they say. On the other nights she hides some of herself in the shadow of the earth, not wanting to be completely seen. In fact, if it were not for me dragging her from her resting place on those nights, she would not come out at all. She would remain hidden, dreaming of becoming a great blazing ball of fire like the sun and illuminating the whole sky. Sometimes, thinking she can't be seen, she will even take herself out in the day to spy on the sun, to see if she can find out his secret.

'Of course, I know that she will always be the moon and could never be like the sun, no matter what secrets she might learn. I know how important her position in the night sky is to me and all the nocturnal animals; to us she is infinitely more beautiful than that glaring show off, the sun. To us, she is soft and gentle. Her light is a comfort to us as we conduct our business in the dark.

'But I could never say all this to her. She must discover it for herself, and then she will shine in all her glory, night after night. Until that time I will continue my duty of carrying her through the night skies, for the sake of all the creatures that awaken when the sun goes down, and most of all, for her, the moon, who I love above all others.'

Hope had been staring at the moon while listening to Ishopa. As he did so he began to view the moon much differently than he ever had before. He was struck by how amazingly beautiful she was, and indeed, by the fact that she was a *she*. He had never thought of the moon being male or female, or having feelings and, more than that - self image problems. Certainly, he thought that she was beautiful and he wished that he could tell her. What he didn't realise, was that simply by looking at her in this new way, he *was* telling her, and she shone just a little brighter.

Ishopa continued. 'I have been carrying the moon for as long as the moon has been in the sky. We came into the world together: we are one and the same, inseparable, and when the time comes, we will leave the world together. In the aeons of time in between, we have, and always will evolve in our own ways. In the beginning I spent all of my time with the moon, coaxing her into the sky in order that all the night time animals who had descended from us, might have light to guide them. As time went by and her confidence grew a little, it came to be that I began to become more independent. Every month I have two nights of solitude. One night each month the moon refuses to come out and on this dark night I am free to roam, unseen in the darkness.

'On the night that the moon is full, such as tonight, I use the bright light she casts to watch over the affairs of the world from high in the skies. The desert where I found you only comes to life on the night of the full moon, and so that is where I watch the closest. Tonight I knew that you would be there, and when I rose with the moon I made my way straight to you; and just in time I might add.'

'How did you know that I would be there?' asked Hope.

'We have been expecting you.'

'Who is *we*?'

'All of us,' she responded simply.

Hope was hit suddenly by a flashback to the story Queen Freassel told of her mother.

'Did you ever find a white tiger in the desert and fly

212

her away to a mountain while she slept?'

Ishopa didn't so much as pause to sort through her memories. 'Yes, of course,' she said. 'That was the first sign of the changes to come. After the wind, it was inevitable that the world would never be the same, and in the search for answers it was only a matter of time before someone tried to cross the desert to find them.

'But that desert cannot be crossed, and so on my free night I always watched over it. One night I spotted her, curled up in the sand, close to death but glowing so beautifully white that she looked as a reflection of the moon on a still lake.

'I took her to the mountain to recover, and whilst there, she found what she had been looking for. After that we knew that in time there would be another, looking for something different. Different, but at the same time, the same. And so I continued to watch and wait. Tonight, you came.'

'Are you taking me to the same mountain?'

'Out here, there is only the mountain.'

There was a pause while Hope pondered on what that meant. It was the phrase "out here" that concerned him. He looked down at the landscape below, but found that he couldn't see the ground at all. The moon was at its peak and the bright light was reflected back to Hope as a thick mist that covered the land for as far as he could see.

'We will be there before morning,' interrupted Ishopa, 'you should get some rest.'

As soon as she had spoken the words, Hope felt an irresistible urge to nestle himself amongst her feathers and drift off to sleep. Which is exactly what he did.

The light of the moon was shut out by his falling eyelids and soon a new light emerged in his mind. He dreamt that the moon descended to the earth. As it drew closer, it moulded itself into the shape of a pure white tiger, settling itself on the very tip of a mountain peak so high that every corner of the land could be seen from it.

In the dream, Hope found himself at the very bottom of that mountain, and as soon as he stepped onto it, the mountain disappeared. He was floating in black, empty space. Still, the tiny speck of light was there, watching him, but he could no longer move towards it, he could only float, motionless, watching.

As he watched, it started to fade slowly until finally, it extinguished completely. Hope was left alone in the dark nothingness, and he dreamt of that empty space for the rest of his sleep.

Hope felt a wind beating down on him as he slept. He opened his eyes to see what might be the cause, but by the time he opened them the wind had departed. His mind was soon distracted from the wind to his surroundings. He realised that he was no longer on the back of the giant moon carrying owl, but laying on a patch of cool green grass.

The light suggested that dawn was breaking, though the sun was yet to make an appearance. The moon had disappeared - so too Ishopa.

Realising this, Hope thought again of the flapping wind that had awoken him and he guessed at its cause. He raised himself to his feet to get a better look at this new setting in which he found himself placed. In doing so, his body responded to the fact that he was awake

214

once more. His insatiable thirst and hunger returned to remind him of how long it had been since he had last eaten or drank. He put his feelings aside for the moment to first take a good look at his surroundings.

He was in a small clearing on the side of what must have been the tallest mountain anywhere in the world; or anywhere else for that matter. Looking down, he couldn't tell how high he actually was because the mountain disappeared into a thick rolling mist that spread out in all directions for as far as he could see, but he was obviously very, very high; but not at the top because, looking up, he could see that the mountain still had some way to go before it peaked. Not too far though, and Hope felt that he could certainly reach it before tomorrow's sunrise, when surely he would find the giant sun throwing elephant on the other side,

For the moment he returned his thoughts to his most immediate needs: food and water. For these, he didn't have to go far; in fact he didn't really have to move at all. He was surrounded by the highest, greenest grass he ever saw and a sparkling stream of fresh cool water cut gently through the middle of the clearing. He needed no invitation and set about feeding his neglected stomach with the delicious spread laid before him.

As he gorged on the succulent feast the light steadily grew brighter around him, highlighting the intense green of the grass and foliage of the trees. His attention was drawn away momentarily by a loud whooshing sound that seemed to emanate somewhere at the top of, or on the other side of the mountain. Startled, his head snapped upwards to locate the source of the sound, half chewed grass hanging from either side of his mouth. Seeing nothing that could account for it, he returned to his eating frenzy. A moment later, unseen by Hope, the sun made its first appearance from behind the mountain.

Hope stuffed himself until he could fit nothing more in. He tried, but as soon as he swallowed, the chewed ball of grass just popped straight back out, landing with a soft 'plop' at his feet. He tried to shoot in more of the delectable and refreshing water with his trunk, but it trickled straight back out, dripping off his lip and down his chin. He was reluctant to admit defeat, but it was clear that he had taken his fill.

His appetite satisfied, he was able to take a closer look and better appreciate his surroundings.

It was truly a beautiful mountain. There was no trace of any brown or withered grass in all of the greenness that covered it. Flowers of every kind were in bloom and had their faces open to the light of the sun. The music of the birds skipped delicately on the surface of a gentle breeze, with not a single harsh or discordant note and no one song trying to overpower another, but rather melding together to form one harmonious tune.

Butterflies fluttered and bees buzzed, never getting in each other's way or fighting over the sweet nectar of the flowers. Squirrels raced up the trunks of the trees, scampered to the ends of the branches until they hung precariously from the tips over the floor below, and then raced back and down the trunks, simply because they had nothing better to do.

Scenes such as this played out wherever Hope

looked. The mountain was brimming with life. The trees shook with it, while the grass danced with it. The flowers rejoiced in it, while the animals immersed themselves in it wholeheartedly. The wind sang of it, and the sun, high in the sky above, illuminated it so that all could see.

It was overwhelming to Hope, such was its beauty.

He allowed himself to enjoy the feeling of peace that filled him then, though he didn't so much allow *it*, as it allowed him. He knew, however, that he must start moving, as he may still encounter any manner of obstacles or delays before he reached the top. And, in fact, there was one coming right at that moment!

Hope heard the distant sound of snapping twigs and cracking branches moving towards him. As it came closer he noticed that it was accompanied by the easily distinguishable voice of an elephant. He listened closely to what it was saying, and he had to laugh as he did so.

'Out of my way blasted trees,' he heard. 'Always jumping out in front of me no matter where I want to walk. Well, let me tell you, if I was twenty years younger, I'd give you a sound thrashing I would, and well deserved it would be too.

'No respect for the elders these days. In my day, I'll tell you….Ahhh!!! What on earth was that? A surprise attack. Well, let me tell you, if it wasn't so blasted dark around here all the time, then maybe you wouldn't be so brave, am I right? I think so.

'Where is that lazy sun anyway? It's been years since I've seen it, and personally I'm a little tired of stumbling around in this dim light, having trees knocking in to me all the time.

'No matter: I have this one last thing to do and then I can rest.......Who *am* I talking to? Is anyone even listening? No one listens any more. No respect I tell you. It doesn't matter anyway. None of you are half as important as you think you are, so kindly get out of my way and let me go about my business, which is three times as important as the most important thing that you could ever think of.

'Thank you.'

Hope was chuckling loudly to himself when the voice, accompanied by the elephant to whom it belonged, emerged into the clearing where he was standing. Hope stopped laughing. The elephant was a tall, thin female, and she was most likely the oldest elephant he had ever laid eyes on. Her face was thin and gaunt, her bones jutting out against her wrinkled skin –more wrinkled than is normal for an elephant, of course- and her feet were big and wide at the end of her long, skinny legs.

She moved, however, as if she were not much older than Hope himself, and she appeared to be in a hurry to get somewhere.

'Hello,' said Hope as she came charging across the clearing to where he was waiting.

She froze, ears flying forwards, trunk shooting up and feet skidding to a slightly awkward, uncoordinated but effective stop. 'Who said that?' she demanded. 'Where are you? Come out from those shadows and show yourself.'

Hope looked around. The sun was quite bright, and the clearing, in which he was virtually in the middle,

218

was well lit. 'I'm right in front of you. My name is Hope.'

'Ah,' she said, 'then I *have* found you. I knew I would. They said I wouldn't of course, but as usual they were wrong. Well, shall we go then?'

Hope took a deep breath. He had become well prepared for things like this. 'Where are we going?' he asked, remaining polite and unflustered, 'and, ah…..who are *they*?'

'*They*?' she repeated back at him. 'They, them, he, she, us, you, we………..um….they?' She paused. 'What was the question?'

'Um,' started Hope, wanting to keep it simple. 'Where are you taking me?'

'To see *him*.'

Hope started to ask who "*him*" was, but thought better of it. He had one more question. 'What's your name?' he asked.

The elephant sprang into a flurry of movement and bounced over to him. 'Oh my word,' she exclaimed, 'how rude of me. I get rather forgetful in my old age.' She reached her trunk out to grab hold of his, but got his ear instead, which she vigorously shook up and down. 'My name is Mae Bia. I'm delighted to make your acquaintance. It's an absolute pleasure.'

She let go of his ear, which by then was very red, very hot and very sore, and turned sharply on her heel. 'Right,' she barked, 'that's the pleasantries taken care of. Let's go. Follow me now, and *do* keep up.'

Mae Bia disappeared into the jungle crashing and banging into anything that didn't agree with her choice of direction. Hope remained where he was, amused and bemused, but unsure if he really wanted to follow an elephant that seemed to have little idea where they were going. He listened and followed the sound of her smashing a path through the thick vegetation, threatening and cursing everything as she went.

Her sound circled around him unseen, until it was on the opposite side of the clearing to where she had left, and soon enough she came bursting through the trees again and charged straight at Hope.

Hope remained silent and motionless as she headed towards him, expecting her to stop when she saw him. She didn't. Didn't stop, I mean. Seemingly she didn't see him, and they collided heavily.

Hope, who was sturdy and strong for his age and size, took the blow well, and was only knocked back a couple of steps.

Mae Bia, who was still fit and agile for her age, physically took the blow well, but emotionally – well, let's just say that she had likely handled things better. Her tail shot up straight in the air, her ears flapped wildly about and she swung her trunk madly at the perceived attacker.

'Who's there?' she cried. 'Come out where I can see you.'

Hope ducked and weaved to avoid the flailing trunk.

'It's me,' he yelled back at her between bobs. 'Hope!'

Mae Bia stopped still. She eyed him suspiciously, but it seemed to Hope that those eyes didn't see very much any more. They were clouded over and seemed to stare straight through him.

'Well,' she said sternly, 'I really am in no mood for these games, young bull. I have very important matters to take care of, and so I shall say good day to you sir.'

She turned and started to stomp out of the clearing once more, her head held high indignantly.

'Wait,' called Hope and he started after her.

Mae Bia stopped and turned around. 'What now?', she snapped at him. 'I am in an awful rush and I have no time for silly little calves, so please say what you have to say post haste, so I may be on my way.'

'Well,' said Hope, a little humiliated at being called a silly little calf. 'Doesn't your important business involve taking me to meet someone?'

Mae Bia was silent and thoughtful for a moment. Hope awaited her response patiently and respectfully.

'Eh, quite so,' she conceded. 'Well, this time, you follow me, understand? And *do* keep up"

Hope nodded and smiled. He figured there was really no good reason not to follow her. At least for a little while.

Mae Bia had already set off at a brisk pace and Hope's little legs had to work hard to keep up with her. One thing he was glad of was that she was leading the way. At that pace Hope would likely have been battered and bruised by the dense jungle, but following behind Mae Bia meant that he always had a path to follow as she very effectively, if unintentionally, cleared the way for him.

He quickly gave up trying to keep track of the direction they were taking as they zigzagged in and out, bouncing off a tree, and taking the direction the tree suggested, before being deflected onto a new path by a helpful boulder which Mae Bia crashed headlong into.

'Keep up,' she would call out regularly. 'There's no rush, but we have no time to waste,' before slamming hard into another obstacle that had been standing there quite still, minding its own business.

'Out of my way,' she would yell. 'Do you have any idea who I am and what important business I am on? If you did, then you would be laying a path of soft flower petals at my feet and not forever blocking my way.'

'No matter,' she would always finish. 'You'll find out one day and then you will search for me everywhere to apologise, but by then I'll be gone.'

Hope wondered at this last remark, but he could make no real sense of anything she said and so he guessed that the poor old dear was losing her mind to old age, as she was losing her sight.

With that thought, and given that they had been racing to and fro and up and down without seeming to get anywhere; coupled with the fact that they had just emerged into a clearing that looked suspiciously like the one that they had started from over an hour ago, Hope suddenly came to an abrupt halt and yelled, '**STOP!**', at the top of his voice. He was panting from what was basically a long chase all over the mountainside that led absolutely nowhere.

Mae Bia swung around to face him. 'I beg your pardon,' she demanded sternly, 'where are you manners young bull? If I could see better where you were hiding I'd give you a swift kick in the backside.' Hope was standing in the middle of an open clearing in broad daylight. The grass wasn't even long enough to hide his ankles!

She continued. 'Now, what on earth are you yelling at me? We really have no time to waste, although there is no rush.'

Hope felt a little ashamed, but he didn't want to waste his day chasing a crazy old elephant to nowhere for no apparent reason when he could be getting himself to the top of the mountains in readiness for tomorrow's sunrise.

'I'm sorry,' he said sincerely, 'it's just that it seems as if we have just gone around in a big circle and we're back to where we started. And I still don't know where we're even going.'

'I already told you,' said Mae Bia, irritated. 'I'm taking you to see *him*,' and then she added to herself under her breath, 'No one ever listens: they hear, but they don't listen.'

Hope was growing frustrated and he was about ready to dispense with politeness. 'You haven't told me who '*he*' is,' he said shakily, barely containing his anger.

'He's right through there,' said Mae Bia gently and calmly. 'He's waiting for you.' She pointed with her trunk through some trees at the edge of the clearing.

That was it for Hope.

'BUT THAT'S WHERE WE STARTED OUR RIDICULOUS LOOP WHEN WE TOOK OFF ON THIS POINTLESS JOURNEY, AND THERE WAS NO ONE THERE' he shouted, 'WHAT WAS THE POINT OF ALL THAT RUNNING AROUND CRASHING INTO THINGS?'

Mae Bia had become calmer as Hope had become

more and more agitated.

'What's the point of anything, my little king in the making?' she chuckled at him. 'If you can answer that, then you know you are on the right track. And yes, this *is* the same clearing as this morning, but if you leave anything, it is never the same when you come back to it. Everything is moving, changing, growing and dying all the time; nothing is ever motionless.

'It's only when you move with it that you can be still.'

Hope was struck dumb by the clarity and gentleness of Mae Bia's response. He had expected a tirade of nonsense and he had been ready to storm off in a huff.

Mae Bia smiled at him. 'Go on,' she said. 'He's waiting.'

Hope could only look at her in bemusement, but he started towards the trees. Mae Bia watched, still smiling at him, but she didn't make a move to follow.

As he approached, the trees seemed to arch backwards to make way and he noticed what seemed to be a scattering of flower petals on the ground. Hope glanced once more over his shoulder to Mae Bia. She smiled encouragingly at him, waving him on with her trunk.

'Go on, go on,' she said with a slight chuckle in her voice, 'Don't keep him waiting.'

Hope smiled nervously back at her and turned back to the trees and fragrant path. He stepped through to the sound of hundreds of animals settling into position to watch what was happening.

Chapter Five
The king

Hope emerged through the trees and was immediately confronted by a scene from his past. A scene he had never expected to come upon again.

'Maximus,' he said, barely above a whisper, almost choking on the mix of emotions that his memories stirred up. Once again, after all these years, he found himself face to knee with the wizened old bull.

At this point in our story it should be pointed out that for now we are only telling one small fragment of little Hope's short, but eventful, life. It may be one of the most important fragments - or even *the* most important - up until this point, but still it is only one fragment, and we simply don't have the time right now to tell it all. For the time being, until the time is right to tell of the years that had led up to this moment, I would like to briefly allude to an earlier period in Hope's life, a period very shortly after Hope had lost his birth mother and had become an orphan, wandering the jungle alone, and a little afraid if we're honest about it. This may come as a bit of a shock to those of you who didn't know this already, because as we know Hope left his family at home in his valley at the beginning of this narrative. You see, Hope did find another family, as is very often the case with elephants who are always most generous in extending their family to include those who need one, and sometimes even those who don't. There's little that gives an elephant more joy than looking after their young.

But to go back a little; at that time when Hope was itinerant and lost, he came across another, younger orphan named Ging Mai, and together they set about exploring, trying to find a family, and generally having a lot of fun. In the course of this they stumbled into - or should I say Hope literally bumped into - a giant of an elephant. A giant named Maximus, who explained to them that there exists a world apart from but connected to this one, a spirit jungle where all elephants would one day return to, and that night in their dreams little Ging Mai was reunited with his mother in the spirit jungle, while the next morning, on awaking, Hope found himself surrounded by a large group of elephants who quickly and gladly became his new family, as if he was their own; which of course he was. The rest of this element of Hope's story should be told another time, when there is enough time to tell it properly, but for now this should serve as a brief introduction to the next chapter in our tale.

Speaking of which; here is the next chapter in our tale.

'It's good to see you again, little Hope,' Max replied evenly.

Max was as tall and stately as ever though he had aged in the time since Hope had last seen him. A thin beard of white hair stretched from his bottom lip. Its apparent aim was to give him a wise and dignified look, but its achieved effect was to give him a slightly comical appearance, which was better suited to the elephant Hope remembered.

'What are you doing here?' was all Hope could think to ask.

'Still straight to the point I see,' laughed Max and the petals from nearby flowers vibrated off their stems and thickened the thin layer at their feet.

'The first reason,' he continued, 'is simply that this is where I am meant to be. This mountain is the final place that every elephant comes to before they depart from this world. It is a mountain free from all the trials of the lands that border it, and an elephant that has been fortunate enough to live her or his life well will make its way here in their final years so they can contemplate in peace before they take the next step. Only one elephant in every generation will come here and be able to return to the outside world. In my generation I was blessed with that privilege, and now it is time for one from your generation to do the same.

'Which brings me to the second reason that I am here. I am waiting for you.'

Hope drew himself to his full height holding his head erect and proud. 'Well,' he said, 'here I am.'

Max placed his trunk gently on the top of Hope's head. Hope relaxed at the touch. 'Tell me,' said Max, pausing a little before continuing. 'What are *you* doing here?'

Hope hadn't been expecting the question and he was forced to think about his answer. His immediate response would have been that he was searching for the giant sun throwing elephant, and certainly that was one of the things he was doing there.

He thought back to that first morning when he had set out to climb that first mountain. At the time he had simply wanted to see where the sun came from each morning, not realising how far the world stretched out from the valley he had grown up in. He had climbed the mountain on that particular morning because he was worried that his freedom was soon to be taken from him with his impending coronation.

Was he here searching for his freedom, he wondered, or was he running away from his responsibilities?

The sun throwing elephant was something he thought he had imagined, yet on his travels he had discovered that not only was it real, but that this was a journey he *had* to take to become the king he had always dreamed of becoming.

The other ambition in his short life had been to be a great elephant warrior, and a few days ago he had met the greatest of them all, and learnt what it really meant to be an elephant warrior. He had helped to liberate all those animals from the monkey cages, he had helped the tigers to realise the error of the way in which they had lived their lives; but more than that, he had been helped every step of the way. By Pu-pa, by Ma and Pa who had freed him from the ivy trap and helped him to overcome his fear of pigs and, of course, had introduced him to Boon Khum. Boon Khum in turn had valiantly fought all of those tigers to defend him. In the desert he had been rescued by Ishopa and carried to this mountain, where Mae Bia had, in her own unique way, led Hope to this meeting with Max.

He had learnt so much on his travels; more than he

himself realised at that moment, and experienced things that he had never imagined he would have experienced.

The question remained; what was he doing here?

Was he searching for the giant sun throwing elephant? Was he running away from his responsibilities, having one last taste of freedom? Was he exploring and getting to know his kingdom, or was he just fulfilling his destiny, undertaking what he had always been supposed to undertake?

None of these questions received a definite answer in his mind, and he rejected them all completely. In the space left behind by the discarded questions, an answer quietly and confidently slipped in and presented itself.

Hope looked up at Max, suddenly sure of his response. 'I'm here to see you.'

Max smiled satisfactorily. 'Good,' he said, 'then let us walk together to the top of the mountain. There is something I would like to show you before tomorrow's sunrise. We can talk along the way.'

The two started up the well worn path to the mountain's peak. The sun was making his way towards midday, but it remained cool and fresh on the tall mountain. The sounds of the jungle around them were gentle and playful, never once intruding on their conversation.

Hope was jolted by the memory of something Max had mentioned earlier, about him being the elephant of his generation who had made this journey before.

'Max!' Hope exclaimed. 'When we met all those years ago, I asked you if you were the king, and you said "no", but you were, weren't you?'

229

'No,' said Maximus, 'I was King once, a long time ago, but not when I met you. At the time I was on my way here. That's not important now though. We have more important things to discuss. First of all, I should like to hear all that has happened to you in making your way here.'

Hope told him his story as they walked up the mountain. Maximus walked with very slow and measured steps, aware of every placement of each foot, while Hope danced around him, gesturing wildly whenever his tale called for it, and sometimes when it didn't.

Max was very interested in everything that Hope had to tell. He was amused by Hope's retelling of his conversations with Pu-Pa, and disturbed when he heard about the monkeys, who he, as we know, was already aware of. He was very pleased to hear of the two pigs coming to Hope's rescue, but most pleased of all when he heard of his old friend Boon Khum. He was angered and distressed to hear of what had happened to his magnificent tusks but greatly heartened to learn of his heroics in saving Hope from the tigers. He nodded knowingly when Hope told of his near call with the carnivorous desert and his timely escape into the clutches of Ishopa. By the time Hope had finished they were getting close to the top. The sun had passed the top of his arc and had begun his descent.

Max was silent for a time after Hope's story finished, but he seemed pleased with what he had heard. As they walked on in silence Hope was suddenly startled by the sound of rustling in the treetops behind him. There were many sounds around them the whole time they were walking, but all of those sounds had seemed to be in their place. This sound struck Hope as being decidedly out of place.

He spun around. Max continued to walk slowly on, with not even the slightest indication that he had heard anything.

Hope stared hard into all the treetops but he could see nothing unusual. He wasn't sure why, but something about that sound had greatly unsettled him. He trundled back to Max, who continued on as if nothing had happened.

'Did you hear that?' asked Hope.

'Of course,' answered Max.

'I think we are being followed,' said Hope. 'I heard something similar in the desert, but I ignored it then.'

'We *are* being followed,' said Max without the slightest trace of concern.

'Do you know by whom?' asked Hope, who *was* concerned, and a little annoyed that Max didn't share in it.

'*You* know by whom,' said Max calmly.

'You mean…..?' started Hope, but he didn't finish the question.

'Do not concern yourself,' said Max. 'He is on his journey, as you are on yours. You should be concerned only with yours.'

Hope respectfully took Max's suggestion and resumed walking alongside the King, as Hope still thought of him. Every now and then he glanced over his shoulder and a chill ran up and down his spine. There was only one more ridge to climb before they reached the summit when Max unexpectedly came to a halt.

'Stop here,' he said.

Hope was compelled to do as Max said, there was something in the tone of his voice, but stopping now, when they were so close, went against Hope's tendency to keep going until he reached wherever he intended to reach. He stopped.

'What is it?' he asked Maximus.

'This is as far as I can go,' said the giant. 'The day will come soon enough when I will cross over this mountain once more, but today, you must go alone.'

Hope's heart sank.

'Since I started this journey,' he said, 'I have been alone. I have met so many new friends, and some old ones, but as quickly as they come, they are gone again.'

'Such is the way of life, my friend,' said Max kindly. 'We come into this world alone and we leave it alone. We make many friends but sooner or later we must depart from them, or they from us.

'The life of a bull elephant is one of the loneliest of them all, but the most important thing you must learn on this journey is that even though you will spend a great deal of your time alone, you are never truly on your own. The trees and the flowers will be your companions; the sky and the stars will watch over you and the wind will whisper stories to when you sleep and, when you learn to listen, when you wake also.

'The rivers and the birds will guide you and the mountains will shelter you. All of the animals shall play with you, and learn from you. You must learn what it truly means to be a King, Hope, before you can teach them. And, of course, your family, which begins with every elephant that walks the jungle, will be there whenever you need them; including me.'

Hope took all of this in. It was a lot for a young elephant to grasp, but at that moment Hope felt - no, he knew - that he was ready. He wasn't quite ready, however, to say goodbye to Maximus.

'When I first met you Max,' he said, 'you gave me some advice on becoming King. Now I am about to fulfil my ambition and I don't know if I will ever see you again. Don't you have any advice for me now?'

Max breathed in deeply and slowly, letting the breath out again evenly. 'Is it your ambition to be king?' asked Max, his eyes locked on Hope's.

'Of course,' answered Hope.

'Then you cannot become King,' said Max.

Hope was stunned. He knew he was going to be King. Everyone had told him so. Everything on this journey has indicated that he would.

'Listen to me,' Maximus interrupted Hope's thoughts. 'You cannot *want* to be King. Ambition is the birthplace of loss, and you must rise above ambition. Indeed, you must rise above loss. You cannot become King. You can only *be* King.

'You do not become King on the day that someone places a crown on your head. That is simply meaningless ceremony. It has its place, but you must already be King before anyone recognises you as such.

'If you pass over this mountain and return again to your valley, then you will be King. Otherwise, you will not be able to return at all. I have passed over, as I have already said, and I could tell you exactly what you will

233

see, what you will hear and what you should do, but I would never do that.

'Nobody can ever tell you what is the truth. It can never be explained to you, it can never be written down for you, it can never be held in your hand or pinned under your feet. The truth can only be discovered by yourself, through understanding.

'Do you understand?'

'No,' said Hope.

'Exactly,' smiled Max. 'But you will. Once you cross over that peak, everything will change. Your old life will be left behind and a new one will begin. From that time on, your life will be new in every passing moment, as it should be. The entire universe is changing from one instant to the next, and any one moment can never be pinned down. It will slip through your grasp as if it never existed. You must move with it.

'When you stood at the entrance of that cave, you plunged into the darkness without a second thought. When you were in that monkey cage, Pu-Pa walked through it without considering that maybe he couldn't. When you failed to find the giant sun throwing elephant on the far side of each mountain, you didn't turn back; you simply continued on to the next mountain.

'Those are the things that brought you to where you are now, which is where you are meant to be.' Max became silent. He looked up towards the mountaintop, distant memories never forgotten flooding his mind.

Hope was staring at the ground, lost in the effort to commit all that Max had said to his memory, but those words were not to be stored there. They would spread throughout his being, becoming a part of him. He could neither remember them nor forget them.

Max broke the silence.

'It's time for you to go,' he said, sounding almost as sad to say it as Hope was to hear it. 'But before you do, there is something you must take with you.'

Hope looked at Max, puzzled. Max turned from the mountaintop and faced the tree behind them. He drew himself to his full height and a presence grew around him that spread over the mountains in waves of power. It was a power that couldn't be sought or gained, it couldn't be bought or sold and it could never be abused.

'COME DOWN FROM THERE,' he commanded to the treetops.

There was not a single sound or movement in the entire jungle. There was no response from the treetops.

Max spoke again, and this time there was a weight in his voice that threatened to crush the very mountain that they stood on. This time the treetops responded immediately. They shook and trembled, and from their dark and hidden interior they expelled a shaken and trembling figure that landed pathetically sprawled at Max's feet.

Hope reeled backwards.

He recognised the figure instantly. The golden fur and the pale blue eyes that had lost most of their coolness, carrying instead now a searing flame of hatred and vengeance. He was thin and gaunt and his fur was matted and dull, but there was no mistaking him. It was Maad!

Though he was sprawled in a most undignified manner, his eyes were raised just above the ground and were locked on Hope.

Hope was shocked and confused. Surely Max had not meant that he was to take Maad with him. Why didn't Max finish him there and then, or even simply leave him up in the treetops where he belonged?

Maad continued to stare at Hope with such hatred that Hope felt himself being sucked into those flaming blue eyes. He found himself surrounded by leaping flames crawling with dark shadows. He could hear the screams and trumpets of tortured elephants, but he couldn't see past the roaring fires that closed in on him, scorching his skin. The black shapes emerged from the flames, clawing and grabbing at him, but they couldn't reach him, and they merged back into the fires, screaming and hissing their frustration.

The sound of Max's voice broke the spell and Hope was released from the hold of Maad's gaze. He looked away.

'To your feet,' commanded Max.

Maad slowly but surely lifted himself from the ground and to his feet, but he kept his eyes locked on Hope.

'Look at me when I am addressing you,' boomed Max, and the jungle, from the tips of the trees to the ground at their feet, shook.

Maad's head involuntarily whipped upwards at Max's command. Max regarded him as one might regard a particularly unpleasant chore that you know you must do, but would much rather not.

'You have come here because your desire for both

revenge and power have taken such a hold of your mind and body that without them now you would simply curl up lifeless on the ground.'

Max was towering over Maad as he addressed him. 'Even now these words cannot penetrate the dark clouds that swirl in your mind, but I say them anyway because I must. You may go with Hope to the top of this mountain. That is what you want, and so you may have it. This is the way it was always meant to be. However, I warn you now, for one of you, there shall be no returning. If you choose not to go, I guarantee you a safe passage back to your mountain. If you choose to go, then I can guarantee you nothing more then what I have already stated.

'Do you understand?'

Maad curled his lips back over his teeth and sneeringly replied, 'We do what we have to do.'

Max dropped his eyes from Maad's and there was a weariness and resignation in his voice as he said, 'So be it.'

He moved slowly over to Hope, who was more than a little distressed at this turn of events. Hope looked pleadingly at Max, wordlessly begging him to change his decision, but Max simply smiled reassuringly at him.

'It is the way it is, little Hope,' he said, 'and that's the only way it can be.'

'More riddles,' cried Hope in frustration. 'I have had it up to here with riddles.' His trunk was raised high up over his head as he said this. 'I don't know what any of this means.'

Max reached his trunk out to calm Hope. 'It's

simple,' he said calmly, 'it's very, very simple. The problem is that it's too simple, and so we don't see it. We like to complicate things so that we can seem really clever when we figure it out. The more important we think something is, the more complicated we expect it, or even want it to be. But really, the most important things are much too simple for the really clever among us to see.'

Only the sound of Maad's rasping, impatient breath broke the silence that followed, as he waited for Hope, already a few steps ahead on the path.

'I must go now,' said Hope quietly.

'Yes,' said Max, and the two elephants, tall and short, old and young, past and future King pressed their foreheads together.

'I will see you again, Hope,' Max said quietly. 'And I will always be watching over you, no matter where you are.'

Hope had no words, but really, he didn't need any.

They stepped back from each other and there was nothing more to say or to do, but each to go their own way.

Max turned, and without looking back, started his slow and gentle walk back down the mountain. It seemed as if the light around Max was just a little bit brighter than anywhere else, and as Hope watched the giant disappear into the trees it felt as if the light around him grew just a little bit dimmer.

He turned to Maad, who seemed most pleased with the present situation. 'You lead the way,' he snarled. 'I want you where I can see you.'

'As you wish, Your Majesty,' mocked Maad, feeble

bow included. 'I wouldn't have it any other way.'

With that, Maad turned and started up the mountain. Hope followed closely, never taking his eyes off the monkey for a moment. The sun was setting and night was on its way. Hope felt very uneasy about the prospect of being alone on the mountain top with Maad throughout the night. He was sure he wouldn't be able to sleep, but all he could say was, that's just the way it is.

Chapter Six
The story of the wind

The distance remaining to the top of the mountain was short and the climb easy. The path was clear and smooth and the evening was cool and fresh. The moon was just making an appearance, and though it was very close to being full, Hope knew that it was hiding a tiny strip of its side behind the earth's shadow. Looking very closely at it, he could almost make out the massive wings that were helping it across the sky.

Maad was very eagerly leading the way up the mountain path and was keeping very quiet, which made Hope all the more nervous. He could only imagine the cunning plots being devised in that twisted mind, but he tried to keep his own mind on more pleasant things; such as reaching the end of his journey and returning back to his family.

Thinking of his family then, he wondered if he could ever go back to the life he had left behind. It hadn't been his intention at the time to leave anything, but he had changed so much in the days since he left that he really wasn't sure if he could ever settle back into the familiar life in his little valley.

Certainly he wanted to see all his family and friends again, but there was just so much to see and to discover, he knew that when this journey ended, it would be really only the beginning of a new and bigger one.

The elephant and the monkey were coming over the peak now, and as they did, a dark figure emerged from over the mini-horizon of the mountain top.

The slender, twisted fingers on the uppermost branches of a great and ancient tree presented themselves against the backdrop of the pale moon. As Hope and Maad drew closer to the peak on which it grew, the tree revealed more of itself.

It was an imposing figure in the half light of the growing evening, its countless branches stretching up, out, and down; twisting in and around each other, snake like in their movements. It was this that struck Hope as he was drawn towards the tree. The branches were moving!

Not moving in the way branches are likely to do when blown about by the wind, but each one moving independently and of its own accord, and as the trunk rose into view beneath, it too seemed to be a writhing pillar of many smaller trunks, coiling one around the other to climb up and out of the ground towards the vast and endless sky.

Hope was captivated and he walked towards it as if in a trance. Maad seemed fearful of it, and he crouched low to the ground, crawling warily behind Hope who was now leading the way.

They were atop the mountain now and the tree was the only thing visible that was distinct from the mountain itself. How distinct was unclear.

The tree was calling to Hope and he was mesmerized by its seductive rhythm. There wasn't a single part of it that was still, but it was almost impossible for Hope to follow any of its movements. It was impossible to tell where its motion came from, or was going to. Its many entwined trunks seemed to be both growing out of the ground as well as back into it, and the ground itself shifted around its base.

Its branches held no leaves, or even buds, and their barren skeletal limbs slipped in and out of one another, their infinite fingertips probing every particle of air that surrounded them.

As Hope watched, hypnotised, the tips of the tree branches started to become agitated. Their movements became more erratic and less coordinated. This affliction spread down the branches to the trunk, and soon the entire tree was moving to a more frantic and disjointed rhythm.

It was then that the wind started!

It started as a gentle and unassuming breeze but immediately started growing, feeding on itself. As they came closer still to the tree, which by this point had whipped itself into a frenzy and was thrashing violently along with the wind, Hope found it difficult to move his legs forward against the building gale. Maad had positioned himself directly behind him, where he was protected against the full force of the wind, though he still held lightly to Hope's tail to ensure he didn't get blown clear off the mountain.

The wind continued to grow in strength. It howled through Hope's ears and threatened to lift him off his feet. He had come to a stop. He could no longer push himself forward and could barely keep his eyes open, such was the force of air that was rushing at him.

Maad's grip had tightened around his tail.

It was then that the voices started!

They started as an indecipherable whisper in Hope's head, as he remained motionless and in danger of being blown backwards off the mountain. Maad, clinging desperately to Hope, was now lifted off the ground and was flapping madly about like a stray log thrown about on the surface of a torrential river. Hope's tail was Maad's only lifeline, and he clung desperately to it, though his hands had started to slip down its length.

Hope was being pushed from the front by the onslaught of the wind, and being pulled from behind by the desperate monkey. All he could do was plant all four of his feet as hard as he could and try to hold his ground. At that moment though, his focus was much more concerned with the voices that were competing for his attention inside his head.

'…..are two jungles….,' '…..is no King…..,' '…..the elephants abandoned…...,' '…..shall be a bird or a raindrop….,' '…..story is a long and sad one…...'

The voices came one at a time and all together, mixing and weaving in and out and making such a confused noise in Hope's mind that he shut his eyes tight and tried to force them from his head. But they were stubborn and continued to pour into him.

'…..little tree…...,' '…..sound of countless branches breaking…...,' '…..never be repeated again…...,' 'the monkey just stared at me…...,' '…..ONLY A LITTLE ELEPHANT…...,' '…..don't be sad…...,' '…..nothing that's impossible…...'

Hope's head was starting to ache. It felt as if it were

243

going to explode from the pressure of all the voices that were cramming themselves inside, and none seemed to be leaving. His heart was beating fast and it seemed to swell with each beat; it was a race between his head and his heart as to which would burst first.

He had a vague awareness of Maad still clinging to his tail, but the grip was now at the very end, and he may have had only the tail hairs to still hold onto: soon, nothing.

The wind was howling mercilessly and the tree was throwing itself about with such fury that it uncoiled itself into many separate thrashing limbs before twisting itself back into one writhing mass: then repeating.

The voices were relentless. Hope tried to ignore them, but there was no escape. They were spilling from his head and crawling under his skin. They were scratching behind his eyes and climbing down his tongue. His trunk was filled by them and his stomach was heavy with them.

All there was now was the voices.

'…..the way it is…..,' '…..do what we have to do…..,' '…..sea puts itself lower…..,' '…..my little brother…..,' '…..my mother…..,' '…..have no family…..,' '…..what are you doing…..,' '…..cannot be King…..,' '…..will be King…..,' '…..universe is changing…..,' '…..birthplace of loss…..,' '…..it's simple…..,' '…..very, very simple……,' '…..they hear, but they don't listen…..'

Hope wanted to scream. Every particle of his being wanted to scream, to run, to fly, to do anything possible to get away from those voices. It was as if the voices were an army of ants that had swarmed over and completely throughout his body, picking him apart a million tiny pieces at a time.

The wind increased in intensity. Hope's feet started to slide backwards, carrying him towards the edge of the mountain. The voices increased in multitude and volume, drowning out the sound of the wind rushing in Hope's ears. The tree was furious in its throes and whipped itself around the mountaintop, brushing over Hope's head. Hope tried desperately to dig his feet hard against the earth, but the earth wanted nothing to do with it and moved with him, leaving deep gouges in front as Hope continued to be pushed backwards. He felt his back feet slide to the edge of the precipice, only his toenails maintaining contact with the mountain, everything behind them meeting nothing but empty air; the same empty air that was now beckoning to him to come pay a visit. Maad was attached to Hope only by the very tips of his fingers, clinging to the very tips of Hope's tail hairs - and then he was gone.

Hope felt the tension on his tail release as the monkey was plucked from him and tossed over the side of the mountain. He reacted instantly and without thought. He spun around and threw his trunk out, grasping at the air behind him. Finding the hairy end of Maad's long tail, Hope's trunk grabbed it tightly. In doing this Hope found himself with all four feet bunched together, fighting for the same piece of ground which was all that remained between himself and oblivion. He was teetering on the brink - the brink of something he was trying very hard not to think about. With a strength and resolve that seemed to belong to someone else, Hope managed to pull Maad back from the void and threw him over his head to the safety of terra firma.

All this happened in a single moment, and in that same single moment the wind vanished, the voices were silenced and the tree pulled itself together and resumed its gentle and continuous movement within itself.

Hope was left breathless, still balanced precariously on the verge of a swift and final descent below. Safe now from the buffeting wind, he started to stretch his body out once more in the direction most suited to his well-being; namely, back onto the mountain, but before he could manage this simple task, he was struck by a new force; a force also intent on seeing him disappear over the mountains edge. It was Maad.

Sensing his opportunity to be done with Hope once and for all, Maad had quickly regained his feet where Hope had dropped him and rushed back at the vulnerable elephant. Hope had just managed to turn around when Maad met him, but was caught off balance. The wiry monkey was surprisingly strong for his size, but would normally have been no match in a test of strength, even against a young elephant like Hope. Catching him off balance and in such a delicate position had served to tip the scales back to a much more even setting.

Maad sent the full force of his body against the forehead of Hope, flinging himself with great determination. Hope felt the impact push him back a few inches; enough to see his hind feet lose the safety of the mountains last few remaining rocks in that particular region. Hope's feet slipped over the edge and he fell to his knees, desperately trying to find a grip with his front feet to arrest the slide. He had some success, but was left in a position where he was no longer slipping further backwards, but also unable to gain any forward momentum.

Maad cackled with glee, bounced a couple of times into the air before heaving his full frame once more at his target. Hope was shunted backwards again. He was using all his remaining strength to try to hold himself up, but he was failing. He searched blindly with his back feet to try to gain a foothold somewhere. His front feet slipped back a further inch. There was maybe one more inch left to them; at best.

Maad was thoroughly enjoying himself. He moved slowly closer to Hope, savouring the moment, knowing that one little shove, one tiny tipping of the scales, and Hope was gone. Hope could only watch, helpless. Maad stopped a foot or so away from him. He raised his hand. Likely, one hand was all he was going to need, though his other hand now reached behind his back, rummaged a while in his fur. From his position Hope only caught the faintest glimpse of something white and shiny, but the greater part of his attention was focused on something else.

Hope's unseen back legs were still kicking wildly, hoping beyond hope that they would find something to hold onto; but they wouldn't. I can tell you, dear reader, that there was nothing down there for Hope's unfortunate feet to grip onto. There was however, something to grip onto Hope's feet. Hope felt that something coil itself snakelike around his ankles and

247

pull like he'd never been pulled before. That was certainly the last of his endeavours to get back to the mountaintop in the normal manner.

From Maad's perspective, Hope had simply lost his grip, denying him the pleasure of a final helping hand, but as the result was still the same to him, and very much to his liking, he shrugged with mild disappointment, before grinning devilishly to himself as he started past the tree to make his way over the other side of the mountain where his destiny awaited.

Unknown to him there was another whose destiny was running perfectly parallel with his; only about four feet deeper.

Maad felt a slight rumbling in the earth below. He stopped, a feeling of familiar disappointment descending on him. Or should I say ascending.

'Oh, what now!' Maad managed to bleat before being upended and tossed unceremoniously high and wide by an explosion directly beneath his feet; an explosion caused by an almost ten year old elephant being thrust up and through the ground with great force by the massive roots of the equally massive tree which had moments before pulled him through the side of the mountain before expelling him upwards to safety.

Maad was sent shooting into the sky which rejected him with as much vigour as the earth had just done, sending him hurtling back down with at least as much velocity, where monkey and ground met each other in a battle which ground won both easily and convincingly, leaving said monkey in an unconsciously bewildered state at the foot of the tree.

The tree recoiled almost imperceptibly for a split

moment, before resuming its delicate meanderings. Stillness fell on the mountain and on Hope. He was left precisely where he had been dumped by his volcanic eruption, in a daze so compelling he really didn't want to think about what had just happened. Or anything else really, for that matter.

Waiting a moment to see if things had really settled down, or were simply waiting for a new assault, Hope bathed in the peace that had descended on him, and the whole of the mountain. Not a single voice, not even his own, disturbed the tranquillity of his mind, and his senses gathered all the information that washed over him without discrimination.

Drawn once again to the rippling movements of the tree, but no longer hypnotised by it, Hope started to slowly walk towards the centre of the clearing. Maad remained motionless on the ground.

Stopping only inches from its trunk, and sheltered completely by its twisting branches, Hope too became motionless, and by their own accord, his eyelids slid down over his eyes leaving only narrow slits where light continued to creep through.

How long he was like that, Hope did not know. Time seemed to not only stand still, but disappear altogether.

Then a voice started in his head once more, only this time it was only one. It seemed to come from the tree, but it was not so much a voice that Hope heard. It was more that Hope became aware of the things that the voice would have been saying, had there been a voice saying it.

This is the story that Hope became aware of:

A long, long time ago, before elephants even walked on the land or monkeys swung from the treetops, the world was divided very simply into one large continent, and one giant ocean that surrounded it. The continent was covered only in rocks and the ocean was filled only by water. The continent and the ocean lived side by side, in perfect harmony, each happy with their place in the world, and they remained like this for as long as can be measured by time.

But as with anything that is measured by time, change is inevitable, and so it was for the continent and the ocean. One day there was a great upheaval within the earth, and the great continent was split into many parts. Those parts were spread over the earth, with great mountain peaks forming where the lands crashed into and jostled one another. The ocean was stirred from its peaceful slumber and it lifted itself into waves higher than the tallest mountains. The waves crashed down upon the divided continents with such force that many of the the rocks spread across them were crushed down to sand. Soil was pushed up from below to the surface, as everything that had been was destroyed.

When the world settled down once more, it had destroyed and recreated itself. The ocean had been divided up into many oceans and seas, and where it had crashed over land, rivers and lakes had been born. The land had been divided into many continents and islands that lay scattered throughout the oceans and the seas.

With the rocks crushed down into smaller stones and sand, and becoming mixed with the soil and water that had come from below and above, a new colour appeared across the land. It was green.

I was the first to break through the surface, and when I did, I was greeted by the light and warmth of the sun above. It breathed life into me, and as its heat spread throughout my limbs, it was as if I had been awakened from a deep sleep. I stretched myself towards the sun, branches spread wide to catch as much as I could of the energy it poured so generously on me.

After a time other trees emerged, and soon the land was covered by them, from one corner to the next. Being the tallest tree, atop the tallest mountain, I stood guardian over the entire land, but the world stretched past every horizon, and I wished to know of all that was happening in every land.

I tried to come down from the mountain to explore the earth, but I could not. My roots were too deep, and in my efforts to wrench myself free, my limbs thrashed and twisted about against the air that surrounded me, in turn pushing the air away. It tumbled down the mountain and across the land, sweeping over the other trees and stirring their branches into motion.

The wind was born.

It rushed away from my flailing limbs and spread across the lands. All the trees in its path swayed back and forth against it, and in turn they created more wind. On the wind was carried the sound of all the creaking branches and groaning trunks of the trees, who were both blowing and being blown by the wind. This became our language.

We started to creak and moan to each other, and the wind carried our stories from one tree to the next.

Every wind started with me, and every wind finished at me. I have held the burden of being the only living thing to know the whole story of the wind from that moment on.

But then something happened that changed that.

It happened a long time ago, but by then all the animals of the jungle had come into being, and the world, in appearance, was similar to how it is today. There was one big difference though, and that was the way in which everything lived in accordance with the unspoken rules of the jungle. There was balance.

What happened was something that upset that balance, and so it remains to this day.

It was a monkey, very similar in appearance to the one who accompanies you here. His hair was the same golden hue and his eyes, the same clear blue, but he was never seen as different by any of the other monkeys, and at that time he never saw himself as different either.

One day he was alone in the jungle and came upon a watering hole. Stopping to refresh himself, he was suddenly struck by the appearance of another monkey staring up at him from the surface of the still water. Curious only of the fact of there being another monkey in the water, he stared at it for a long time.

Then it happened.

A small bird landed on the monkey's shoulder. He felt it land on himself and, at the same time, he saw it land on the monkey in the water.

That's when it struck him.

He reached up slowly and watched as the monkey in the water followed his movement exactly. He grabbed hold of the bird swiftly, and the other monkey mimicked him perfectly. He hurled the bird at the water, and the monkey disappeared beneath the ripples of the disturbed pool. When the water settled back down the other monkey reappeared and he now recognised it not as another monkey at all, but as the reflection of his self.

He returned to his family and friends and brought them to the watering hole. He showed them what he had discovered, and soon they all recognised themselves in the water. Suddenly, they saw all their differences.

The first monkey saw how he was markedly different from all the others, and he thought of himself as special among all the monkeys. He decreed that he should be their ruler, and he gave all the other monkeys names that reflected their differences.

He named himself One, as he saw himself as the original and first monkey, and said in fact that all other monkeys, and indeed all other animals, were different from him; never the other way around.

This idea spread through all the monkeys and each one found a way to distinguish his self from another, and so hierarchy was born. This in turn spread over time through the jungle, and all were affected by it. Division erupted: between one species and another, between one animal and another. No one was untouched by it, and even the trees started to speak of themselves as being an oak tree or an elm tree, a big tree or a small tree.

Greed became a way of life as each individual catered first to their own needs. Hatred and jealously formed in some animals minds when they saw others with more than they had. This in turn bred violence as these ideas became actions.

The way of life in the jungle changed completely, and the stories that the wind carried back to me became darker and heavier with each passing day, until I could stand it no longer. My leaves started to brown and fall at my feet. I watched as they withered and crumbled around me and were blown away by the wind, no more than dust. My branches ached from the weight of the story that blew endlessly on every breeze. I was dying, and with me would die the story that I alone held in its completeness, and so I stopped it. I stopped the wind.

I can't explain exactly how I did it, but as the source of the wind, it is enough to say that when I wished it to stop; it stopped.

All of the winds that had sailed back to me no longer found a place to tell their stories. Instead, they gathered around me while I remained in the centre, motionless, and when the pressure of all the gathered winds, laden with their untold stories became too much, they burst forth throughout the jungle. Their combined force swept across the land with such fury that the jungle was once more turned upside down.

I have heard no more stories from that day forth. The wind no longer passes this way, but continues to pour around the world, forever gathering more stories. One day, perhaps, it will find a way to tell its tale and unburden itself, so that it can blow freely once more.

I have remained in silence from that day forward. Once in a while, a visitor will pass through. When they pass to the other side of the mountain, I know that they will never return. Others that have come, always with a specific purpose, have returned to the jungle and I have never seen them again. All of them, I have expected.

There was one, however, who came unexpected and unannounced; who passed me without stopping, who made his way to the far side of the mountain and who never returned. He seemed to have a great purpose and conviction, and it was only seeing him that tempted me to once more open myself to the wind. I desired to know what his purpose was, for I recognised him immediately. It was the monkey, One.

I resisted the temptation and remained still: until now. When I saw you arrive, it was not unusual, because it has been expected. But when I saw the monkey that travelled with you, I could remain still no longer. I needed to know how it was possible that after such a length of time, the very same monkey could appear once more before me.

The wind that blew through told me all I wanted to know, but when I wished to stop it, I found that I couldn't. It was too strong.

You would have been blown clear off the mountain had the wind not stopped when it did.

And what stopped it?

You did. At the moment that you risked your life to save the monkey that accompanies you, you were thinking of nothing else but what you had to do. It was this selfless act that stopped the wind and quietened the voices that tormented you.

The monkey who had passed me all that time ago was not the same monkey before me now, but his ancestor, and so they are indeed connected, perhaps somehow following the same path.

The first monkey, One, as he called himself, did indeed have a purpose that day. Over time he had come to believe that the difference between him and the other monkeys was so great, that there must have been a higher purpose for him, and so he set out to find it. His search led him to this mountain and beyond. What befell him after that remains unknown.

The story ended there.

Hope remained motionless for some time afterwards as he absorbed all that he had become aware of. Not a single thought stirred in his mind for some time, until one quietly and politely presented itself. That thought was – it is time to go.

He gathered himself together, and slowly, movement returned to his body. The light over the mountain was growing as dawn approached. Realising what this meant returned a sense of urgency to Hope. He had to get to the far side of the mountain before the sun came up.

Silently bidding a farewell to the tree, Hope was already on his way when he suddenly remembered something. Maad! He turned back and there, sprawled in the same position that Hope had tossed him to, was the unconscious monkey.

Hope of course had no desire to take him with him, he would quite happily have left him there to wake whenever he might, but there was something that made him think that there was a reason that Maad was here in the first place and perhaps, a reason why Maad should continue the journey to its end.

He made his way back to the prone figure, scooped him up in his trunk, and placed him over his back. He turned once more and began his descent down the far side of the mountain. The light was bright enough now for Hope to be able to see clearly the path in front of him, and he rushed down it. Across his back, Maad's limp body was stretched and motionless but, unseen to Hope, who was focused intently on the path, his eyelids first flickered - and then opened.

Chapter Seven
Three heads are better than one

Hope was only a short way down the mountain when it started. The light was still a pale grey, but Hope could see clearly into the distance beyond the mountain. Or at least he would have, were it not for the thick mist.

The mist gathered at the bottom of the mountain and stretched up like a curtain for as far as Hope could bend his neck back to look up at it. Inside the mist, there was not a single shadow or light that moved; it was uniform in its greyness and yet, as Hope stared into it, it seemed to possess an infinite depth.

He stopped to look upon it more, and he found that despite its featurelessness and lack of any colour or movement, it nevertheless struck Hope as incredibly beautiful. He was overawed by it.

It was then, as I mentioned before, that it started.

From the very centre and the very depths of the mist, a black shadow appeared. It was very small at first but quickly grew. And grew. And continued growing.

Hope's heart quickened. His skin tingled and his breath decided it would rather stay in the familiar warmth and darkness of his chest.

The black shadow continued to grow until it

seemed almost as big as the mountain itself. It was starting to take on a distinct shape, and Hope felt that he recognised its form, but there was something different about it. Besides its size, that is. The only thing Hope had ever seen that big was a mountain and this, Hope was sure, was no mountain.

Despite the mist - if indeed it was actually a mist and not just something Hope imagined as a mist because he had no other way to describe it - despite it having no apparent form or dimension of its own, it certainly appeared to Hope that the black shadow was emerging from it.

Hope's breath decided it would like to see this after all, and he exhaled.

Realising that he wasn't going anywhere any time soon, Hope reached up and, surprisingly gently, pulled Maad from his back and laid him on the ground beside him.

Maad's eyes remained closed as Hope did this, but as soon as Hope resumed watching the mist, his eyes crept open and he too watched.

The black figure stopped growing and became motionless. It seemed to be right at the point of stepping through the grey curtain, but for the moment paused.

Hope waited for something to happen.

And then, something did happen!

All around the black shadow, a faint orange glow appeared. It seemed to be coming from the figure itself, but it was its effect on the grey mist around it that was most striking. The grey was immediately set aflame by the light, and as it grew in intensity, Hope's entire world at that point became a flickering, dancing sea of yellows, oranges and reds.

He could hear the crackling sound of the sky as it burned, and yet there was only the faintest breath of hot air that blew over him.

If that wasn't spectacular enough, what happened next certainly was.

Out of the flames, the black shadow emerged.

As if a part of the inferno that surrounded it, the head of an elephant so incredibly massive that it could have swallowed Hope without even noticing, (and Hope wasn't sure that it wouldn't), pressed through the searing mist.

Its skin; (and I should mention that we're using familiar words here to describe something totally unfamiliar), was the colour of pure gold, and it flowed over the head like melting honey. Dark blemishes of deep crimson red mixed with black, erupted over its surface in spectacular explosions that sank back into the molten river of its hide as quickly as they appeared.

The eyes were completely black. As black as black can ever be before becoming some other undiscovered colour. There were no pupils, and no white surrounding them; only two great orbs of shining black glass that cast no reflections.

The trunk was a great waterfall of golden lava and at its end the elephant's breath blasted massive balls of steam over the mountain with every exhalation.

Down one side of the trunk stretched a tusk of gleaming white ivory, so long that it could have stabbed through one side of the mountain and easily emerged out the other. Its perfect and unblemished whiteness contrasted with the flowing river of golds, reds, oranges and black that was the surface, or shall we say, skin, of the elephant.

It continued to reveal itself from the wall of flames around it, and its movements were accompanied by a sound of creaking and groaning so terrifying, that you might have thought that the earth and the sky around were splitting and cracking apart.

As more of the elephant's head approached, it became apparent to Hope that it was not alone.

On either side of it there appeared another head, each identical to the first, only slightly smaller and without any tusks. The most unusual thing about this was that the three heads could only have been held so close together if, in fact, they all belonged to the one elephant. And, as Hope soon saw, they did.

The elephant's front legs appeared beneath the heads. First the left, and then the right, as the elephant stepped forward. Covered in the same golden liquid fire as the heads, as each foot came down, sparks as big as trees shot up in the air and the ground beneath instantly melted into magma footprints that bubbled and hissed around them.

With its three heads, two front feet and half its body now visible, the elephant stopped. The rest of it remained hidden in the flaming wall behind it. Or possibly, the rest of it *was* the flaming wall behind it.

There was a pause, and the only sound in the air was the spitting and crackling of the flames, accompanied by the ssssshhhing steam of the elephant's breath counting the moments as they passed.

It seemed an eternity to Hope as he waited

261

expectantly to see what happened next, but after seven inhalations and seven exhalations, all sound disappeared.

The centre head of the elephant lowered itself, its chin tucked into its chest and its tusk pointed directly at the ground in front of it.

It held this position for only a moment before plunging its tusk with incredible force, and amazing ease, straight through the earth's surface, as deep as the tusk could go, until the elephant's forehead was pressed against the ground.

The elephant then slid the tusk back out to the sound of ivory screeching against hard rock, and the head once again took up its position between the other two, where they all remained, motionless and impassive.

The head on the elephant's right hand side now started to move. It reached its trunk down over the neat hole left by the first elephant's tusk, and inserted the tip into the opening. The second head held its trunk like this for a short time, and seemed to be sucking something from inside the earth.

Hope watched open-mouthed. The elephant hadn't given any indication that it had seen Hope at this point, and Hope had no desire to make himself known as yet. Maad continued to watch secretly, but his mind was spinning together a cunning plan; but plans, as we shall see, and should already know, tend to have a life of their own and really don't like to be told what to do.

The second head seemed to have taken what it needed from the earth and it withdrew its trunk from the hole. It took up a position once more alongside the other two, though the end of its trunk continued to twist around on itself, as if mixing something inside.

The cavity in the ground started to exhale puffs of black smoke. Soon it began to spit showers of rock and burning embers and, finally, a pool of molten lava welled up inside and belched forth, pouring out each side of the hole.

Almost instantly, the lava cooled and began to harden once more into stone, and so the gaping wound that the elephant had opened in the earth was sealed once more.

The second head had continued to stir up whatever ingredients it held within its trunk, and now reached its trunk out to its left, holding it in front of the central head with the trunk's end pointed up.

From the nostrils of the elephant's trunk, the same oozing lava started to bubble up. The elephant was blowing very gently and deliberately, pushing the lava from its trunk, and as the liquid fire emerged, it formed a bubble around the air that the elephant was breathing into it.

Small at first, the glowing red sphere started to grow as the elephant very delicately blew more and more air, and at the same time, slowly released more and more lava that it still held within its trunk. Soon it was almost as large as the elephant's head, and here it stopped.

The elephant continued to balance it on the end of its trunk, held out in front of the centre head as if it was an offering.

It was now the turn of the third head to take part in the ritual.

It reached its trunk out towards the sphere, which appeared to be already hardening slightly in the cool air. Holding the end of its trunk just at the edge of its surface, it drew a deep breath in, and when it was filled to capacity by the air, it stabbed its trunk into the heart of the ball and released its breath with a great blast.

The sphere erupted into flames and expanded with a great rush that engulfed everything Hope could see. Its very edge rushed to meet Hope and a wave of heat swept over him as flames licked at his face. The light was blinding, and he could only barely keep a tiny gap in his eyelids open so as that he could see what was happening.

As quickly as it grew, it shrank back once again. Despite being at the very heart of the explosion, the giant elephant appeared unharmed and completely unmoved by it.

Shrinking back to its previous size, the huge ball of fire remained balanced on the end of the second head's trunk, only now it was a raging inferno of orange and yellow flames that rolled and crashed in waves of fury over its surface.

The sun had been born.

The centre head moved quickly and purposefully. It reached up with its trunk, which it wrapped around the sun. Only just able to contain it, it lifted the sun off the second head's trunk, which then swung away to hang obediently out of the way.

The giant sun throwing elephant, with the sun held eagerly inside its curled trunk, bowed its head forward, keeping the flaming ball tucked beneath its chin and pressed against its chest. Then, with a massive whooshing sound, it threw its head forcefully but gracefully upwards, flinging its trunk up and over its head and releasing the sun from its grip.

The sun sailed majestically into the sky, revealing itself from behind the mountain and was greeted by a rousing chorus of birdsong.

It was a new day!

The ending of everything

Hope was thrilled, from the tip of his trunk to the tip of his tail, and everywhere in between. He could do little more than stand there in amazement, vibrating excitedly on the spot with his mouth spread wide in a boyish grin, while his eyes almost exploded from their sockets as they followed the sun through the sky.

He had seen it!

The giant sun throwing elephant had stood before him and had proved to be more fantastic, more impressive and, if he was honest, more terrifying than anything he had ever imagined.

Now that the giant sun throwing elephant had performed its daily task, it started to retreat once more into the haze behind and around it. The flat grey colour had returned, which only served to highlight the fiery golden skin of the elephant. Noticing that the giant sun throwing elephant was disappearing once more to where it had appeared from, Hope awoke from the dazed stupor he had fallen into.

'Wait,' he cried out suddenly.

The giant sun throwing elephant stopped. It seemed startled and confused by the sound, but also curious. Only the three heads were visible on Hope's side of the grey screen. The rest of the elephant was an indistinct black shadow enveloped in the mist. The three heads were swivelling back and forth, the six ink black eyes scanning the landscape for the source of the voice.

'Eh,' called Hope sheepishly. 'I'm over here.'

He raised his trunk in the air and waved, suddenly feeling incredibly tiny and insignificant in front of such an enormous being.

The centre head found him first, and the other two immediately followed suit. The three sets of eyes stared down at the little elephant and the golden monkey laid out next to him. Hope then heard three distinct voices address him, though each sounded almost exactly like the other. The conversation that followed proved fairly difficult, and at times frustrating for Hope to follow. To stay true to the story, I will present it in the way Hope experienced it and I hope you will forgive me if you too find it difficult, and at times frustrating, to follow.

'Yes'

'What do you want?'

'Don't you know how cold it is out here,' was the manner in which Hope was addressed by the three voices.

'Umm,' started Hope, taken by surprise. 'My name is Hope. I have travelled a long way to see you and have been through many dangerous adventures to get here. You see, I am going to be the next King of the jungle and I thought maybe you might, you know, have some words of…..eh…..advice...or something like that. Maybe,' he finished weakly.

'Advice?'

'How about, be nice to your mother?'

'Or; don't go for a walk just after eating.'

'You mean; "don't go swimming just after eating,"

not "don't go for a walk." What if he's eating while he's being chased by a swarm of bees?'

'Well then he wouldn't be walking, he'd be running, wouldn't he?'

'Same thing.'

'No it's not.'

'Of course it is, only faster.'

'Eh, sorry,' interrupted Hope. 'I kinda meant more like some advice about being King. If you have any, that is.'

'King, hey. Well, don't you think highly of yourself, heh?'

'Leave him alone, there's nothing wrong with having big dreams.'

'And what would you know about dreams? You've never even been asleep.'

'I'm not talking about those kinds of dreams.'

'Oh, oh, I see. You mean like your dream of one day being a delicate little butterfly and flying over this mountain to see what's on the other side. You mean like that?'

'Shut up!! I knew I should have never told you that.'

'You never told *me* that. If you became a butterfly, how would we make the sun with only the two of us?'

'He's not going to be a butterfly. He's just being ridiculous.'

'How do you know? You're going to be very surprised when you come out one morning and I'm gone. What will you do then, huh?   Well?   Well!!?

'Ahem,' coughed Hope to remind them that he was there.

268

They stopped arguing, and Hope spoke quickly before they started again.

'Do you have a name?' he asked, and then added, 'I mean besides the giant sun throwing elephant, which is what I call you.'

'Giant sun throwing elephant, hey. It's a little obvious, and not very catchy, but I like it.'

'I like Fred. Nice and simple. Makes me feel normal, just like any other elephant.'

'You're far from normal.'

'You be quiet. I've had just about enough of your…..'

'What about Madeline? It's such a pretty name, like a delicate little flower.'

'MADELINE!!!! That's a girl's name.'

'And what's wrong with that? How do you know we're not a girl? Have you ever checked? I mean, it's not like we have anything to compare with now, is it?'

'There's nothing wrong with that, but we're not a girl, because I say we're not!'

'Who made you the boss?'

'Now look here; I'm the biggest *and* I'm the middle head. I'm the one who throws the sun in the sky day in and day out. That makes me the most important, and so what I say goes, got it?'

'Now who thinks highly of themselves, hey?'

'One more word out of you and I'm gonna…..'

'You're gonna what?'

'Stop it you two. Why don't we just settle on Fred. It could be short for Frederick or Winifred, so really it's neither a boy's name *or* a girl's name.'

'Fred's a boring name.'

'Oh, right, and Madeline is just the sort of name that every warrior or adventurer would give themselves.'

'Why not?'

'Oh you're just a…..'

'Hey!!' yelled Hope. They were quiet. 'Why don't you just let people call you whatever they want to call you?'

'Yeah, I guess.'

'You're probably right.'

'I agree. As long as it's not Madeline.'

'Now why did you have to say that? You always have to have the last word. Just like that time when…..

'ENOUGH!!' yelled Hope. He surprised even himself with the authority of his voice.

'There's no need to yell at us.'

'Yeah, I mean we're only still here because you wanted us to wait.'

'That's right! Do you know how cold it is out here?'

'Sorry,' apologised Hope. 'It's just that I can't seem to get a single answer that any of you agree on.'

'Well maybe you should ask easier questions.'

'Right, like what's 2 + 2?'

'What!' said Hope.

'Or maybe, what's the sound of one hand clapping?'

Hope was really confused, but he went along with it.

'What's the sound of one hand clapping?' he asked.

'How on earth should we know? Do we look like we have hands?'

Two of the heads burst into laughter, finding this very funny. Hope didn't see the funny side at all. The third head seemed to be thinking very hard about the question, and when the others stopped laughing it asked 'Wouldn't it just be half the sound of two hands clapping?'

'Don't be daft. How can one hand clap?'

'Well if I had one hand I could show you.'

'Is the other answer 4?'

'What!'

'What's 2 + 2? The answer is 4, right?'

'That depends. If it's 2 elephants plus 2 elephants, then the answer is 4 elephants. But if it's 2 elephants plus 2 giraffes, then the answer would still be 2 elephants plus 2 giraffes…..See?'

'Yeah. That's pretty clever.'

'That's why I'm the middle head, and why you'd both do well to listen to me!'

'How can we not listen to you? It's not like we can just walk away to somewhere where we can't hear you any more, is it?'

'Well, if you don't like it, then maybe I just won't say anything from now on.'

'Promises, promises.'

'Mock all you want, but you'll see where you end up without my advice to guide you.'

'Considering we're all attached to the same body, my guess is I'll end up exactly where I always end up. Right next to you.'

'He's got a point.'

'Who asked you?'

'I thought you weren't going to say anything from

now on?'

'Shut up.'

'You're still talking.'

'You're still talking.'

'Oh, you're copying me now, are you? That's really mature.'

'Oh, you're copying me now, are you? That's really mature.'

'Stop it.'

'Stop it.'

'Stop it.'

'STOP IT.'

'STOP IT.'

'STOP IT.'

'WILL YOU ALL JUST SHUT UP!!'

They all fell silent. Hope was exhausted just from listening to them. He'd heard enough, but there was one more thing he had to ask the giant sun throwing elephant before they parted ways.

'There's one favour I would like to ask of you, if possible,' he said. 'You see, I'm a long way from home, and I'm really tired, and tomorrow I'm going to be crowned King. I really don't want to be late for that. Do you think you would be able to throw me back to my valley, the way you throw the sun, which must be much heavier than me?'

'Oh, sure.'

'No problem.'

'Let me just calculate the angles, and the wind speed. How heavy are you, if you don't mind me asking?'

'Will you stop that.'

'What?'

'Always overcomplicating things. It's an easy throw.'

'What if we miss?'

'We've never missed yet.'

'Sure, but we've never thrown an elephant.'

'It's the same thing, because he's much lighter than the sun, but we're throwing him a much shorter distance. Same thing, see?'

'I really don't think that actually…..'

'It's okay,' interrupted Hope. 'Close enough is just fine.'

'And how about if you just stay right here? Is that also fine?' It was a voice that hadn't taken part in the conversation up to that point, and Hope had wished it had stayed that way. It was a voice he had forgotten about completely, but now he was forced to think of it once more. It was Maad's voice.

Hope spun around to face him. Maad was on his feet, an evil grin spread across his face, and there was something held in one of his hands. Hope couldn't quite make out what it was, but the way in which Maad held it told him that he would soon find out.

'So here we are,' sneered Maad. 'You at the end of your journey and me, well, if I have my way, this is just the beginning of mine.'

'What do you mean?' asked Hope. He was nervous of the sinister tone in Maad's voice.

'What do I mean?' repeated Maad back to Hope. 'WHAT DO I MEAN!!? Have you not been following your own little story? All this time you're on this cute little journey to find this giant sun throwing elephant and, lo and behold, you've actually found it. And now what happens? You go back to your little valley and, just like that, you become King of the jungle.'

Hope wasn't sure how to answer, and so he didn't. In any event, Maad wasn't waiting for a response and continued on, becoming more agitated as he went.

'Who says that's the way it has to be?' he demanded. 'Why should it be you? Your oversized friend back on the mountain said that only one of us will return, and my guess would be that the one who does will be King. That's the whole point of finding this big buffoon here; correct me if I'm wrong.

'I didn't think so. Well, I'm not going to wait around to see which of us that will be. Something tells me I might regret it if I do, and so I'm simply going to take what's rightfully mine. Now do you see what I mean?' To emphasise his last question, Maad raised his hand over his head and Hope saw what it was that he held.

It was a pure white dagger, just like the sharpened stones Hope had seen the monkeys use, only it wasn't made of stone. Hope instantly recognised what it was made from, and his stomach twisted in revolt.

'Boon Khum's tusk.' He could barely speak the words, but Maad knew well enough what he said.

'Ironic, isn't it?' jeered Maad. He was taking great pleasure in the moment, and he slowly moved in on Hope.

Hope was rooted to the spot. It wasn't from fear; Hope had faced so much on his adventures that fear would have to try much harder from now on if it was going to get to him. It was an overwhelming sense of horror at the situation that paralysed Hope. Thee thought of Boon khum's tusk, which had been so violently stolen, being used for a purpose such as this, at a moment such as this, to achieve an end such as Maad envisioned; it was too much for the little elephant.

Maad was standing over Hope who was on the lower end of the slope, and seemed puzzled at how easy his plan was coming together. He had expected more of a fight, but he wasn't complaining. He licked his fangs in anticipation and holding the ivory knife in both hands, he raised it high above his head, ready to plunge it down upon Hope who seemed resigned to his fate. How could he fight against someone so filled with hatred and wickedness?

The sun was high over the mountain and partly obscured by a cloud that was passing in front of it, casting its shadow over the mountain. At that exact moment the sun's light came out from behind the cloud and landed on the spot where Maad and Hope were standing.

Neither of them noticed it, but the giant sun throwing elephant, who seemed surprisingly impartial to the events taking place in front of it, did notice. Or more correctly, it noticed the flash of light that reflected off the polished ivory of Maad's weapon. Seeing what the monkey held in his hands, the giant sun throwing elephant became enraged.

'**STOP**,' roared all three heads at once.

Maad had started to bring the knife down already, but the force of the command froze him on the spot. The knife's point was halted only a hair's width from

Hope's skin. A tiny flea, directly under the razor sharp tip, breathed a sigh of relief and sprang from Hope's back, vowing to stick to cats and dogs in the future.

Maad turned his head upwards to where the order had come from, and found himself pinned under the weight of six fierce pitch black eyes, each bigger than any tree he had climbed or wall he had built.

His hands started to tremble, his legs turned to jelly, his teeth chattered in his head and his heart turned to stone. The knife dropped harmlessly to the ground. As soon as the sound of ivory clanging against rock rang out the middle head of the giant sun throwing elephant lashed out its trunk, scooped up the petrified monkey and, in one amazingly swift manoeuvre, tossed him over its head into the grey mist behind.

Hope watched as the flailing figure of his nemesis disappeared into the fog, became a black shadow that faded quickly, and then, just like that, was gone.

There wasn't a single sound. No scream, no final curse, no grunt of effort or satisfaction from the elephant. Nothing.

It was done. Maad was gone. Hope was stunned.

'Where has he gone to?' he stammered.

'Into the unknown,' replied the head.

'What's the unknown?' asked Hope.

'Well if I told you that, it wouldn't be the unknown now, would it? It would be the known.'

'Is that where you came from?' Hope pressed.

'It's where everything comes from, and where everything goes to.'

'That's not a real answer,' said another head.

'Well you try and explain it better then. I'd like to

see you try.'

'You can't explain the unknown; that's the whole point.'

'Well at least I tried.'

They were off again. Hope sighed. 'Can I go in?' he asked.

'One day.'

'But not now.'

'When the time is right.'

'It's very painful if you're not ready.'

'Was Maad ready?' queried Hope.

'Er, no, I dare say he was not.'

'Yeah. That must have hurt.'

'Something like being pulled apart slowly, piece by piece, and then being stuck back together, only to be pulled apart again.'

'Don't scare him. You'll give him nightmares.'

'He's a big elephant. I'm sure he can handle it.'

'I'm fine,' interjected Hope, 'but I'd appreciate it if I could go home now.'

'Oh, right, the throwing thing; of course. Are you ready?'

'As I'll ever be,' laughed Hope. The middle head reached out its trunk and gently lifted Hope. It was so big -the trunk I mean- Hope could have spent the rest of the day exploring it. But he was done with exploring for the moment.

The giant sun throwing elephant lowered Hope down and under itself, and with an effortless swing sent Hope flying up into the sky.

'Goodbye,' called Hope as he was propelled from the trunk. Behind him he heard three voices call out;

'Goodbye.'

'Good luck.'

'Come back soon.'

'What'd you say that for? You know that when he comes back again it'll be for the last time. Do you really want that to be soon?'

'I didn't mean it like that. I just meant that I'd miss him, that's all.'

'You're a buffoon.'

'You're so mean. Why are you always so mean to me?'

'Because you're a buffoon.'

'Stop saying that.'

'Will you both just be quiet.'

The voices faded into the distance as Hope sailed over the mountain. Soon he would be safely back in his valley. He had started this journey because he had wanted to see for himself where the sun came from, but also because he was afraid of losing his freedom. Now he had seen more of the world than he had ever dreamed even existed, and as he soared across the sky, gazing down at all the places he had been – the mountain where Queen Freassel lived; the mountain where Pu-pa was teaching monkeys to have fun; all the way back to his home where his family awaited him- he felt a freedom he never knew he could feel.

It was the freedom simply to be. And what Hope had decided to be, was King.

The sun flew high in the sky, and just below it, only visible to those on the ground who knew exactly what to look for, was a tiny little speck in the shape of a little elephant.

It was Hope, King of the jungle, looking over his Kingdom.